T0381452

Beautiful Flowers

GENESIS

ISRiAL d'LOCURA

BALBOA.PRESS

A DIVISION OF HAY HOUSE

Balboa Press books may be ordered through booksellers or by contacting:

Balboa Press
A Division of Hay House
1663 Liberty Drive
Bloomington, IN 47403
www.balboapress.com
1 (877) 407-4847

Edited by: Everett Michael James

Scripture quotations marked (NLT) are taken from the Holy Bible,
New Living Translation, copyright © 1996, 2004, 2007 by Tyndale
House Foundation. Used by permission of Tyndale House Publishers,
Inc., Carol Stream, Illinois 60188. All rights reserved.

Print information available on the last page.

ISBN: 978-1-9822-3906-0 (sc)
ISBN: 978-1-9822-3907-7 (e)

Balboa Press rev. date: 11/21/2019

Contents

Chapter 1   April 1st, 2044. 3:00 P.M.
            Jacksonville, FL..1

Chapter 2   April 1st, 2044. 3:25 P.M. Houston TX....3

Chapter 3   April 1st, 2044. 4:00 P.M. Empire
            Aoks I.S.D. Houston, TX.......................13

Chapter 4   April 1st 2044, 4:25 P.M. Houston, TX....19

Chapter 5   April 1st, 2044. 4:50 P.M. Houston, TX...23

Chapter 6   April 1st 2044, 9:10 P.M. The City,
            Guerra, Texas. 33

Chapter 7   April 2nd, 2044. 10:00 A.M.
            Houston,TX. 37

Chapter 8   April 2nd, 2044. 2:00 P.M. The
            City, Guerra, TX......................................45

Chapter 9   April 2nd, 2044. 5:00 P.M. Houston, TX...51

Chapter 10 April 3rd, 2044. 7:05 P.M. Houston, TX...55

Chapter 11 April 4th, 2044. 3:00 A.M.
            Houston, TX. 81

Chapter 12   April 4th, 2044. 5:00 A.M.
Houston, TX. 89

Chapter 13   April 22, 2044. 6:00 p.m. The City,
Guerra TX. 95

Chapter 14   May 16, 2044. 3:00 P.M. The City,
Guerra, TX. 103

Chapter 15   May 20, 2044. 11:00 A.M.
Kingwood, TX. 109

Chapter 16   May 20th, 2044. 6:00 P.M. Outside
the Shady Oaks Housing Complex,
Kingwood, TX. 127

Chapter 17   May 20th, 2044. 7:00 P.M.
Kingwood, TX. 133

Chapter 18   May 31st, 2044 3:00 P.M. Shepherd
TX. 145

Chapter 19   June 1st, 2044. 6:00 P.M. Dallas, TX. 161

Chapter 20   June 1st, 2044. 7:30 PM. Shepherd, TX. ... 167

Chapter 21   June 22nd, 2044. 10:00 A.M.
Dallas, TX. 181

Chapter 22   June 25th, 2044. 5:00 P.M. The
Alta Vista Ranch. Shepherd, TX. 185

Chapter 23   June 26th, 2044. 5:00 P.M. Agua
Nueva, TX. 191

Chapter 24   June 30th, 2044. 6:00 A.M. Shady
Oaks, Kingwood, TX. 195

Chapter 25 July 1st, 2044. 12:00 P.M.
Livingston, TX..203

Chapter 26 July 2nd, 2044. 12:00 P.M. The
Alta Vista Ranch. Shepherd, TX. 209

Chapter 27 July 2nd, 2044. 8:00 A.M. The Alta
Vista Ranch. Shepherd, TX. 213

Chapter 28 July 4th, 2044. 1:00 P.M. 10
minutes outside of Fort Hadknot,
New Orleans, LA 223

Chapter 29 July 23rd, 2044. 10:00 P.M. The
Alta Vista Ranch. Shepherd, TX. 231

Chapter 30 August 1st, 2044. 2:00 P.M. Dallas,
TX. 237

Chapter 31 August 10th, 2044. 10:30 P.M. Fort
Hadknot, New Orleans, LA. 241

Chapter 32 August 15th, 2044. 10:00 P.M. The
Alta Vista Ranch. Shepherd, TX. 255

Chapter 33 August 30th, 2044. 8:00 A.M.
Kingwood, TX. 263

Chapter 34 September 30th, 2044. 8:00 A.M.
Fort Hadknot in New Orleans, LA. 265

Chapter 35 September 30th, 2044. 3:00 P.M.
Shepherd, TX. 269

Chapter 36 October 15th, 2044. 4:00 P.M.
Austin, TX. 273

Chapter 37 October 15th, 2044. 11:00 P.M.
            The Alta Vista Ranch. Shepherd, TX... 279

Chapter 38 October 16th, 2044. 10:00 A.M.
            The Alta Vista Ranch. Shepherd, TX... 281

Chapter 39 October 16th, 2044. 3:00 P.M.
            Shepherd, TX................................285

Chapter 40 October 25th, 2044. 12:30 P.M.
            Austin, TX.................................289

Chapter 41 October 31st, 2044. 10:00 A.M.
            The Alta Vista Ranch. Shepherd, TX... 293

Chapter 42 November 1st, 2044. 10:00 A.M.
            The Alta Vista Ranch. Shepherd, TX... 295

Chapter 43 November 5th, 2044. 7:00 A.M.
            Just outside the city of Houston, TX.....299

Chapter 44 November 6th, 2044. 12:00 P.M.
            Dallas, TX.................................303

Chapter 45 November 7th, 2044. 6:00 P.M.
            Houston, TX...............................305

Chapter 46 November 10th, 2044. 5:00 A.M.
            Conroe, TX................................309

Chapter 47 November 12th, 2044. 11:00 A.M.
            Houston, TX...............................315

Chapter 48 November 14th, 2044. 3:00 P.M.
            Houston, TX...............................319

Chapter 49   December 1st, 2044. 7:00 P.M.
             The Beacon of Hope Compound.
             Houston, TX. 323

Chapter 50   December 20th, 2044. The Beacon
             of Hope Compound, Houston, TX. 325

Chapter 51   December 21st, 2044. The Beacon
             of Hope Compound, Houston, TX. 327

Chapter 52   December 22nd, 2044. 11:00 A.M.
             The Beacon of Hope Compound,
             Houston, TX. 331

Chapter 53   January 1st, 2045. The Beacon Of
             Hope Compound. Houston, TX. 337

Chapter 54   February 2nd, 2045. 12:00 P.M.
             The Beacon of Hope Compound.
             Houston, TX. 341

Chapter 55   February 15th, 2045. 10:08 A.M.
             Tingleton Howard International
             Airport. Houston, TX. 347

Chapter 56   February 15th, 2045. 11:00 A.M.
             Dr. Sherman's Laboratory. The
             Beacon of Hope Compound. 353

Chapter One

"Luther, Luther, Luther, Luther," the crowd chanted as he walked to the wooden podium positioned in the center of the stage and as he stood before the mass of people a crooked smile crept across his dark brown face.

"How can a child sense unfairness when his brother is favored over him?," he asked.

"I believe that all conscious beings are all born with an internal sense of justice that calls out from the depths of their souls when one tastes the bitter essence of bias," Luther stated while gazing at the people staring in awe.

"Men and women of every shade are flocking to the way of the Zodia and its many teachings, and now is the time my conscious brothers and sisters that we burn our misled siblings in a baptism of fire so that our cries will be neglected no longer," he screamed while slamming his fist onto the face of the podium.

"The immigrants have been banned from entering the land we call home, yet you convicted felons are not considered for the jobs they left behind because you refuse to work for the crumbs offered by the mouse's trap," Luther said as the crowd erupted in cheers of admiration. "White-collar exploitation is a crime against humanity itself and we must purge the American society of this, for we have been subdued by it for far too long. Let the pigs die to the twelve!" he yelled.

"The police that is appointed to protect us hunt us like dogs in the streets in our metropolitan areas, and I say to you in attendance and those watching at home; let us hunt them as well," he said as the crowd began to applaud.

"This is not a call for peaceful protest or political action! Like many other groups of our time, we have tried that, and have seen that the leaders of our nation do not hear our pleas; this is simply a declaration of war," he stated while lifting his voice to speak over the ocean of people now chanting his name once again.

"And to the citizens of the United States of America, we will hunt you, we will kill you, and we will remove the flesh from your bones lest you yield to the teachings of the Zodia and join us in our Novus Ordo Seclorum," Luther said while raising his voice again to be heard over the mob of people.

"The stars have aligned in our favor, let us cut off the head and set the body ablaze. Let the Zodia reign forever," he screamed; basking in the glory of the crowd's veneration while lifting his hands toward the cosmos.

"Luna, Martis, Veneris, Lovis, and Mercurii," Luther exclaimed before turning to his right and finishing, "Saturnii, Urani, Neptuni, don't be like the treacherous Plutonis; cling to the teachings of the Zodia."

Chapter Two

Turning the crystal doorknob, Elijah entered onto the dance floor of Club Atlantis. He had been working there for four years, working his way up the ladder from a security position in the parking lot to co-manager of the club. Although the club was one of the hottest attractions in downtown Houston, most of their money came from the red cards dealt beneath the round table. Not all of them were crooked, nonetheless, prosperity was their main goal. His boss Isaac had owned the club for thirteen years, thus the Club Atlantis was a giant machine that had been fixed up through years of operation and they had expanded from a small building around the corner to a vast empire of alcohol, money, sex, and drugs.

Elijah thought his life to be always on the go. He was always busy doing something hardly leaving him with any free time left for himself or his family. Running the Atlantis seemed to be like a twenty-four-hour job. The smell of sweat, perfume, and perspiration filled the air of the dimly lit room. *Tomorrow is payday*, he thought as he weaved his way through the dancing mob. Large speakers mounted onto the walls blared as white strobe lights pulsed in sync with hypnotic music.

The DJ of the hour went by the name of Christopher Wallace, however, Elijah referred to him as "Eddy." He was one of three DJs that worked at Club Atlantis throughout the week. His excuse for calling him Eddy was that it was much easier for him to remember his name.

"Eddy, my man, what do you have for me?," he called out to the man inside the DJ booth. Christopher then looked up with a cheesy smile with eyes that were low and bloodshot red. He wore a long grey jacket and baggy black sweatpants; in which he always held the "special of the week." The club DJ's were well known for providing a gateway to psychedelic experiences. While Christopher shook his hand, he passed him a small bag containing two circular pills.

"For the ten-thousandth time, my name is not Eddy! Call me Christopher Wallace, Mr. Wallace, Chris, or Medicine Man," he said with a smile.

"Yeah, I like Eddy better," Elijah replied.

"So what is this?" he inquired inquisitively while looking down at the pills.

"Well one's a blue dragon and the other one is some new fire I just got in," Christopher started running his fingers through his hair. "I call it a paintbrush," he finished.

"Yeah the name needs some work," Elijah said while backing away from the DJ booth while exclaiming; "but

I'll let you know how it comes out." Elijah then put the pills in his jacket pocket and pushed open the door before starting toward the parking lot. He had dinner reservations with his fiancée at La Casa Bistec, the finest restaurant in the Houston area. The sun began to beat down on his light brown skin.

"You got somewhere important to be?" asked his co-worker Jonah as he passed her in mid-stride. Elijah did not answer but nodded his head as he walked briskly toward the parking lot. His phone suddenly began to vibrate frantically in his breast pocket. He reached into his jacket and pulled out his cellular device and swiped the button to answer the call.

"Hello," he stated plainly.

"Hey babe, did you make reservations at the restaurant?" his fiancée asked. She often wondered would · they ever get married. They had been engaged for a little over a year now and were unhappily unwedded, but still, she had hoped for a better future. His fiancé's family would always ask him in their thick southern accents, "when are you and Simone going to tie the knot?"

Elijah would always laugh it off, but they did not know about the problems that had destroyed the bridge of communication that once bonded them together and this was the reason he disliked her family. Perhaps he had over-extended himself by asking her hand in marriage. But also, there was another side of him that wanted something different. He did want forever but lost the map to get to their destination. Their relationship was on a downhill spiral and he knew it. But he held on with the hope that it would return as it once was.

"Yeah, I got it all taken care of," Elijah replied.

"I have an appointment with Mr. Heartside today. What time do you want me to meet you there again?" she asked.

Elijah began to tune her out while he patted himself for his keys.

"You dropped something?" a voice called out behind him. He spun around like a madman to see that it was Jonah's voice resonating within his ears. He looked deep into her light blue eyes. They seemed to melt away his frustration as lustful thoughts began to conjure in the depths of his mind.

"Babe I'm going to call you back, just meet me at La Casa Bistec at four o'clock," he said before hanging up the phone. He watched as his keys dangled from her fingertips. Elijah checked his watch, it was now 3:35.

"Dinner plans?" she asked while passing him the tarnished metal keyring with three keys on it.

"Yes, my fiancé and I are going to a Mexican steakhouse tonight," he said with a tooth-filled grin.

"Oh that's a change from your usual acts of having relations with our coworkers," she jeered.

His eyes then flared with disbelief. He thought no one knew. "I didn't know what you are talking about," he said as the lie slithered from his lips. Sweat began to perspire from his bald head as humidity filled the air, making his white dress shirt stick to his skin.

"Don't play me for stupid," she said in a bashful tone. Elijah's eyes darted to the golden charm bracelet on her wrist. A golden beveled cross dangled from it as the sun's vibrant rays reflected onto her black blouse.

"It's fascinating how you convince yourself of these lies," he continued. A puzzled expression suddenly came over her face. Instantaneously, she grasped hold of her position in the conversation.

"I saw you, I know you are lying," she said. "I won't report you to the manager. I'll pray for you. You have a family at home," she said with disgust. "You deserve to lose everything, maybe then it would teach you how to appreciate what you have," she screamed.

"Is that all you have to say," Elijah asked, "I don't come to work to be slandered in public," he retorted.

But her frustration made her voice grew even louder, "I'm going to pray for you!" Then she stormed off in a vortex of exasperation.

Elijah then took a long look at his keys. "Thank you!" he shouted from behind her watching her hips sway as she walked toward the entrance of the club and he chuckled to himself as he entered his car.

"Some things you just have to laugh off," he said to himself.

Besides what was it to her if I was having sex with my co-worker?

Though he wondered if she had seen them amid their fornication, or if she had convinced herself that it had occurred by the way he interacted with certain faculty. Regardless of the matter, it was, in fact, true, and he felt no guilt whatsoever. He simply did not care enough to quit, *It was like having a drink after a long day's work.* "Puerto Rican Vodka", he said while laughing to himself. He ignited the engine and put his automobile in reverse.

I really should be more careful, Isaac and I are close but I am unsure if he would stand for the skeletons in the corners of my closet.

He then rolled the windows down and turned the radio on, "And in today's top story the protest demanding justice for the brutal death of Bradley Thompson are popping up like wildfire across the U.S! Be advised."

But in the middle of the hosting podcast, he switched the station. "And this is the top hits on Jeje The Point," the speakers blared. The music began playing in harmony with the ambiance of sounds coming from the downtown city streets as he turned at the corner onto North Main Street. Traffic was not typically bad at this time, but in this particular instance, it was much worse than usual. This traffic is terrible, I should probably stop and get flowers for her to sweeten the blow of me being late, he thought.

Elijah then checked his watch, "3:45. Yep, I'm going to be late," he said. As he pulled over in front of parking meter "Eh, it will only be a few minutes there's no need to pay," he said to himself.

The crowded street was backed up to the intersection and it inched forward like a caterpillar on an oak leaf. Elijah pulled out one of the pills from the small bag from his jacket pocket and swallowed it before exiting his automobile.

"One a day keeps the doctor at bay and extra for good luck," he said as he threw the second pill down his throat. He locked his car door and then started for the flower shop around the corner. The shop was titled Beautiful Flowers. It was the best flower shop in town and close to his job. Elijah strolled past the cars honking their horns at the seemingly motionless traffic. He was nearing the corner of Scott Street and Bell and then suddenly a tall woman walked from around the corner. She wore a cheetah printed shirt and a blue skirt that stopped just before her knees. The shirt's shoulder straps were worn and tattered. Her face was chiseled and her dark brown skin glowed in the shining sun.

She smiled and glared at him with lust in her eyes as she neared him, revealing her yellow teeth in a tooth filled grin. As Elijah's stomach began to turn she exclaimed while walking past him, "hey."

"Well, it looked good from a distance. But I prefer egg whites instead," he said to himself.

He then turned the corner to see an old man sitting on the ground in front of a closed down theatre which had been boarded up several years ago. The old man looked up at him with dirt in his yellow-tinted eyes and his clothes were filthy, reeking of perspiration. He sped up his pace, walking briskly past the old man without haste, for he had no morsel of sympathy for the homeless and forgotten. As he looked into the poor man's plastic cup he said, "It isn't my fault people are lazy."

A mob of people were standing amid the street with signs labeled with "Stop The Violence," as they chanted frantically; marching back and forth in front of a group of officers holding black batons in one hand and riot shields in the other. Elijah was almost to the door of the flower shop when a man holding a charity bucket stopped him. "Excuse me, sir, what's your name?" he inquired.

"Elijah," he replied.

"Ah a Christian name, do you know what your name means?" the man asked.

"No, but I need to get going. I don't have any money to give you," Elijah said.

"Are you a Christian?" the man asked while looking into Elijah's eyes.

"No I'm an Atheist," Elijah replied. "What are you going to try to do, convert me?" he mocked.

"Well I believe if the Lord wants to, he will reel you in like a fish on a string," he stated. Elijah's expression then altered.

"I do not believe your God exists," he said before walking into the store, leaving the man and the mob outdoors. The scent of sweet freshly cut flowers was in the air, and the pills he had taken had finally begun to kick in; sending a tingling sensation throughout his entire body.

"Hi, welcome to Beautiful Flowers," the attendant said. She wore a black dress shirt and pants with diamond studs planted firmly in her ears. Her long red hair contrasted with her ivory skin, which stopped just before her name tag that had, "Anastasia" inscribed in the center. She was a very beautiful woman. After sitting down the blue bouquet of white roses onto the grand piano, she approached him and asked, "What can I help you with today?"

"I need flowers," he exclaimed, as he entered a state of complete euphoria.

She paused for a second while staring at him then chuckled softly. "Well those on the rack are half off," she said while pointing to a giant glass display case.

"You are really beautiful," he stated.

"Thank you," she replied cheerfully. Suddenly, the mob of people outside began to chant louder as the second group of policemen ran by the large glass window in front of them.

"Do you think this protest will continue if the policeman who killed that kid walks free," Elijah asked as he moved closer to the glass window.

"I'm not sure. People aren't just accepting it anymore, something needs to change," she stated as she moved beside him.

BOOM!!!!

Elijah then flew backward as he watched the glass window break before his very eyes and the sounds of car alarms and people screaming suddenly filled the air. He staggered with incoordination as he rose to his feet, looking at the ground to see blood oozing from the back of Anastasia's skull. Beautiful Flowers had been vandalized. He peered out of the broken glass window and saw a burning car surrounded by charred bodies. His legs were paralyzed by fear, but seconds later he was able to charge down the street through the hostile surroundings. People were afraid, it looked as if hundreds of flies were scattering from a piece of burning flesh. As Elijah reached the corner where he had seen the old man he noticed that people were running through slews of vacant vehicles in every direction; while the drivers who remained in their cars drove on the sidewalk, hitting mail dispensaries, signs, and parking meters in the process. A barrage of sirens suddenly attributed to the ambiance of chaos.

I am not going to be able to drive out of here, he thought to himself before expressing aloud; "I have to get to my daughter." But as he attempted to cross the intersection he was hit by a speeding car. His body flopped onto its silver hood before he fell onto cement earth striped with white lines. Without haste, the woman inside the vehicle ran out to him. It was Jonah! His head beamed and his ears rang, while a pain shot through his rib cage.

"Oh my goodness," she screamed, "are you ok?"

"I need to get to Empire Aoks Elementary," he shouted curled up in a fetal position.

"Get in," she said as she ran to the driver's side of her car. He staggered up with aching bones and settled himself into her automobile.

"So what happened to La Casa Bistec?" she asked as she mashed on the accelerator.

"You didn't hear the blast!" he shouted.

"All I saw was people running," she stated as she weaved through the people running against the flow of traffic. Elijah then pulled out his cell phone, but its screen was cracked on its edge from his impact with Jonah's automobile.

"No signal, that's odd," he said to himself as he put his hands on his side and closed his eyes shut.

Chapter Three

"**A**re you sure you don't want me to take you to the hospital?" Jonah asked with apprehension. "I already told you I'm fine," Elijah replied in a nonchalant tone of voice; his body was riddled with pain and he tried to grasp hold of himself. There were more important things at hand. He couldn't wrap his brain around what had just happened. Was it an accident or a terrorist attack? These thoughts circled his brain like a fresh brew in a steaming hot cauldron. His head began to beam and he felt the blood pulsate through his ribs.

"I hope no one was seriously injured in that car bombing," Jonah said; but Elijah pursed his lips and chose not to respond. He knew better, he had seen the burning bodies outside of the flower shop. Not to mention the smell of seared flesh was still simmering in his nostrils. "The school's just around the corner," Jonah exclaimed as she attempted to break the aura of dead silence.

The pills he had taken had begun to make him perspire abundantly and he felt as if he was on the moon, his thoughts were eager to dance from the tip of his tongue. What a way to bring my high down, Elijah thought; Eddy always has the best drugs. He never liked being high around his daughter, but it was a dire emergency. He wanted his family all together again in a safe location.

Jonah brought the car to a stop as she pulled between the yellow lines of the parking space. "So do you want me to go in with you?" she asked.

"I have this under......control," Elijah responded in an exuberant struggle.

"Oh my goodness, are you high right now?" Jonah said while exaggerating her voice and slapping her forehead.

"We will talk about this when I get back," he stated while reaching for the door handle.

"That's strike one," she yelled as he slammed the car door behind him! Elijah's legs wobbled while he stood and started for the front entrance of the school. As he neared the awning covering the front door he noticed a black cop car with its emergency lights on, and in the front seat sat a reddish-brown woman with her hair pulled to a knot on the top of her head. Their eyes met just as he ascended the cement ramp, putting him under a ward of shade beneath the metal covering. Suddenly, he began to find himself immersed in the sound of rushing water from a nearby fountain while attempting to divert his attention from her gawking fixation. Besides the blue entrance door lay a silver panel containing a black button and speaker.

"You got this Eli," he said before pressing the round button. Seconds later an attendant's voice projected through the speaker, "Hi, how can I help you?"

"Oh yeah, my daughter Sequoia is enrolled here and I'd like to check her out for the day," Elijah responded.

"I'm sorry I can't let you do that, due to current events we are currently on lockdown until the President gives further instruction," he called back.

"So when am I supposed to be able to pick up my little girl?" Elijah asked with frustration.

"We will notify you when we hear any changes from the administration," the attendant stated in return.

"I don't think you understand, I want my child now because my phone isn't getting any signal. You won't be able to reach me," Elijah said with a dash of anger surging within him.

"The answer is no," the man stated rudely before the speaker cut off.

"Give me my child now, I'm not going to play this game with you," he screamed while beating on the tinted glass window! Suddenly a chocolate man burst out of the blue door, making a thud sound as the door hit the door stopper beside the brick wall. He wore an all-black police uniform with a name tag labeled Cpl. Brady.

"Is there a problem?" the officer asked as he pulled his .45 magnum from his waist and held it to the top of Elijah's skull. Elijah threw his hands in the air and attempted to sober up as fast as he could. But during the excitement, he felt as if he lost control of his bowels, and he closed his eyes in the sheer act of utter embarrassment.

Upon reopening them, the officer pushed his head back with the gun while screaming in his face, "Back up!" Elijah took a deep breath before taking several steps back in the opposite direction. The slamming of a car door forced his eyes to dart toward the police car. The reddish-brown woman had exited her vehicle and was now sprinting toward them with her gun at the ready position. In sheer terror the thoughts of what was to come grew inside him. However, it seemed as if his biggest concern was their discovery of one of his favorite habitual pastimes.

His throat became depleted of moisture as she asked Cpl. Brady, "What is going on here?"

"This boy was disturbing the peace. He was hitting on the window like a pissed-off gorilla," he said while squinting into his pistol's sight.

All of a sudden, Jonah's voice called out from the distance, "Officer, please don't shoot!" Cpl. Brady then looked up from his gun sight to see her running under the awning. "I'm sorry about my friend, he took today's attack a little hard and wasn't thinking clearly," she stated while standing before them both. The officer peered at her then looked back at Elijah with fire in his eyes.

"Do you think we should take him in?" he asked the policewoman in a low tone of voice. Seconds felt like minutes as Elijah glanced at the participants in the triangle of conversation.

"Well judging from the current circumstances, I think we will let you slide on this one, but you have to leave the premises," she said while holstering her weapon.

"Cpl. Brady I'd like to have a word with you indoors," the woman said before they both shut themselves into the school.

Jonah immediately burst into a spur of laughter. "Ok, now that was strike two," she said aloud.

"Shut your mouth," he snapped as they walked back toward her car.

"The least you could say to me is 'thank you for keeping some guy from blowing my brains out today," Jonah stated.

"It's cool though. I'll take you home," she exclaimed. Elijah's jaw began to clinch while he attempted to respond, but his thoughts were like an endless message of mixed emotions.

"You know, this is exactly why I asked you if you wanted me to go with you," she teased.

"Jonah, can I be honest with you?" he asked while wrestling with his speech.

"Sure, what the heck. Why not," she responded.

"I feel like when we interact it's almost as if you hold a wooden gavel behind your back. To be completely honest; the sting of the scorpion's telson doesn't hurt as much while I got my fix," he exclaimed while looking in her direction.

"I see, so is this why 95% of the time I work with you, you're on the pill of the week?" she asked.

"It's not 95%, more like eighty-eight. But the best solution for a man in a dark room is to turn on the flashlight of inebriation and I don't think you understand that" Elijah explained.

"That may work for you, but Jesus is all the light I need," she stated as they both entered her silver sports car.

"I guess everyone has their remedy for the storms of life," Elijah said as he buckled up his seat belt.

"Are you sure you have a remedy because it sounds like you are trying to fill a void?" she asked as she pulled the car onto the road. Elijah then sat back and turned on the radio, Jonah immediately returns it to the off position.

"Something smells like, ugh, check your shoes," she stated while engulfing two sniffs of air in the pith of cold silence, and gagging on the unpleasant aroma that stabbed at her composure.

"Uh, that's not what you think it is, I think I kind of pooped my pants when I was held at gunpoint," Elijah whispered while looking out of the passenger side window. Jonah then glared at him before bringing the car to a screeching halt.

"Get out. That's strike three!" she stated firmly and though Elijah attempted to plead he was cut off by her repeating the same cadence.

"If you stained my seats you will detail this car inside and out," she said in frustration. Elijah gave a deep sigh before opening the car door and exiting the vehicle.

He smelled the rubber burn as the tires whirled against the asphalt beneath them. Elijah's head began to sulk and his feet began to shuffle down the freeway as he prepared himself for his journey home, covered in his filth and adorned in a coat of shame he felt.

Chapter Four

"**Y**ou know what? I think today, let's just talk and not follow the schedule," Mr. Heartside said.

"Ok that's cool," Simone replied.

"So how are you feeling?" he asked.

"Well, I'm fine I guess," Simone stated firmly.

"Remember it's important to take your medications as prescribed," he said. "Though I know this may seem a bit cliché, I feel inclined to ask you for your safety; what are the voices telling you?" he asked.

"I try to ignore them, I've learned not to give it much attention," she said.

Her black leggings scratched against the cotton fabric of the chair as she situated herself in discomfort. The scent of sweet vanilla puffed into the air from the air freshener positioned at the top of a wooden shelf.

"Well schizophrenia is a serious, but manageable condition," he stated. "Many of the individuals that I have counseled have said to me that it is impossible to ignore them and that it is a daily struggle to maintain sanity," he said, "what exactly are your views on that?"

Simone played with her thumbs and looked down at the ground before responding, "Well, I feel as if as long as you don't believe what you are hearing and keep in mind that it is just an illusion, you should be fine," she stated. She brushed her black curls from her eyes and looked at the counselor's face.

"The hardest part you have to go through is coming to grips with the fact that everything you heard and did was in vain," she stated.

"I did not try to hurt anyone when I believed what I heard, but I stripped myself naked and cut myself with razors because it told me to, it said that I needed to be punished," she said as she raised her sleeve to show the whelped scars that lay on her forearm. The counselor sat up in his seat and pushed his glasses onto his face.

"My fiancée found me on the kitchen floor, passed out from the amount of blood I lost," she whispered as she returned her eyes to the ground.

"Do you feel shame from the things that you did during this period of your life?" he asked while sitting back in his chair.

"Well, my actions were definitely out of character," she said with a sigh. "When I was younger I was suicidal, but never tried to hurt myself. But I do feel ashamed for all the things that I did in vain," Simone concluded as she gazed into his eyes.

"Do you have any symptoms of depression?" Mr. Heartside asked while jotting something down on his plastic clipboard. All of a sudden, the room went pitch black. The windows blinds shielded what little light that peeked through there seams. "Must be a power outage," he exclaimed. "I have a flashlight in here somewhere in here," he said as he began to rummage through his giant wooden desk.

Simone attempted to gather herself, for she never really liked the dark. She often wondered if it stemmed from the emotional and physical abuse she endured as a child. At a very young age, she often recalled her father, drunk with rum and depression, locking her in the cupboard beneath the kitchen sink while she listened to the sounds of him beat her mother and making matters worse, their little house in the fifth ward of Houston had giant rats. She recalled hearing them gnawing and scratching behind the paper-thin walls that separated the two until her father released her from her dreaded cell. She stood to her feet as he fumbled about, grabbing her black leather purse and began to feel her way to the door. Knocking over Mr. Heartside's prized crystal globe to Counselor Of The Year, she found the heavy wooden door. As the sun's rays shone brightly through the building's front glass window. Simone made her way toward the exit in the corner of the waiting room.

"That's odd I don't have a cell phone signal," she said as she checked the time on her phone. "4:45. Well, I'm already late," she stated; "Elijah will understand." A dark blue van pulled to a screeching halt behind her as she walked to her car. Instantaneously, three masked men exited the rear of the vehicle. They grabbed Simone and she struggled to escape from their iron grip. She twisted and turned in a failed attempt to break free, as the streets seemed lifeless. His grip left a handprint on her light brown skin. One of the goons was bulky in appearance, she stared into his dark eyes for a moment before he punched her in the face. Leaking blood from her nose as they drug her to the back of the van, throwing her in with little regard for her safety.

"Don't rape me!" she cried as they slammed the door shut.

Chapter Five

Pain riveted through the soles of Elijah's black leather shoes and defecation began to cling to the fabric of his undergarments, forming a cake-like solution that soiled the rear of his trousers. It seemed as if elation had died into the horizon with the setting sun. He knew truly, that his subjugation to his euphoric bliss he longed to preserve had crumbled at its very foundation. While yearning for a chaser of his liking, a white truck whooshed by him. Its brake lights illuminated the shoulder of the street before him. He wiped the sweat from his brow while envisioning the lavish sensation of a steamy shower and clean clothing upon his back. He turned to face the driver inside the truck window. A familiar face brought a smile to the corners of Elijah's lips. It was his companion Cezar, he had been Elijah's close friend ever since he moved to the Camel's Port subdivision; he also happened to be the one that fed their upscale neighborhood with hemp that was sweet to the senses.

"When did you get a new truck?" Elijah asked inquisitively.

"Last weekend. Where are you headed I'll give you a ride?" he inquired while pushing his black aviators back onto his nose.

"I'm on my way home, but I honestly don't think I should get in. I'll ride in the back," he said while grabbing hold of the truck bed's rim. Elijah planted one foot on the tire and swung one leg at a time before easing himself down in a squatting position. Cezar then turned up his reggae music, blasting the soulful sounds of Francis Dixon as he gently pressed the accelerator and turned onto Paradise Lane. Elijah waved to Erin as they crept past him. Erin had just been released from prison for domestic violence and ever since had worked in the neighborhood mowing lawns for what seemed like spare change. Cheap labor meant more coins in the resident's coffers so no one complained. As they neared Elijah's alabaster house he prepared to hop over the postern gate of the truck bed.

"Is it cool if I come by in a few minutes? There's something I want to speak to you about?" he asked as Elijah walked up the driveway.

"Sure thing," he responded while holding up the peace sign over his back. Bewilderment consumed him when he noticed that Simone was still not home, sounding an internal alarm in the epitome of his gut. One thing he knew for certain was that she did not possess the virtue of patience. On previous occasions, she had dropped plans with family and friends because there was no forewarning. He slid in his key, opening the front door and heading up the carpeted stairs to the master bedroom. After flicking the light switch several times it became evident that the power was out.

You have got to be kidding me, he walked over to the window to open its velvet curtains, allowing a small amount of light to gleam through the window and into the avenue of the master bathroom. His fingers caressed the stiff plastic buttons that held his shirt together, undoing them one by one while looking into the mirror positioned upon the roof of his dresser. He touched the purple bruise on the left side of his ribs as his shirt dropped to the floor. He gave a loud sigh of sheer anguish as he removed the rest of his clothing, throwing his underwear in the wastebasket as he entered the bathroom. The sound of metal shower hooks scraping against a bronze rod accented the shout of water drizzling from the showerhead.

"Just enough water pressure," Elijah said to himself while getting into the tub. As the warm water embraced the hairs on his chest, he reached for the bar of soap and began to sing to himself; "Sweet baby I do love you, sweet baby my love is true." He then put one hand on the wall in front of him while bowing his head to allow the withering stream to flow over the apex of his scalp.

It soothed his thoughts of the atrocities committed outside of Beautiful Flowers and the troublesome worries of Simone and Sequoia. However, this rejuvenation of thought was short-lived as the dying stream perished from the plane of view.

While Elijah exited the shower he grabbed a turquoise towel embroidered with gold trimmings and dried himself thoroughly. Just as he began to wrap its dampened fabric around the corners of his waist he heard the faint sound of someone knocking at the front door.

"Just a minute!" he shouted while dashing into his bedroom to throw on deodorant and presentable attire. He hurried down the steps with fresh garments and an elegant essence drifting behind his path. As he pulled the door open Cezar stood before him.

"About time, a second longer and I would have heard roosters crowing," he said while pulling off his black aviators, revealing his hazel eyes and dense eyelashes. Elijah closed the door after he entered and walked behind his Eskimo flat-screen TV. It often was handy during unfortunate hurricane seasons but because the cable company manufactured the device, a late bill would leave its owner to twiddle his thumbs in the dark. Elijah grew up using archaic antennas and cords whose colors resembled your nearest ballpark's condiments. When he got his first job at Nugget's Cafe he decided that an upgrade was overdue and purchased his first Eskimo. There was no denying that the picture quality was the best in the industry. He unplugged it's portable battery from the lifeless wall socket and fitted it into the back of the satellite television. The luminescence of the contraptions loading screen filled the dimly lit room as he marched to the liquor cabinet, grasping his stash can and a Cuban cigar from the bottom shelf.

"Can I have a beer?," Cezar asked while Elijah sat down on his brown leather couch.

"Yeah, look in the freezer," he stated. Elijah pulled the lid off of the container, emptying two grams of ground hemp onto the glass coffee table. All of a sudden, the satellite television projected imagery through high definition. Cezar plopped onto the leather recliner beside him with a chilled brew pressed against his pink lips.

"Do you want some of this?" Elijah asked while preparing to combust the hemp blunt he held between his fingers.

"No, I'm good," Cezar stated after giving a hard swallow. Elijah then leaned back, propping up his feet onto the coffee table with his blunt hanging from the edge of his lips as he switched the channel to Live Stream News.

The screen portrayed President David Alexander sitting behind his desk in the oval office, "Hello America. Earlier today there was an attack on American citizens who simply wished to express their liberties and freedoms granted to them upon their birth into this great nation." "This act of terrorism is a direct attempt to strike fear in the hearts of the American people, and it will by no means be tolerated," the president exclaimed while staring into the camera while Elijah discharged a cloud of smoke into the air. "The conspirators behind this cowardly act of calamity are believed to be Luther White and his cult of Zodia extremists. Due to this, we have entered a state of civil war," he stated while poisoning his hands together with five points of authoritative power.

"Immediately following the attack, I ordered that all preliminary and secondary educational institutions be put on lockdown to protect our nation's future. At precisely 5:30 P.M. the military will have been deployed in all major metropolitan areas and the cessation will be lifted. All legal guardians will have until 7:30 P.M. to pick up their child before the contraflow plan is enacted in the cities of Houston, Philadelphia, Chicago, New York, Los Angeles, and San Antonio. Until then there will be mandatory security checkpoints at specific locations around the Houston area to ensure that no arms or explosives are entering our points of interest," the president exclaimed while returning his hands to their prior locus. "At 7:30 P.M. martial law will be enacted and all children not picked up will be turned directly over to child protective services. May God be with you, and God bless America," he stated before as his message began to repeat.

"The world seems to get crazier every day," Elijah said while turning off the television.

"That's kind of what I wanted to talk to you about," Cesar stated while placing the beer onto the coffee table.

"As you know already, I and my girl have been talking for a while now, but today's attack made me think about a lot," he said with seriousness ebbing from his tongue like a vessel immersed in troubled water.

"If I were to lose her I really wouldn't know what to do, I think I want to propose. I was wondering if you had any advice for me? `` he asked while staring at Elijah.

He then smashed his blunt into the coffee table as laughter bellowed from the crevices of his entrails.

"You picked the strangest time to think of love, but if that's what you want, I support you," he stated. Elijah then removed his phone from his pocket to check the time before asking, "Do you want to take me to go pick up Sequoia?"

"Sure," he responded after chugging the remainder of his alcoholic beverage.

"So what happened to your car?", Cezar inquired as they left the house. Elijah locked the door behind them on the way out.

"I'd rather not talk about it. But on a lighter note how do you think marriage will change your relationship?," Elijah asked as they entered Cezar's truck.

He pondered for a second, "It's deeper than sex and as real as the truth. Though commitment doesn't grow on trees. I can't find a better way to show her that I mean the three words I say to her at the end of every day," Cezar stated while backing out of the driveway. He slid back on his shades before he continued, "Honestly, I believe that it will get rid of the voice that tells her to slow down when her heart pulls me closer."

"You can't just get her a box of chocolates and call it a day?" Elijah inquired with a smile. Cezar then chuckled to himself while entering the highway and declaring, "You know, I might be jumping the gun a little bit, but I was thinking we could honeymoon in Mexico somewhere. Maybe sit on the beach with a few margaritas and watch the sun go down."

"It sounds like you put a lot of thought into it. I hope it works out for you," Elijah responded.

"How's your mother?," Cezar asked inquisitively.

"Old and dusty. No, but seriously, it's getting harder because her Alzheimer's is getting worse," he exclaimed.

"Last week she accused the nurse of stealing her medications, but it isn't like she can live by herself because she is classified as a fall risk," he explained.

"Man I'm sorry to hear that, but just remember hard times come in seasons and as the world turns, the snow will melt and a flower will bloom," he stated while putting on his turn signal and exiting onto the feeder.

Elijah peered out of the passenger side window in awe of the colossal Castle Rock Hospital of Houston. Then all of a sudden, a ball of fire shot out of one of the third-floor windows sending debris in every direction. Elijah jumped back with alarm as Cezar sped through the intersection afraid for their well being. They were nearly broadsided by a car before he jerked the wheel hard to make a right turn onto Fulton Street, forcing both of them to lean with the force of momentum.

"Did you see that!" Cezar squeaked as they flew through the business sector. The sound of bullets piercing the side of Cezar's truck echoed as the automobile slowly began to weave uncontrollably. It lifted into the air and escalated over the ditch, making Elijah scream at the top of his lungs. They then bounced into the parking lot of a Rent to Own furniture store before the truck came to a halt. Elijah felt as if someone had snatched his soul out of his chest as he peered at the devastated windshield in front of him. He heard the sound of Cezar cough before looking to his left and viewing the horrific sight of his best friend choking on his blood. Elijah's eyes grew to the size of cue balls while he watched his friend ebb into demise.

Suddenly, he heard a man scream in Latin. With terror in his heart, he pushed the truck door open and ducked for cover behind a cement pillar in front of the store. He poked his head around the corner and saw a short thick man approach the driver side of the vehicle with an assault rifle in hand and a hockey mask covering his face. The truck shielded his actions from view, but the gunshot stained the pages of Elijah's memory as blood splattered onto the cracked glass of the windshield. Elijah ducked back behind the pillar holding his breath and refraining from motion. The rebel then looked in Elijah's direction, but Elijah was relieved when he heard the man's footsteps move away in the opposite direction. He dashed into the furniture store sick to his stomach and afraid of his life. It seemed like his nightmare was just beginning as he crawled beneath the front desk and hid.

Chapter Six

The van's back doors swung open, revealing Simone as the three masked men hopped out of the automobile's posterior. Her hands shielded her face while she wept softly on her stomach. She savored the grains of salt in her tears as they ran down her ebony cheeks.

"I'm going to go tell Nightmare we are back," one of the goons proclaimed. The bulky man turned around toward her and removed the ski mask from his head.

"Get out!" he barked over the sound of a generator in the distance while brushing the hair from his dark eyes. However, Simone did not move. She was distraught and felt as dirty as a tail of a dusty broom. He tucked his mask into his pants and grabbed her by the leg, ripping her out of the van as she attempted to clinch the back seat before her. She thudded against the dusty earth at his feet, tarnishing her pink shirt. "Shut up," he exclaimed as he grabbed Simone by her hair, dragging her into the shanty house in front of them as she began to scream. Her feet kicked from left to right while she gritted her teeth with pain. She begged him to let go. But from the pain that shot through the top of her skull, it seemed as if he pulled harder with each petition, making her grit her teeth so hard they nearly cracked in its foundation. Her screams oscillated down the hallway as they entered a dimly lit room. The ceiling fan whirled violently, forging a draft that bustled the hot air and rattled the screws in its foundation. He grabbed a silver roll of duct tape from the shelf beside the dirty window stained brown with the filth of neglect and placed her in the chair positioned in the center of the room. He quickly bound her arms and legs as a constrictor would its prey. As he walked out of the room Simone's eyes scanned her surroundings with desperation. The flesh on her wrist bulged was the tape ceased to extend and gloom seemed to consume her as her whimpers fell upon deaf ears.

"I love the smell of fear," a woman said upon entering the room behind her. Chills surged down Simone's spine as the sound of heels clicking against the tile flooring drew near. She felt the cold touch of the woman's fingers grasp the sides of her arms, turning her around toward the door. It gave off an ear-piercing screech as the chair scraped against the floor. "I'm Daisy", the woman said after squatting down before her. "Sorry I had to let the boys have a little fun, the Family has to keep the soldiers happy. I hope you understand," she exclaimed. Her words made her sob louder than ever before as the ashes of pain rekindled their flame. "I wouldn't do that if I were you,

Nightmare doesn't like it when the captives make a lot of noise," she stated in a reassuring tone of voice.

"What do you want from me?" Simone inquired while gasping for air. "Well, we have what we need. We just need you to cooperate, but if you don't we have our ways of getting what we want, `` she responded.

Simone said while peering into Daisy's dark brown eyes, "I don't understand."

Daisy exclaimed while chuckling to herself, "If I had a nickel for every time someone in your position has told me that." "We're going to sell you at the slavers market, but don't take it personally, it's strictly business", Daisy stated as plain as copy paper.

"Please, have a heart. As a fellow woman surely you can sense my pain", Simone cried out with teary eyes.

"My heart is dead and gone, but don't fret about it too much. A pretty thing like you will sell for at least (17 K)," she said while resting her arms on Simone's bound legs. She lifted her gaze from the dark windows of Daisy's soul to see a fair-skinned man enter the room. He wore a navy blue suit and black tie, with one golden earring hanging from his ear.

"I thought I told you to help unload the trucks," he said in a thick Spanish accent. Daisy instantly rose to her feet and turned around with a sense of urgency.

She bowed the crown of her head and stared at the ground as she responded with a shaky voice, "I was just looking at the new captive, I'll be on my way now." She gave one look back in Simone's direction before leaving the room in awkward silence.

"Welcome to The City," he said while stretching out his arms with pride.

"My name is Nightmare, I bet you are wondering right now if the dice will roll in your favor. But what you probably do not realize is that I control the winds of your fate," he stated while removing his black jacket, revealing a butcher knife that rested in a leather sheath on his chest. He withdrew it slowly with his left hand, breathing deeply like a lion in its slumber.

"Where is your family?" he gently whispered in her ear while lightly dragging the blade down her cheek.

Her lip began to quiver as she turned her head away from the tip of the knife.

She mumbled with hesitation, "I don't know what you are talking about."

Nightmare's eyes flashed red with anger as his head slowly cocked to the side. He then reached into the pocket of his pants and removed a picture of Elijah, Sequoia, and herself dressed in fine clothing.

"I found this in your purse. So, lie to me again," he said while hunching towards her.

Chapter Seven

April 2nd, 2044. 10:00 A.M. Houston,TX.

Elijah's eyes drooped with exhaustion as he sat motionless beneath the front desk. His mouth was like desert sands under the merciless sun. He crawled out on bent knees with a hunched back that ached from the arch he held as he perched beneath the desk all night. After peeking his eyes over the top of the desk, using his perceptive analysis to sense any signs of oncoming danger. The sweet sound of silence assured him that the coast was clear. Elijah raised to his feet with trembling bones and walked toward the back door. Along the way, his eyes caught a glimpse of a small corridor. His feet stopped dead in their tracks when he saw the sun's rays pierce through the window, revealing a vending machine stocked with candy. Elijah placed his hands on the glass and stared at the powerless beacon of hope. Just as his stomach began to grumble, he grabbed one of the black metal chairs seated at the grey table and smashed the glass shield that protected its goods. The shattered glass crunched beneath his shoes as he slowly inched closer.

The chair clanked onto the ground as he dropped it to his side with his fingers widened with eagerness. With handfuls of Precious Brand chocolate bars and strawberry flavored gummies, he licked his lips with delight. He tore open the packages and engulfed it's contents one by one, leaving behind a pile of wrappers on the carpeted floor. Then he stuffed his pockets to the max and sat on the wooden counter and pulled out his dead cell phone. Upon realizing that it was truly a dead-end solution to the problem at hand, he tossed it onto the rose countertop. Elijah rubbed his face with the palms of his hands and pondered what he should do. With a shielded face his eyes began to water as the activities of the day before crept into his mind. Then it hit him like a bolt of lightning from a black cloud.

"We will go to Mexico," he said aloud," I doubt we will make it all the way there on foot though."

Although he was afraid to venture out into the urban jungle, he pulled up his bottom lip and dried his watery eyes while his feet marched towards his destiny.

The metal push bar clinked against the steel door, and he stepped into the moist air; the smell of garbage-filled his nostrils. Elijah held his breath until he heard a rustling sound coming from inside the container. As he stepped closer to it, a golden cat lurched from inside it onto the pavement. It paused briefly before scouring off between the hedges at the edge of the parking lot. Elijah breathed deeply and began to head to downtown Houston. The back of the building was drenched in red graffiti, it hung on its grey bricks like ornaments on the tree. But one aspect of the mural caught his attention the most. Labeled in the center of the wall was the tag of the infamous Angels of Death. They were most notorious for their recent turf war with the Slumlords, a high profile crack gang that originated from the Greater Heights, in which many innocent civilians were caught in the clinches of its crossfire. But the question that pestered Elijah's conscience was if they would still be active during a time like this. As his feet shuffled away from the furniture store he noticed a thick cloud of black smoke pouring into the air. Although it looked a great distance from his location, it was in the same direction as his destination. Elijah knew the streets of Houston well. Upon entering the intersection of Hogg park he began to truly see the destruction. At the gas station across the street stood an army of Slumlords.

They turned and looked in his direction, making Elijah's heart pound like a hammer to a steel anvil. He tried hard not to make a scene, proceeding to walk past them. But through his peripheral, he saw one gang member walk towards him with an assault rifle in hand. His pants hung to his knees and with one hand pulled the bandana wrapped around his face to the bottom of his chin. He stopped just a few yards away from Elijah's path, with eyes following him as he walked by. The air was still and tensions were stiff. Elijah then went back onto Fulton Street, trying hard to not give the gang members a second eye for reevaluation.

"I guess the underground never sleeps," Elijah whispered to himself. With each step, he drew farther down the street. His beating heart began to soften into a pool of uncertainty. The smell of smoke filled his nostrils, with the aura of dead silence. In a few miles, he discovered where the soot originated. Orange flames poured from the windows of the Brothers Delight meatpacking company. Inside it's gated facility hung a man in a blue suit and tie, whose body rotated slowly in the gentle breeze. Elijah stepped closer to the front gate, turning away with disgust that seemed to bubble within him. His consciousness became infected with the parasite of pessimism. It was almost as if Elijah believed his nightmare would never end. I've never seen a dead man that was not in a casket, and now I can certainly say I've seen my fair share, he thought to himself.

"They just lay there with their eyes open and cold lips, with no story to tell," Elijah whispered with a grim tone in his voice. Step by step he migrated down the asphalt path and stepped into Hogan Street. Just before he turned the corner he became alerted by the sound of commotion.

"Aequitas Equitas," were the words rang from a group of Zodia warriors as they turned into North Main. Each soldier possessed the mark of the number 12 painted on their shirts that were cut at the abdomen, exposing the bare skin on their stomachs. Elijah dodged across the street and ducked behind a building before peering back at the Zodia members.

"I have to be careful," he said to himself while looking up at the sky, "hopefully they didn't see me."

He sprinted through the buildings like a rat fleeing from its predator, but within a few minutes, his lungs began to burn.

"The ills of the smoker," he said aloud as he stopped in an alley to catch his breath. He placed his hands behind his head while breathing heavily through his mouth. All of a sudden he heard the sound of boots rushing across the earth. U.S soldiers adorned in metal-plated suits moved briskly towards him. He dropped to the ground and as their footsteps drew near, struggling to respirate as he laid on his stomach with his face on the alley floor, If they think I'm dead they will leave me be, he thought to himself. He tried hard to hold his breath as they passed, but curiosity killed the groundhog and that evoked him to see what was going on. He slowly lifted his head and saw a group of American soldiers trotting by in urban camo. This is not good, he thought after the last soldier ran by. Elijah pushed himself up from the ground and sprinted down the street. He was running off of the fumes of an empty tank, but the fact that he wanted to live drove him to push forward like a rocket toward space.

"That didn't look like regular equipment," Elijah gasped. As he drew near to the flower shop where the bombing occurred, he saw his car in view. To his surprise he saw a dark-skinned man with one hand to the glass, attempting to peer through its driver side window.

"Hey, get away from my car," Elijah shouted as he dashed toward the man! As the man turned around and threw a right hook at the bottom of Elijah's chin. After ducking beneath it, Elijah bumped into the car door and spun around with a fist of ire; only to be socked in the jaw by a straight right punch. Elijah fell onto his back and rushed to get up, charging for the man's feet. As he tackled him like a trained fighter his head rose underneath the man's armpit while lifting his weight from the ground and driving his back into the driver's side window. The glass shattered from the impact causing both men to let out a cry of sheer anguish, and Elijah instantly realized he had a laceration that extended from the apex of his left temple to the bottom of his cheekbone. Blood rushed from Elijah's face and covered his fingertips as he caressed the fresh wound, smearing the blood that gushed from his head to the skin surrounding the affected tissue. The dark-skinned man then staggered to his feet and pulled out a chrome pistol, pointing it at Elijah's chest. He turned the gun sideways and gripped it tighter with his finger on the trigger. Elijah was like a deer in the headlights, his frozen bones were like cold glaciers in the arctic caps. The crimson gore began to leak down the side of his face as he stared down the barrel of the chrome 9 mm pistol. Fear radiated from within him, as it tingled from his chest and dispersed throughout his physique like a can of spilled paint pouring out onto a battered canvas.

"I'm sorry I have to do this to you," the man exclaimed with seriousness destroying Elijah's hope that there would be a way out of this dire situation. A split second later Elijah saw a wooden bat crack against the back of the man's skull, forcing him to drop the gun and ebb to the ground below as dark-skinned woman in blue jean overalls and short natural black hair tied up in a red bandanna. Kicking him in the face, and struck him with the bat with intentions to break the strongest of bones. Elijah quickly scrambled to his feet and joined in the action, giving him a few additional kicks before a barrage of gunfire erupted nearby and he attempted to start his car but was left hanging onto false hope as the battery clicked to the turnover of a dead battery.

"We have to get out of here, stay as close as you can," she exclaimed while grabbing the pistol from the ground and sprinting off with Elijah leaving the car and struggling to keep up the pace.

She ran fast like a white rabbit at the greyhound race. The blood was still flowing from his temple and began to build up to drip from the bottom of his chin. Turning corner after corner, they rushed through the streets with their eyes searching for danger until they passed the last high rise building in the downtown metropolitan area. Elijah was at the back of the train trying to survive, watching the woman's hair flutter in the wind and she relentlessly charged beneath the underpass out of the area. It was not until they reach a shrouded grove of trees about a mile away from the war zone that they stopped to take a rest. When Elijah caught up to her position, he leaned against a small tree while desperately gasping for air.

"Thank you for what you did back there," he exclaimed. But the woman did not respond as she sat on the ground and breathed slow and heavy, only the sound of respiration rung in both of their ears. "So what do you want me to call you?" Elijah inquired.

"Call me Gayla," she said while standing to her feet to continue, "that cut looks pretty bad. There is a supermarket around the corner, ill see what I can find to get you cleaned up and hopefully they will have something edible as well. In the meantime, you should go look for some sticks to start a fire with."

"Be safe", Elijah exclaimed as he sat onto his button and leaned against the tree, wiping the dripping gore from his face and leaving a red stain smeared across his light brown skin.

Chapter Eight

April 2nd, 2044. 2:00 P.M.
The City, Guerra, TX.

The glass heels of Daisy's shoes clicked against the flooring with each step she took. The savory smell of a fresh plate of seasoned eggs drifted behind her as she made her way to Simone's chamber. She strolled past door after door with a swing in her narrow waist until she finally entered the last door to the left. Simone lifted her head from the ground with exhaustion that was permeated from within. She had been harnessed to the chair all night, with dried blood resting below her nostrils. She glared at Daisy's ice-white teeth, through a warming smile she threw on after entering the room.

"I thought you'd be hungry," she stated while sitting the plate down in Simone's lap. "Now before we start, let's get something straight," she stated while pulling out a black pistol from behind her back.

"I like you, but if you try anything funny I won't hesitate to show you how I earned my bones. Do we have an understanding?" she asked.

"Understood," she whispered with exhaustion while nodding her head.

"Fantastic!" she exclaimed with a voice coated in pep. She withdrew a dagger hoisted at her hip after returning the gun to its original position and sliced through the binds that held Simone in the seated position.

"Do you guys feed all of the captives like this?" Simone asked while picking up the warm plate.

"They typically get cold beans," Daisy stated while turning her head to the side. Simone then picked up the plastic spork and tore into the meal presented before her. As she gobbled it down Daisy gently ran her fingers through Simone's kinky hair and stated, "if you only knew what I had to do to not have one of my brothers to not follow me here."

Afraid to elude her touch she shifted her gaze from the near-empty plate and into Daisy's eyes and after a hard swallow she whispered, "What makes this occasion so special?"

"The Family transports captives to the slave market every three months, so we will have some time to get acquainted; but I just wanted some time alone with you and believe me, I always get what I want," she stated while withdrawing her hand from Someone's hair. "I know it may seem like we are heartless, but we aren't bad people", she insisted before continuing, "but our partnership with the Zodia is essential to our survival."

As her words swirled in Simone's ears she lost her composure and from the depths of her gut she declared, "Your family took me from my mine. Then beat and raped me like lawless souls of darkness, and you have the nerve to wash your hands in front of me like it never took place."

"You know I've always thought the touch of another woman could heal any pain," Daisy responded. Simone's eyes then widened with the evident truth of Daisy's intentions.

"I have to say I disagree," she exclaimed. The brief moment of honesty was abruptly interrupted by the wooden door swinging open, followed by an Asian man dragging in a pregnant woman by the arm. With blood running from his left ear, he pulled her into the room and professed, "watch out for this one, her husband bit me."

"Where is he?" Daisy inquired while turning around. "We executed him," he responded.

"Put her in room B," Daisy stated after turning back to face Simone.

The goon pulled her close to his side and said, "she'.s going here. It's Nightmare's orders." After the man left the pregnant woman in the corner of the room Daisy returned towards Simon.

"I'm going to see if Nightmare will let you be under my watch for a while," she stated while shifting her weight to one side. "You know I've never been one for love, but rest assured I'm going to make you mine," she said as she leaned in to kiss Simone. As she jerked her head away from her lips the pregnant women suddenly blurted out, "you know in the old testament the Bible says that homosexuality was punishable by death. I'm just telling you because it seems as if we choose to recognize certain parts of the greatest book ever written while turning a blind eye to the parts that taste bitter on our tongue."

Daisy stopped dead in her tracks, then licked her lips and looked in the woman's direction."The Bible is an outdated document," she exclaimed.

The pregnant woman crossed her arms then replied, "Isaiah 40:8 says, the grass withers and the flowers fade, But the word of our God stands forever."

"Well I'm bisexual so it's not the same," Daisy exclaimed.

"If you like same-sex it's considered an abomination, the subcategories are nothing more than man-made ways to feel special. I pray for your soul, homosexuality does not put you on the bus towards the eternal fire, not washing your robes in Jesu's blood and having no relationship with God does," she stated.

"No, pray that we don't sell you below value; two for the price of one," she said with a laugh.

"I'll be seeing you soon," Daisy exclaimed to Simone before starting for the exit. The woman put her hands on her stomach and broke the silence by saying, "Be strong, I know you scared and the truth is I am too. But you can find strength in our Father in heaven."

"What did you mean by abomination?" Simone inquired.

"It is the ornament of repugnance, it's another way of saying it's disgusting to God. It means to stink as if a musty person wrapped their arms around you," she exclaimed. "It was explained to me as a child that there is a desired way of healthy living God intends for us, and that shouldn't be in our diet, she exclaimed.

"The best part about falling short with God is that there is forgiveness, all we have to do is ask for it," she said before continuing; " Matthew 12:31 says, So I tell you, every sin and blasphemy can be forgiven—except blasphemy against the Holy Spirit, which will never be forgiven."

"No one will ever be perfect because our nature is to sin," she expressed before exclaiming, "when Jesus died on the cross he paid for all of our wrongdoing by shedding his blood to free man from his ultimate fate. But it's up to us to accept that payment."

"I can count on one hand the number of times I've prayed in my life. Can you teach me how?" Simone whispered while looking in her direction. A large smile crept across her ivory face as she walked towards her and grabbed her hands.

"What is your name?" Simone asked.

"Jessica", the woman retorted before closing her eyes.

"Abba, God of the heavens and the earth, we ask that you show mercy on us and towards our captors, forgiving us of all of our disobedience to your will. Help our captors to see the error in their ways," Jessica professed.

"Show the one who has no faith that your word reigns supreme in this life and the next, because you alone are the one true God," Jessica professed with shards spirit and fruitful passion.

Simone's eyes gazed up from the floor as Jessica began to grip her hands tighter. "Please give us the strength to not be afraid and to resist the pits adorned in temptation, and be with us. Finally, I ask that you bless my child so that it does not have to grow up in the jaws of barbarity. If it is my fate to be a slave I ask that you make him free, hold him in your hands until the day he dies; Amen," Jessica whispered.

"That was beautiful," Simone whispered.

Chapter Nine

Gayla stood in front of the Brooklyn Brothers supermarket with red brick in hand. Her black gloves separated the skin of her palm from its rough texture while allowing her fingers to feel every indent and blemish it possessed on its surface. While lifting her hand above her shoulder she launched it at the window like a pitcher from the home plate and hopped into the store like a ninja ready for battle. Watching not to cut herself on the broken glass, but since all the doors were locked she felt as if she was left with no other alternative. The confiscated pistol possessed two bullets that she hoped she did not have to use. The inside of the market was vacant, it was almost as if civilization had forgotten about it entirely and the inside looked as if a secret riot had taken place inside. Shelves were leaning against each other, and other empty. Goods, baskets, and everything that she was not looking for seemed to clutter the aisles like a landfill in a field of chaos. Step by step she made her way towards the store's pharmacy, holding the gun low with the wooden bat positioned as a shield and one finger on the trigger, she made her way through the store with a cold expression of an alert huntress, hardened through years of battle and savage warfare. She was about business and was on a mission to find anything that could be of use. The humidity inside the store forced her ebony skin to perspire and leak down her chiseled contour as her head swiveled from left to right looking for potential threats. The dark interior of the supermarket only seemed to heighten her sense of alertness, her ears perched to the sound of her black combat boots compressing against the ground with each step she took. She was determined to let nothing come by surprise, and nothing takes her down. It was her love for humanity that told her that the mission was worthwhile and with never having taken a life before, she had no intention of blood spilling due to her hands. Though in the back of her mind, thoughts generated of the potential scenario where the self-defense would come into play and how she would react.

When she reached the pharmacy department, she peeked behind the counter to see that some of the prescription medications were still on the shelves. After dropping the bat on the other side and hoping over the countertop, she heard the sound of fumbling pills in plastic bottles that made her reassume her defensive position.

Breathing deeply she followed the origin of the commotion to the back of the store and turned the corner towards the fire exit to see a caucasian man on one knee shoving pill bottles into a forest green backpack that rested on the floor. He threw up his hands in the air and slowly rose to his feet, expressing with a shaky voice, "please don't kill me, I am just trying to get medication for my son. He is almost out of all the prescription pills he has." Gayla then cocked her head to the side and squinted her eyes down the gun sight.

"You can have anything else in here, just please let me go about my way," he exclaimed. While lowering her guard she motioned her head towards the exit with a quick twitch that gave the man enough confidence to break the iconic statue of a plea for mercy and dashed for the exit without a second glance in her direction. While returning around the corner to the assortment of pills, she noticed a problem. She had no idea what would be beneficial, so she searched for the most infamous names of pain medication and scooped the pills into a plastic grocery bag before hopping back over the counter and searching the rest of the store.

Along the way, she grabbed what was left to bandage wounds, peanuts, a lighter, water, and a few cans of mixed fruit, but noticed that she lacked items to disinfect wounds. It seemed as if alcohol and peroxide were taken off the menu before she had gotten into the store. But it wasn't until she ventured into the back of the store and looked into the store manager's office that she found the golden goblet. Inside the middle drawer of the metal desk lay half a bottle of scotch, it brought a smile to her face and a sigh of relief as she reached for it and placed it inside the plastic bag.

"Thank you, Father God," she whispered as she made her way out of the exit in the back of the store and headed back to Elijah and the small grove of trees down the street.

Chapter Ten

"You're losing a lot of blood, we need to get you cleaned up," Gayla told Elijah as she sat the plastic grocery bag onto the ground.

"Is that really necessary, I think you're just trying to get close to me," Elijah exclaimed in a flirtatiously. Gayla rolled her eyes to the back of her head and scoffed at his failed attempts to impress her with fizzled words and a flashy smile.

"Look i'm not going to play with you anymore, before this country went to crap I was an emergency medical technician. You need to take my word for what it is, if you keep losing blood at this rate it won't end well," she professed while using her hands to gesture the seriousness of the situation.

With a heavy sigh Elijah raised his head to the night sky, "Ok, do what you have to. I really hope this thing doesn't leave a scar," he stated while reaching to touch the oozing lesion. Gayla's eyes morphed into pink sprinkled doughnuts before Elijah's dirty fingers had the chance to caress the skin on his temple. She slapped down his hand instantaneously with a heavy hand that moved as swift as a professional fighter.

"Ow," Elijah yelled as he glared at the imprint of vasodilatation she left on the crust of his wrist.

"Don't ever touch an open wound with hands that look like that. Look at your nails, they are filthy," she snapped. Elijah straightened out his fingers and examined the specs of black dirt beneath the white tips of his long fingernails. "Endospores and helminths might be in the dirt, you don't want those hatching like eggs inside you," she said while reaching down into the bag and pulling out a white t-shirt, rubber gloves and a bottle of scotch.

"Yea, I honestly have no idea what you just said," Elijah said with a bewildered expression.

"Don't worry about it. Before I begin, do you know if you are allergic to latex," she inquired?

"Not that I know of," he responded.

"Excellent," she said while pouring some of the liquor onto her hands and sliding on the gloves onto her hands before pouring more of the solution on them. Elijah silently watched as she continued to prepare to assess his wound. It seemed as if he became more convinced that she was telling the truth about her past life the more she prepped, eliminating all doubt when she removed a needle and thread from the white grocery bag, sterilizing the small silver needle as if it was his own hands she condemned just moments before.

"This is going to sting just a tad bit, but i need you to stay still," she exclaimed as Elijah resituated himself so that his back was leaning on the tree behind him with his feet stretched out onto the earth and his buttox planted to the patches of weeds beneath him in the grove. Then she slid the needle into his skin. He then tried to hide gritting his teeth as she gently stroked the cut. It felt as if his eyes began to lightly spasm, with each oscillation she performed with the touch like a feather.

"I bet you saw some crazy things as an EMT, I would imagine that this must be a cakewalk to you," he stated while trying to draw attention from the pain he felt succumbed to.

"Most definitely, but I loved it. I seen my fair share of nightmares and horror stories. But it was my job to make sure they lived to tell the tale. I don't think you can ever prepare yourself for what you will see. I would try me best and say a prayer for them as soon as we got the call," she exclaimed while focusing precisely on the lower end of the cut.

"What is the worst thing you ever saw?" Elijah inquired while trying to relax. Gayla remained silent for a few seconds, then took a deep breath and ceased to proceed in sanitizing Elijah's laceration.

Before glaring into his brown eyes she looked down at the earth before returning her gaze back into the windows of his soul, "We got a call on New Year's Eve that their had been an accident on 290 West. I knew that it was going to be bad when I heard the radio. When we got to the scene, the fire department was already there. The car was on fire, but the people were still inside it, a man with two children in the back seat. When you're put in a situation like that time is of the essence, but in reality we were both too late to save them all. We got out the kids first, thank God that they did not endure anything other a few bumps and bruises. I remember the little girl asking where her Dad was, so I told her we were going to get him out too and not to worry about it as I pulled her close to my chest with a reassuring hug. As the firefighters went back to the vehicle, the blaze got out of control. They told them to get away from the car, but one of them didn't listen and charged over to the car with ears of stone. He yanked open the door and pulled out his burnt body and dashed over to the ambulance just before the car exploded. The blast was so loud it hurt my ears, and shrapnel from the car hit a few of the firefighters that helped him carry him to safety. They screamed to me to get the children out of the area but it all happened so fast and I was still green. By the time I scooped them both up and ran in the other direction they caught a glimpse of his steaming body, fresh from the clutches of the closest thing imaginable to hell fire. He had third degree burns on the majority of his body, and looked like a melted candle stick with wax about to drip on the pavement below. I always wonder what the mental state of the children are, or if they had to go to therapy," she said while removing her gloves to wipe her watering eyes with the collar of her shirt.

"I can see that you are very nurturing. Are you a mother?" Elijah asked with sympathy in his words and affection in his eyes.

She sighed to herself and sniffled her nose before giving a hard swallow and putting on a new pair of gloves, "Once upon a time, but the pregnancy ended in a miscarriage," she professed before continuing; "when I saw the look on there face it left a bruise on my heart."

"I didn't lie to her, but had I acted sooner she wouldn't have seen it. All I could think of was if she was mine, I'd wiped the tears from her ivory cheeks but it seemed as if the rivers just never stopped running. The news later reported on the accident, saying that he had been drinking and got into an argument with their mother. He was so intent on proving a point that he almost destroyed everything he built. Selfish decisions will destroy any family," she exclaimed with words that seemed to pierce Elijah's chest.

He seemed to tune out her actions as she stuffed the thread through the eye of the needle like a master seamstress. It was as if a surge of past actions flashed before him, a bitter taste from the mixture of all the women he did wrong, but primarily Simone. It was like a sandwich she fed him that looked delicious to the eyes, but her conversation left an aftertaste that brought sorrow to his soul the more he reflected. He gazed at the filthy hands that caressed the girls he met before her, and all of the women that he crossed paths with at the club, even Simone's sister before he stooped to one knee in front of the woman he proclaimed he wanted to keep for the rest of his life.

"What's on your mind?" Gayla inquired while starting to sew the cleansed wound shut.

"I was just thinking, if a place like hell really does exist; there is a special place in the bottom for people like me," he exclaimed while lowering his head to the earth below. Gayla looked at his state of mind and physical disposition and lifted his chin with the tips of her fingers while shifting her tongue to protrude the skin just below her bottom lip.

"That's only true if you believe that John 3:16 doesn't apply to you," she whispered to him.

"You don't know me though, I've lied, cheated more times than a kid hitting the restart button on a video game, and denied your God for the majority of my existence," he professed while resituating himself closer to her.

She sighed to herself and looked him deep into his eyes while he watched the words flow from her dark brown lips, "I know but do you."

The moment was interrupted by Elijah's screaming in Gayla's face, "Get out of here, he's got a gun"! Gayla spun around like a twister from tornado alley, but was shocked to see the firearm pointed directly at her skull.

"I wouldn't do that if I were you," a man in an orange jumpsuit said while staring through the sight of his shotgun while watching her twitching fingers, though they ceased to inch towards retaliation and he confiscated the pistol. Seconds later another man came from behind Elijah and the tree, hoisting a pistol to his head in a similar fashion.

"How are you this lovely afternoon," the gunman inquired in Elijah's ear wrapping one arm around his neck like a boa constrictor about to consume its prey. Elijah's slowed his breathing due to the grip, and wheezed under the pressure that felt as if it would crush his esophagus.

"What do you want?" Gayla inquired with frustration.

"How nice of you to ask. Well you can start by handing over all of the weapons you two have, I don't care if its a stick you sharpened to pry the old meat from your pretty white teeth," the gunman who held Gayla hostage exclaimed. She began to reach for the pistol slowly with her right hand.

"Careful, I've never really liked jokes," the man near Elijah stated as he cocked the pistol in the awkward silence. She lifted it from her waist and gripped it by its barrel, then tossed it onto the ground before the gunmen.

"This is our only means of defense," Gayla exclaimed with irritation.

"Thanks for being a good sport," one of them stated in a peppy tone of voice. The man behind Elijah then let him go, giving him a shove forward so that he was positioned by Gayla's side.

"I'm really getting tired of getting held at gunpoint. I must say, this is getting rather oldm" Elijah confessed to Gayla; but she gave no sign that he even existed. He felt the man behind him begin to pat him down with as if he were searching for something of interest. He pulled out Elijah's wallet and confiscated the candies he took from the vending machine at the Rent-to-Own Furniture store.

"Well what do we have here?" the man asked while walking in front of the two of them, tossing them to the head gunman. "I am so thankful for your contribution to the Quondam Caged Bird Association," he said with a smile.

"So what are we supposed to eat?" Elijah inquired with a juvenile expression.

"That is a very good question. Tell you what, since you two were such good sports i'll make you nice people a heck of a deal. We will keep the candy, you can't blame us for that one though. You don't exactly get to trick or treat behind those dense bars and cement walls," the head honcho exclaimed.

"You got that right," his henchman exclaimed with a cheeky grin while spitting onto the ground. Gayla looked at them with disgust. Perhaps it was her gentle nature or simply just the fact that the country reeked with a bouquet of potpourri crafted from the blossoms crisis.

"How can you two live with yourselves. Isn't it bad enough we can't defend ourselves against these blood thirsty wolves, now you plan to succumb us to deprivation of the few goods we have and force us into deprivation," she professed with courage as if she was an angry drunk who had taken six shots of the strongest whiskey.

"You can always eat bugs, I hear the here beetles are pretty juicy. Just make sure you savor the flavor," the henchman hissed at her. "Now we can't just do them like that, after all they did do what we asked of them and I didn't have to waste any of my shells," he exclaimed while lifting the barrel of the shotgun in the air and propping it on his shoulder and continuing; "my friend Cecil caught a glimpse of a few squirrels in a tree this morning, fortunately for you I will allow you to have some of the scraps."

"How generous of you," Gayla exclaimed with objectivated sarcasm. Cecil puffed a rush of air from his nostrils and stood beside his acompinance. Looking at the corner of the white of his eye he asked, "So what's next Patrick?"

"I think you should take our two friends a little deeper into the woods to go get some sticks for a fire. I'll cut up the game and get the meal prepared for us," Patrick stated. Cecil twitched the pistol deeper into the grove of trees after pointing it at Gayla. As they both walked through the thicket of pine and oak trunks planted firmly into the ground, picking up the fallen branches and twigs along the way; Elijah asked to Gayla, "What does John 3:16 say?".

Gayla reached down to pick up a mossy limb and inquired, "You don't read the bible?"

"No, not really", he called back.

"For this is how God loved the world: He gave his one and only Son, so that everyone who believes in him will not perish but have eternal life," she professed while gazing into the distance in thought."

"So Jesus is the Son of God, I assume he has a father as well?" Elijah questioned.

"Well that's the funny part about the story. He only has one father and he is heavenly, though to hazed eyes it could seem illogical, `` she said as Elijah grabbed another twig.

"But just think about it. If a man has sin, how can he be the spawn of God. But Jesus never sinned. Some people think that there is a distinction between him and his father; but in reality they are the same. Jesus said in John 14:9 that, Have I been with you all this time, Philip, and yet you still don't know who I am? Anyone who has seen me has seen the Father! So why are you asking me to show him to you?," she exclaimed to the sound of the henchman spitting onto the ground once again.

"But how they both be the same," Elijah inquired with bewilderment.

"Well, try not to confuse yourself. There are two things that you have to understand before you ask a question like that. Number one, would a God who created the essence of existence be limited to the things that apply to us like time, space and location. You can't forget number two as well, if they have the same goals, aspirations, wants and desires are they not one body with different functional parts?" she asked.

"I guess i've never heard it put that way," Elijah exclaimed.

"You may hear people put a distinction between them, but I wouldn't pay too much attention to it. Have you ever heard how the story ends," Gayla asked him while the henchman turned an open ear toward her lips from her posterior.

"I don't believe I have," Elijah exclaimed.

"My Lord, Jesus Christ will set up a kingdom on Earth possessing peace and harmony called the Messianic Kingdom. There will be no weeping nor sorrow or even marriage for that matter; our sole purpose is to praise the Father and have eternal life," she exclaimed while looking into Elijah eyes.

"Are there any requirements needed to join this club of his," Elijah inquired.

Gayla chuckled to herself before responding, "of course you have to play by the rules, But if you learn what is asked of you, and you walk with God long enough you will start to see that it's impossible for you to ever be able to get it right all the time. If you were never wrong, you would be Christ himself walking right next to me. But don't ever let someone fool you into believing that they are Jesus, for the next time the Son of Man returns he will come for those who have met the true test in life; to have a real relationship with God as its described in Romans 10:9, "If you openly declare that Jesus is Lord and believe in your heart that God raised him from the dead, you will be saved."

"I would first work on that if I were just putting my roots in Christian soil," Gayla exclaimed while shifting her sticks to one arm to pick up another with one hand, stacking it on top of an armful of branches pressed against her bosom.

"That's enough for what we need tonight, let's head back and see if Patrick has those squirrels ready," Cecil exclaimed. As their feet marched back to where Patrick was Cecil broke the midst of silence with words that shocked the two flesh feathered wagons, "I'm sure glad we did not kill you, I may do my fair share of ills, but I believe what you said about my friend back their," Cecil proclaimed to Gayla before they entered the area were Patrick stood next to a stump with his back turned to them both.·

Turning around with a bloody pocket knife in one hand as he grinned and turned his head to the left and stated, "I've taken the liberty of cutting them into pieces. Have a look for yourself." "Yall will also see that they are in groups. I did my best to play fair," Patrick stated as Elijah dropped an armful of tree branches onto the ground. Gayla quickly strolled over to the bloody clusters of squirrel cuts with the fur still bound to its flesh.

"I want this one," she said while pointing to a pile of meat. Patrick chuckled to himself before stating plainly,

"I'm sure you do, but if you look on the ground you will see your piece of the pie." Elijah gazed at the earth beneath the stump to see the gory innards of the dead rodent. Gayla gave a hard swallow and began to fill with muffled rage as she said, "I'm not hungry." Cecil gazed at the heap of guts in the dirt, a black fly with green eyes buzzed frantically from one end of the pile to the other. It fluttered away as Elijah stooped down to pick up one end of an intestine with one hand. As he stooped to acquire his portion, Gayla watched her surroundings from the corners of her eyes, Patrick piled up the sticks and commenced to ignite them with a few pieces of newspaper, Celil stood in the distance with his pistol in hand; as if he was awaiting to see if they would really accept the handouts that they were dealt in exchange for a chance to live and consume a hot meal.

"Wait a minute," Cecil exclaimed after he spat onto the ground yet again, "they can have some of mine." Patrick walked over to the pile of wood and grabbed a twig, and he began to stuff the chunks of meat onto its far end.

"Very well, I see you all became friends," he chuckled. Gayla's attention seemed to be captivated on how quickly he performed the task. Your everyday store bought meat was acceptable in Gayla's eyes, but this was a wild rodent. In her eyes this was a whole different ball game and a violation to one of the cutest creatures to walk the earth. Patrick then started towards the fire that glowed in the darkness, with Elijah and Cecil trailing behind him to mimic his process. Being the last to move towards the stump that they were on top of. Gayla glared at his meal for the night. "Patrick, the fur is still on it," she exclaimed with hopes he would remove it from the equation. Patrick glared at her with a blank expression but did not respond. After sighing deeply at the lack of empathy towards her disposition.

"I'm sorry," Gayla whispered softly as she put on the first piece of meat. After her first few pieces she caught the rhythm of her three predecessors, but it was short lived. As she picked up his pace she became less cautious due to envisioning her stomach away from the ladder of famine it sat at the bottom of. When she reached for the last piece it slipped from her fingertips and landed in the weeds beneath her. Gayla exhaled heavily as she bent down to pick it up and shove it onto the edge of the stick, but stopped as the thought of all of the microscopic organisms that might dwell there; and left it behind unnoticed and join the others by the small fire. But something seemed suspicious to Patrick, and upon noticing that their was another piece by the stump, so he strolled over to it and added it to his collection before returning to the campfire. As they sat around the scarlet blaze with their meal hoisted into the flame; Elijah lysed the silence, "So where are you headed?" Elijah asked Patrick.

"Home, Dallas Texas," Patrick said with a grin.

"You're a long way from home, what did you do to get incarcerated?" Elijah inquired.

"I got caught trying to set my house on fire. I wanted the insurance money," Patrick casually replied. Gayla tried hard to muffle his giggles but unfortunately he failed, bellowing a roar of laughter that echoed off the walls of his steel gut.

"I'm glad you find humor in the situation," Patrick exclaimed.

"How did you get caught?" Elijah inquired.

"I had been scheming the whole ordeal months in advance. I tried to figure out everything, from where I'd live to what I would say. But what I did not anticipate was for a policeman to roll through my neighborhood just as my master plan was about to unfold. Long story short, he saw the smoke and came to the back yard while I was squirting more fuel on the flame," Patrick professed while laying on his side and switching his shishkabob from one hand to the other. "I was truly in a struggle, at night I mostly ate microwaveable noodles and canned meat," he continued while smiling at the recollection long hard memories, "Vienna sausages were my favorite."

"What about you?" Gayla inquired to Cecil

"Armed robbery," he exclaimed before exclaiming, "I've never been one for sad stories though, so I'd rather keep my peace."

"You all must understand that my friend here is a man of very few words," Patrick stated. "But in conclusion to what little has been expounded, a great man once told me there is a blackness in the hearts of all of us. If it isn't murder it's something else that is just as dark whether we are aware of it or not. The question is the person conscious enough to see it? That is my definition of self awareness, it simply shows the honcho in perspective that we have truly missed the bar and that we all need God's grace and mercy."

"I bet it really feels good to be out," Gayla exclaimed while attempting to change the subject.

"I agree, that had to be the longest eighteen months of my life. You definitely don't come out the same as you went in," Patrick stated. Elijah gazed at Patrick as he withdrew his stick from the flame. They watched him pause for a second with closed eyes before beginning to tear into the steaming game. Curiosity foamed inside of him like a well shaken soda, stories of the incarcerated seemed to always perplex him in a strange way.

"I've been to jail but I've never been to prison," Elijah exclaimed while picking up his shishkabob with intent to savor the roasted rodent.

"It's a rather awful place, they take a bunch of screw ups and lock them in cages, there's more prisoners than guards. Who do you really think is in control," Patrick asked. Without giving Elijah time to respond he continued his speech, jumping back into the driver's seat of their conversation. "I remember the night they brought me to the cell. There were 25 beds in one room, and trouble was always lurking," he said with a film of emphasis in his voice. "The guy who bunked above me was a Latino named Josue. I of course am a caucasian from an upper class suburb, people had fountains in front of their houses. But there, it's a whole different world," he exclaimed while Gayla began to eat as well, lightly smacked on the roasted meat.

"Josue told me the rules of the game, stick with your own race, watch out for the guard named Geralds, keep your head down and stay out of gangs if you're not in one already," he exclaimed to Elijah while savoring sweet memories of his conversation with Josue. "Once they see that you are affiliated, there is no turning back," Patrick said while pulling off a piece of charred meat at the end of the burnt stick.

"Man, I never knew it was that bad," Gayla gently whispered.

"Trust me my friend, it gets a lot worse than that. The third night I was there one of the cell mates got jumped after lunch. He was notorious for sprinkling bodily fluids on the toilet seat and leaving the scene like a bank robber who pulled bag over the head of his own country. I guess they just got tired of it," Patrick said with a mouthful of meat. After a few seconds of the combination of sounds from chewing and the fire crackling he joined in and exclaimed, "You have to think about it though. We only got one roll of toilet paper per week. If we are using a nice chunk of it to soak up a grown man's urine, i'm sure you can see how it could cause some of the guys to get a bit agitated. Nonetheless, he never did it again and when the guards started asked questions, it was funny how everyone instantly got a whiff of improvised amnesia," he concluded. "The guards were just gimps in clown suits, handicapped by their bigotry and dressed in garments no one behind bars took seriously. Sergeant Gereld was the ringleader of the royal jesters, he walked with a limp between the cells looking for bad apples that were up to no good. He always addressed us in a demoralizing manner. One time he shouted a Christmas list of racial slurs while rushing us to get out of the shower as if he was driving cattle to the slaughter house. We only got two baths a week, and frankly we only had enough time to get the good parts, but to do that you had to be on a mission. Do you catch my drift?" Patrick inquired. Elijah and Gayla nodded their heads back and forth like a bobble heads as Elijah laid on the ground with the remnants of his dinner laying in the palm of his hand.

"So, did you worry about being raped in there?" Gayla asked as Cecil chuckled to himself.

"Man I am not even kidding, there is not even the need that type of act because there are so many homosexuals. But I do not dabble on that side of the equation," Patrick exclaimed.

"On a serious note, the rehabilitation classes they required us to take within the prison's barbed wire fence did nothing. Barbaric order is the government of correctional institutions and violence is always customary. Now, Josue had been there a while and the longer I rotted behind those walls the more we became friends," Patrick exclaimed.

"Sounds like he broke rule number one," Gayla interjected.

"I guess you could say we both broke that number," Patrick professed between chews.

"So what happened to him?" Elijah inquired.

"Well, one evening I witnessed three Caucasian men pin Josue against the wall. Their stares laid inches from each other, im sure they could even smell each other's breath; personal space was non existent. I couldn't help but overhear the confrontation as I laid in bed with my back turned and ears fluttering for something juicy. At first I thought it was just a joke. But when I heard them ask if he had any affiliation with any racial faction as they scanned his body for tattoos, it was then that my thoughts bubbled with distress. I started to get a bad feeling of what was to come," Patrick stated while Elijah resituated himself.

"A week or two later I captured a glimpse of a crime against humanity that is still caught in my chest like mucus in your chest from an infection. We were about to be released for rec time and the infamous guard Toney Gerelds was placing shackles around all of our wrist and feet. Typically, there would be an acompinance with the person performing the task. We referred to that guard as the rifle buddy. They would always walk behind us, whistling, humming, or chewing a plug of tobacco as we scuttled to the jingle of the steel chains and heavy shackles. Our neon orange jumpsuits all possessed our cell block number on our tops and bottoms and I wore my Loco Carmesis like jewels on my feet, he stated while pointing to the white pair of shoes he had on. But on that day a rookie guard named Victor had the rifle and a reputation for pulling a pillowcase over his head in exchange for information he deemed useful to the advancement of his career. Although, some of those times it was at the expense of the well being of another individual. There was always rumors of the some racial party beating on someone after Victor strolled down the hall slowly to scout to see if the coast was clear. He cared nothing for the gangs themselves and no more for the people that represented them. The only race he recognized was the chase for currency. Promotion after bonus he hopped, skipped, and jumped down the aisles of the prison just in time to stop the occasional inmate using a contraband or sneaking in a late night cell phone conversation with a special someone in tones as faint as a whisper. I thought it was rather odd when only about half of the usual guys were chained and Toney told the line to get on the move on and pursued them from behind after giving a wink with his left eye to Victor. With only twelve guys left in the cell, I stood there a bit confused," Patrick stated.

"Victor approached me fast and hit me in my stomach with the butt of the bun. I fell onto my knees gasping for breath and rolled onto my back to see Victor's pink lips pursed with restraint as he gripped the gun tightener with veins bulging from his forearms as if they were bread baked with yeast," Patrick professed before continuing, "If it was a front to make me stay down, it was rather persuasive," he exclaimed.

A giant bubble of thought boiled from his dry mouth as he inquired, "Wait a minute, Toney and Victor were white men?"

"Well, Victor was more of a toasted honey glazed biscuit with a hint of a testosterone amplifier and Toney was hard nosed man whose reputation was darker than his complexion," Patrick hissed before continuing, "the bulk of the prison population was the non minority of American society."

"Interesting, please go on," Elijah exclaimed with infatuation.

"From the peripheral of my purview, six men of my tincture approached Josue and held him down. One of the goons pulled off a blanket from one of the bunks and shoved it into his mouth while another inmate struck Josue in the face and withdrew a razor blade coated in rust like sugar on the rim of a margarita. He stared deep into

Josue's dark brown eyes and sadistically stated, "I made sure to keep it in a cup of water for you."

Josue's eyes widened to their limit as they tore into his flesh, carving out the tattoos on his skin to the sound of muffled screams and pinned limbs frantically tapping softly onto the cement floor beneath him. It was something I do not believe I will ever forget", Patrick professed as Elijah gazed in awe.

"When the deed was all said and done, the four men who pinned down his limbs, then the stifler and the butcher rose to their feet as if nothing had ever happened. The cutter reached into his pocket and withdrew a folded piece of paper and handed it to Victor with the tarnished blade pressed against it. It stained the parchment with crimson callous as it pressed against the pleated page. After wiping his hands on the blanket gouged into his victim's mouth he crossed both hands over one another and stated plainly with a lack of emotion, "now you all know that Anemia runs this institution. Any other faction is inferior to the elite supremacist at the top of this food chain. With that being said, hopefully we won't have to do this again. But if we do, just know that your discomfort won't go in vain because your pain will feed fear into the inferior creatures that run through the cell blocks like roaches in this rotting cupboard. Victor backed away one step after another before turning for the exit without a glimpse of sympathy for my fallen companion," he exclaimed.

"Man that sounds rough," Gayla said in a soft tone.

"It's truly was a sight to see, but had it not happened I wouldn't be the man I am today. It wasn't until a few weeks later that I saw a posting that a prison ministry group was coming to speak about the greatest superhero to ever walk the face of the Earth," he stated as he noticed his words seemed to spark the attention of his audience, making Cecil give a small smirk as he laid onto his side and attempted to get some sleep.

"So I went, I had nothing to lose and I was looking for a sense of direction in the midst of a world of darkness. I had tried other routes before, but never truly felt as if they heard me, if you will. I sat in the room with eight others who were covered in tattoos, you saw some of everything in that prison but these guys were from my cell, so it will only tell you part of the story. I remember one of the three men gazed into one of the prisoner's eyes and examined his markings in awe. On the knots of his skull sat two eyes, one on each side. When the deacon asked what it meant the man responded, "So I can see everything, but I was a fool to think I was a superhero too."

Giving no response or emotional discharge, he made his way to the other side of the room and leaned in towards another inmate and asked him the same, but his answer seemed to jab him in the chest or it must have been that his breath was just simply repulsive.

"I got the black rays of the sun inked across both of my lips to remind me of my family that isn't welcomed here," he stated coldly while crossing his arms, forcing a flushed look to run across the face of the deacon that seemed to be pestered with questions.

As he near the last inmate before he began their ministry, a smirk to crept across both of their faces; "Im sure you knew what I would ask, what does the tattoo on your eyelids symbolize", the deacon inquired?"

"I got black rainbows tattooed on me so I will always remember what the rainbow's forgotten meaning is," he exclaimed.

"By far my friend, I must say that your tattoo is my favorite of them all," the deacon stated while shaking his hand and presuming to begin their presentation.

"Well I hope you all enjoy what he have to offer you this evening, I must say I'd say it's rather of a nice treat," he exclaimed while clasping his hands together in front of the projector screen. The image projected across his body, distorting the words it was intending to display until he stepped to the side and began to click through the slides one at a time.

"So let's get this started. I know we are running a bit late so I'll just try to hit the main points, but hopefully when we come back we will have something else for you to take away from this. First off, does anyone have any idea who the Greatest superhero to ever walk the face of the Earth is, or ever will exist in any form of book ever written?" he inquired.

"I'd throw my dice towards Jesus if I was a gambling man, too bad I've never cared much for the casinos I've been to," said one of the inmates with three roman numerals tattooed beneath his left eye, each totaling to the equivalent of mark of the beast. The deacon giggled softly to himself and began to continue through his presentation, not giving much attention to the man's attempt to disturb him of his element.

"Jesus is the greatest superhero, and that's one thing I want everyone needs to understand from the jump. To have only done good, but to be accused of accusations that were really just a manipulation of public opinion to achieve a selfish desire mixed with a lack of faith is what he was forced to endure. Jesus performed miracles like feeding multitudes of people, healing the sick and raising the dead. My favorite part about the last point on the topic of miracles is that his was different than any other like it's kind. If you have time you should read the story of Lazarus and see what I mean. Christ paid the ultimate price that no one could have atoned for because we as humans are soiled but he is perfect. He is the one true Son of God that was ordered to be put to death by his own people. Without him, there would be no eternal life," he exclaimed while staring directly at the roman numerals under the man's eye, moving his gaze into his pupils as if he was searching for something he knew was there.

"See, most people just hear that he was beaten and nailed to a cross; but what they don't think about is how demoralizing a death like that is," he exclaimed.

I sat there thinking to myself while he went on to discuss brutality of his death, *if I had been beaten to that extent and forced to go through the same end I would have quit, and for that reason I am glad that I am not nor will ever be God, because if I where for just a day mankind would have been screwed. The fact that the Son of God was killed so we could have eternal life, and in the same room as me stood a man with the mark of the beast on his face told me a lot about myself. My love for the people in this world must have not been the same as the love Christ had for us,* Patrick exclaimed with Gayla and Elijah still hanging on to every word.

"I like to think of it as someone who did you wrong in the past, and that person struggled to forgive them for whatever they did and marinated on it day and night, or even reflected back to it on occasion and got a sour taste in their mouth from just the essence of the thought, because if that occurs, I would raise a question as if the person truly forgive them for the wrong they have done. In a sense, it's something like you just said; if he can forgive us for not accepting him and not hold anything against us at all, then the least we should be able to do is try to move forward and do the same with others. But it just goes to show us that we aren't fit to sit in that seat of power, and like you my friend I share the same belief on the issue, `` Elijah exclaimed, forcing Gayla to turn her head and stare in awe of the words that were just stated.

"Before I went to prison, I was the pastor of a local church. I am a man of faith who has dabbled with what is right and wrong, but I would like to ask you a question that seems to burn within me," Patrick professed.

"Sure, ask away," Elijah exclaimed.

"Have you accepted Jesus as your Lord and personal savior, and if you haven't would you like to tonight?" Patrick inquired.

Gayla was instantly put in an awkward disposition. *Truly this man would have been touched to show a testament of faith after experiencing the things we have today;* she thought to herself as she held her breath and awaited an answer.

"These past couple of days have been the worst I have ever seen in my entire life, I don't know how I am going to make my life get back on track. But something tells me that following your God is my best shot at even getting close to what he has in store for me at this point, I've spilt my fiance's ice cream in my lap, wore a mask to hide the true color of my lips, and have fallen far from worthiness of the club that the greatest superhero to ever live desires to create," Elijah whispered while staring into the dying flame.

"Repeat after me," Patrick exclaimed while reaching for the two of their hands. "Lord Jesus Christ, I come to you today to say that I am unworthy of your goodness. I believe that you are the Son of the one true living God, our father in heaven. In my mind I have accepted that you were raised from the dead and your words are true. I give you my soul, my life, and anything of me you wish to use, let it be a testament to you that all can see, even if no words are said at all. Remember us on the day you return, and never let us get too far away to fall short of the Kingdom of God," Patrick exclaimed with Elijah's words following closely behind.

"So I assume the innards are for breakfast," Gayla exclaimed while looking at the pile of guts on the earth.

Patrick smiled at her with admiration and stated, "no, by the time you wake up we will be long gone. You can have them if you like, and I'll be sure to leave your possessions as we took them before we depart."

Gayla smirked in a reassuring tone of voice, "I'll believe it when I see it. I've learned not to put my trust in mankind, because they are bound to slip if you stand on the confidence they drop in the palms of your hands."

Giving a hard swallow Elijah got up from the ground and said, "I'll be back in a few minutes I'm going to go take a walk." As he walked into the darkness, leaving Gayla and the others behind to find ease of mind. But on his way into the woods his ears perked at the million dollar question.

"You never told us how you all managed to get free?" she asked.

"The Zodia attacked the prison, killed the guards, and demanded we all join them and worship the stars. But Cecil and I made a break for it as soon as we could, why turn away from a God like ours?" he asked.

Chapter Eleven

As Elijah stepped into the street, analyzing the man he used to be and what he would promise to never do again. He stuck one hand into his pocket and with the other hand he rubbed the scalp of his head. He exhaled heavily with a heart weighed heavy with emotions that diffused through his veins like oxygen into his capillaries. He felt them rush back and forth through his skull with each beat in his chest, making his nose feel as if it were stuffed with wet cement, a sickening congestion. He turned his head to the side and stared at the vandalized buildings of the city he once called home. His feet stepped down the road of destruction, with a mind filled with worry and regret, his lips began to quiver.

Stuttering words that felt like futile speech, "God, I haven't prayed in a long time, but I don't know what else to do. So I'm going to pour out my heart, and all I ask that if you are real, that you listen and do what you have to do to make a difference in my situation." Elijah's feet stopped dead in their tracks as he took one more deep breath while hanging his head before beginning to commence his walk with God.

"I don't think I'll ever understand how someone could love me, even Simone? I cheated on her at least five times. There was a Hispanic woman from work, but I feel like that was just throwing dirt into an empty grave. No life in my body and the same for her, we were just hungry to feel. I took advantage of her, and we both knew it; but to her I was Rico Suave," he exclaimed while looking towards the night sky, to see the stars amid the powerless light post that stood like dead beacons towering above him.

"That name use to boost my head up higher than a bag of ecstasy, but now it seems like a black stain on my soul," he professed.

"How could anyone want to be next to someone as vile and putrid as I?" he stated as pain like a nail went into the right side of his heart, pouring out more emotion that perforated from the seams of his wound.

"I wake up in the morning and hate my existence, I think back to that island girl, Cidni; and all that I put her through. I was deceitful, lustful, greedy, unmerciful, and selfish. The hole in my chest ate everyone and everything it could to fill the void, so she was just a passerby that got sucked into the black pages of my history that even I dread to read. I was a slave to lust, it wiped me with a Gladiator's Retarus that tore into my flesh; spilling lies onto the people beneath me," he said after exhaling heavily as another nail sliced through the flesh in the foundation of his heart. His vision blurred as a tear appeared in his right eye while he reflected on the man he used to be, while his nose gave way to small sniffles that accented the sound of his footsteps. The small drop drizzled down from his long eyelashes, down his light brown cheeks, until it splashed onto the cement beneath him, leaving behind a watermark.

"How could someone want to build something with a monster like me?" he asked in between distant gasp.

"Monster's have no emotions, they care nothing for the people in the world around them, and have no smudge of compassion for the sanctity of life or how anyone else in their life feels. They are zombies and vampires that sap the life out of everyone they see with it in them. What makes me different than the Zodia? Sure yea, they kill mothers; but to you i'd say i killed them too. Caprice was a prime example. I leached her dry, sucked all of the life from her rose colored lips and left her family at home like a ripped piece of paper that I licked the ink from before I balled it up and threw it over my shoulder. That man was furious, and I didnt care that he kicked her out because I had Simone at home to keep me warm. You would think that after all these years this kind of stuff wouldn't still be on my brain but it is! I live with regret and I am haunted by the darkest shadows of my past. I'll never be looked at the same way, because my blood has dried on the flowers and their hasn't been a rain hard enough to wash it off and I don't think there ever will be," he exclaimed.

"But that's besides the point, I get sick when I look in the mirror. I see a man with a head that was split in two, glued back together, and forced to look at the scar his life printed on his face from his past. It's invisible to the naked eye, but a closer look at my soul and anyone can see that I am in critical condition. It feels like i'm on a road of destruction, or if i'm not it sure seems that way to me. The spewed guile has me low on bodily fluids, the lust left my skin charred, the deceit showed me that I was nothing more than a crocodile under water; I cared little for the women I stole from other men, and when they were in need I neglected them because I had my fill of their fruit," he said.

"So can you tell me, how on earth can someone desire to stay in my life with all i've done? When I look into the silver goblet, I see a fiend to feel something other than pain, and I reached under my wooden mask to get the itch I couldn't scratch, but my skin flaked as it came off like layers like cake. I would peel back the falsified face to reveal the monster I was and when I found a damsel to my liking, she would be mesmerized by solid black eyes that glittered like gold as I attempted to devour their soul because mine seemed non existent. I thought I knew who I was, but I guess it never really dawned upon me until now," he professed softly as the final nail pierced through the left side of his heart.

"If anyone could love me, can you put them in my arms. If you know what love is, can you teach me how? So that way, maybe I could love them as much as humanly possible. Can you show me who you are, and take my filthy soul and craft it into what you see fit, will you be the carpenter of my life?," he inquired while opening his palms to the sky while they dangled at his side. After hanging his head once more with slight sobs and immense sorrow, he turned his head to an angle to see a church on the corner of the street with illuminated stained glass windows perched at the top of the building. He dried his pink eyes and wet cheeks as he made his way across the street, pushing open the door of the chapel to enter a dark white tiled lobby. A silver water fountain rested in the corner of the room near the entrance of the women's restroom.

When he pushed open the door he was surprised to see a man dressed in a black suit on both knees, surrounded by a shroud of candles that were clustered around the pulpit to illuminate the front of the church.

"Well hello, is there anything I can do for you," he asked Elijah in a lightly cheerful tone. His red tie accented his cream shirt beneath it, and the candlelight waved illumination over his back. Elijah stared at his grey hair and wrinkled face as he walked down the center aisle towards where he sat in the middle of a wooden pew. He placed his hand on the back of the row in front of him and rested on the velvet cushioning padding their dark brown wood.

"What brings you into the house of the Lord?" the man inquired.

"I was just taking a walk and saw the lights. Why are you here?" Elijah asked him with a perplexed expression.

"This place is comforting in my time of distress, it's all I have left. I've ushered here for about 13 years," he exclaimed with a smile.

"You aren't married," Elijah questioned while turning his gaze from the dimly lit floor boards to the man's smirked expression.

"My wife died many years ago in childbirth, unfortunately the child was lost as well. So many years, I spent life wasting away in the bottom of a bottle. I was angry at the world and at God, and for a long time never understood why he took away the one person I thought I would spend the rest of my life with," he stated while leaning forward and putting his hands together; interlocking his right hand around the base of his thumb.

"So how did get over it. You seemed to be dealing with it much better now, or that's how the picture looks from this angle at least," he professed.

"I am dealing with it better now. I haven't had a drink in years, but I had to come to a few realizations. Life is in God's hands, so who are we to say who should and shouldn't die and eternity in the world we live in would be hell on earth. So I see death differently now, I dont recomend suicide but i've been down that road as well. But to be taken and expire isn't all that its put up to be, death is more of a gift to us. It's selfish to want to keep someone here because you love them, because I assure you God loves them more. On the other hand, I had to see the selfishness inside of me in the desire to keep them both with me. I cried the night I heard that sermon and begged the heavenly father to forgive me for being angry with him, it was a fight i'd never win no matter what I threw into the air. It was a test, and I passed but only after the biggest failure of my life. Thirty six years of bitterness that corrupted my soul from within, but God's way of dealing with guilt is forgiveness," he exclaimed while looking into Elijah's eyes.

"During my walk I wrestled with how anyone can love me with the things that I have done. So how could God love a man like me to even care about what I go through," he inquired to the man with small swirls circling in steaming emotions.

"Well lets just see," the man exclaimed while reaching for one of the books in front of him. After licking the tip of his finger he flipped through the pages and handed the book to Elijah and exclaimed, "read this."

"Job 3:20. Oh, why give light to those in misery, and life to those who are bitter? They long for death, and it won't come. They search for death more eagerly than for hidden treasure. They're filled with joy when they finally die, and rejoice when they find the grave. Why is life given to those with no future, those God has surrounded with difficulties? I cannot eat for sighing;my groans pour out like water. What I always feared has happened to me. What I dreaded has come true. I have no peace, no quietness. I have no rest; only trouble comes," Elijah said aloud before handing the book back to him. He swiped through the pages like a smartphone before putting the book back in Elijah's hands.

"Here is another eye opener," he exclaimed.

Holding the book closer, Elijah's eyes widened as he thought he read what the man was trying to say; "Romans 14:8, for if we live, we live to the Lord, and if we die, we die to the Lord. So then, whether we live or whether we die, we are the Lord's," he exclaimed while sitting the book down slowly in his lap.

"There is one more. Everytime I read it cracks the stones in my heart," he exclaimed while grabbing the book and performing the same routine.

"Isaiah 43:2, When you pass through the waters, I will be with you; And through the rivers, they shall not overflow you. When you walk through the fire, you shall not be burned, Nor shall the flame scorch you," Elijah said aloud. "I don't get it," he exclaimed.

"Even in my anger and bitterness at the one that gave me life, he was with me. It tickles me to think of how big of a fool I truly was," he exclaimed before continuing, "like I said, it was a test. He loved me, and always will so he never left my side."

"He loves you too; it doesn't matter what you did in your past or what test came your way," he finished. Elijah looked into the man's pupils and handed the book back to him but he held up his hand to reject it. "Keep it," he exclaimed.

"Thank you," Elijah responded in a soft voice while holding the Holy Bible in his hands and staring at its black leather.

"I have to go now, but I wish you the best. I really appreciate your words of wisdom, "he exclaimed.

"No problem, I'll be praying for you brother. Take care, "he said while reaching out his hand towards Elijah. After giving him a firm grip he rose to his feet and walked down the aisle with a holy weapon in hand.

Chapter Twelve

Gayla slept on the ground with hands tucked beneath her head as she dreamed of living color. She dropped into the darkroom, landing in a wooden chair with a desk in front. Above her head shone a bright spotlight that illuminated its immediate surroundings. As Gayla looked around the room she noticed a wormhole opened in the ceiling, dropping a blue man onto the table before her. From behind his red shirt that possessed a large yellow smiley face with unfilled eyes, he pulled out an oversized hot dog, loaded with mayonnaise. It seemed almost as if she seemed nonexistent by the way he paid her no attention. With each colossal sized chunk he shoved down his throat, the more the mayonnaise got around the corners of his Royal blue lips; it dripped down onto his baby blue and white striped pajama pants leaving a white clump of condiments on it satin fabric.

"Excuse me," Gayla exclaimed while raising one finger in the air in an attempt to get his attention. His eyes shot open to an obnoxiously abnormal size, then he turned his head to face her before spinning his body in her direction and throwing the hotdog behind him and straightening his baby blue sleeping cap.

"Well hello madam," he exclaimed after sticking out his pink tongue and licking the condiment from his lips like a dog who just finished a bowl of hot gravy.

"Who are you?" Gayla inquired.

"I go by a lot of names, but let's just keep this as simple as we can. Call me Meme, nothing more nothing less," he exclaimed.

"Let me just cut to the chase and not hack around the bush with a pickax. You have a decision to make my dear," he stated while reaching into his pocket as if he were searching for something deep in its depths with his eyes pointed diagonally towards the bright light.

"Ah hah, here were are," he said as he removed a black wand and flicked it at the floor below, making a red cloud of smoke that engulfed his body. Gayla jumped back at the sight but leaned back in when it cleared and she saw him once again but this time he was draped in a black cloak as if he had to be ready for his grand finale.

"So if you look around you will see three doors," he exclaimed as if he were presenting exhibit A while flicking the wand behind her and appearing from the red smoke beside it. "You can try, but you won't because you can't, this door is unfortunately locked my lady," he professed.

"What's behind that door?" she inquired.

"Oh, a little of this a little of that, but mostly pain. Not a scary movie, It's your past and your soon to be present, there is no going back," he stated while putting his arms behind his back, leaving the wand sticking out from behind his side", he stated.

"There is no going back?" she questioned with a puzzled expression.

"Yea, I don't think I need to explain why. Typically most people just accept this and move forward because you would be wasting your time trying to pry it open, I welded it shut," Meme said rudely and finishing with a smile before he vanished into a cloud of smoke and appearing on the wooden desk again.

"You sure are an active creature," she exclaimed.

With a cartoonish alarmed expression he exclaimed with a hint that he had taken it as an insult, "my princess I am not a creature, I am a character, simply a...," he professed before stopping dead in his tracks to calm himself and reroute to a different subject with the clearing of his throat and shaking his blue head before straightening his sleeping cap on his head.

"As I was saying, there are two other options. But you won't like one and the other has potential, but that's the test you will face in life. Can you swallow your beans without making a bigger mess of the spilled milk," he said while two different lights appeared over two different doors behind him.

"On side B we have another decision," he said while disappearing into a cloud of smoke and reappearing with a trident in one hand and a crystal ball in the other. Gayla stared at the red light over the door, something behind it beat against it; but the chain kept the monster behind the door.

"What is that?" Galya inquired with fear in her voice. Meme then chuckled to himself.

"That's opposition, rather disgusting really," he insisted as a large claw stretched from behind the chained door.

"Do not tamper with it. Now, revenge is a funny thing, who does it belong to is the question I pose?" Meme asked while swirling the trident over the crystal ball until Elijah's face shown in it.

"Why is...?" Gayla started before being cut off by Meme in mid-question.

"Ah ah, I wouldn't even mention that name if I were you, you're asking for a fall. Now, where were we? Oh yes, door C," he said while vanishing again into a cloud of red smoke.

"This is perhaps the better option for you," he exclaimed as he opened his cape and released four doves, striking his wand to release an orange beam at the last to make it turn into a caucasian man who fell onto the floor and disappeared when landing into an aura of sparkling dust. Then the dove appeared in her fingertips with her eyes gazing on it. She stroked the top of its head as it ate the seed that appeared in her hands as well.

"I won't tell you what will happen if you go in there, but just remember it's never too late to catch a dove," he exclaimed while poofing again into his original attire.

"But what about Elijah," she asked, and immediately fell into a hole in the floor. She tried to grab hold of the edges of the hole but was sucked into blackness as it closed over her while Meme waved a cheerful goodbye.

As Gayla jumped out of her sleep, she awoke to Elijah wrapping the pistol in the fabric she once wiped his wound with.

"You ok?" Elijah inquired.

"Yea, I just had a weird dream," she exclaimed while putting her hand on his forehead and rubbing her dark brown eyes, exhaling heavily in relief to see an end to her slumber. "So what's your plan?" she inquired.

"Survive," he stated plainly while placing the bible on to of the pistol before folding up the sides of the garment.

"Mind if I join you?" she asked.

"If you want to tag team in this deathmatch you'll have to keep up with my pace," he said as she rose to her feet and brushed the dirt from the back of her pants.

"I guess those guys told the truth," she exclaimed as she looked around her to see the gun but no sign of Patrick or Cecil.

"Yea, let's just hope we don't have to dance with death again. I'm getting tired of getting held at gunpoint," he professed.

"I'll be sure to have the next aimed at me," she exclaimed as she picked up her bag and they walked out of the grove into the rising sun.

Chapter Thirteen

April 22, 2044. 6:00 p.m.
The City, Guerra TX.

Nightmare stood in a dimly lit bathroom with the moon's luminescence etching its way through the dirty glass window above the bathtub. He stared into the mirror with a towel wrapped tightly around his waist while the sound of a running faucet accented the noise of him tapping a straight razor in the sink that held the shaven hair from his face. As he turned his head to the side, to check the other side of his face to see a chinstrap of shaving cream. Once the razor had been washed in the warm water he poised it to his face once again, humming his favorite tune he heard his father sing to him as a child. It was a cold tune, a symphony of madness in murder. As the Underboss of the Family, Nightmare was responsible for taking more lives than he could count, but it was justifiable in his eyes. For when he lived in Mexico as a young boy his dad had taught him the rules of his trade. His dad was the Don, and a man of great respect throughout his country of Mexico.

While he hummed the soliloquy of sadness, he rubbed the smooth skin of his left cheek before washing his face and reflecting on the sweetness of his childhood. His father was never much for emotional expression but the love he did show transcended into Nightmare's heart. He often recalled short talks he had with the Don that taught him valuable lessons in his life. Talks that altered the way he looked at things like drugs, women, money, power, and later life.

"In the world we live in these things are like candy. Once you pick one up and try it, it's hard to only taste it's essence one time," he recalled the Don stating while he sat in a chair in front of him with an assortment of drugs placed before him. As he drifted deeper into recollection with more memories dancing across his brain as his thoughts stood on hot coals with nylon socks.

"Have you ever done drugs?" his dad asked him. After a few seconds of silence, he pushed the packages of drugs towards his son and exclaimed, "I've tried them all. So id is a hypocrite if I told you not to do them, but I will tell you what they do, and afterward, if you want to try them we will try them together." Although he was just a child, the freedom to this door was open for him to decide; and for that reason, he never used substances, but drank after the atrocities he committed in the Family's name.

In truth killing was something he never liked to do, the Don would always say to him; "violence is the last option. Only use it to protect yourself and to protect the Family." All in all, that philosophy had enabled him to be a Soldier who gunned down the men who waged war with their mafia, and the Underboss who ordered men to be made into fajita meat to send a warning to the governing body that they were not playing games with them. A wicked smile crept across his face as he reflected how their voice sounded once they had figured out their favorite restaurant served them their colleague on a steaming platter. Nightmare's home was in Texas, Mexico belonged to the Family, in truth, there was hardly a place the sun did not shine that the Family did not reside. As he grabbed a pink towel to dry his face there was a knock on the bathroom door.

"What is it?," Nightmare called out.

"The Don is here to see you," a man's voice called back from behind the door.

"Ok, I'll be out in a few minutes," he said. He flicked his fingers in the sink to throw off the water dripping from his fingertips and exited the bathroom to put on his clothes. As he dressed he heard Don's voice grew louder as he approached Nightmare's room. The aura of commotion made Nightmare rush to put on his attire, before long it sounded as if they were a finger's length away.

"Get out of the way. I changed that boy's diaper, he doesn't have anything I haven't seen before," he exclaimed in his thick Spanish accent. Just as Nightmare slipped on his pressed black slacks the door burst open and the Don walked in.

"Nightmare, you have more security than an airport. How is it going, son? I've missed you," he exclaimed while stretching out his arms for a hug.

"Papa!," Nightmare responded while meeting him near the entrance of the room, wrapping his arms around the Don and pressing his bare chest against his suit. He felt Don's lips kiss his forehead as he did when he was young.

"I brought your cousin with me, Pablo. He is my new Consigliere and I am pleased with his progress," the Don professed. Pablo then approached them with his hands clasped over his groin as he entered the room in a maroon suit and black tie.

"I like the suit," Nightmare said to his cousin Pablo while reaching out his hand to shake.

"I know you do. I like it to," Pablo exclaimed while popping the collar of his shirt and rolling his shoulders forward; ignoring the hand extended to him as if he was blind.

"I came to talk business with you," the Don said to Nightmare.

"You should have told me you were coming," he professed back.

"You know I don't trust cell phones. You shouldn't either," he retorted.

"The boss is right on that one," Pablo said in a co-sign that sickened Nightmare's stomach.

"Let's play some bones, I thought dominoes would be a good mood setter," the Don professed.

"Sure thing," let me finish putting on some clothes first.

"Excellent, I'll be waiting downstairs for you. Be sure to bring Daisy with you", the Don exclaimed while they left the room. As he walked down the steps with Pablo they passed the bodyguard standing by the door.

Pablo stopped dead in his tracks as one bodyguard's eyes yes met the Don's. "I'll cut out what binds you to this family if you ever look at the Don that way again," he exclaimed in a serious tone.

"It won't happen again sir," the man stated in a shaky voice; forcing the Don to look back from the middle of the staircase.

"Pablo, let's go," he yelled. When they reached the bottom of the staircase they found another soldier leaning against the wall, dressed in a black v neck and dress pants.

"Bring us something strong to drink," the Don exclaimed before continuing, "Four shot glasses and something strong".

"Make that three, I'm going to pass on this one boss", Pablo said to them both. After glancing at Pablo he turned back to the man and continued to walk down the hall. They entered a small room filled with leather couches and a table positioned in the center, with chairs positioned beneath it. As they sat in the assorted chairs at the table the Don pulled out a cigar and poised it to his lips. Pablo then pulled out a box of matches and lit it for him, exhaling the smoke and removing it from his lips to reveal its wet tip.

"Always remember Pablo, violence should never be the first answer. I built the Family from bribes and business, it wasn't until resistance from our rivals and prices hanging over my head like the blade of a guillotine that violence came into play," he exclaimed while he tapped the cigar over a nearby ashtray.

"I know boss, it just simmers my nerves to see someone disrespect you," he professed.

"I have to ask you though, how many deaths are you responsible for?" Pablo inquired.

"More than I can count. The life we live puts us in predicaments where you have to do what you have to do," the Don exclaimed as Daisy and Nightmare entered the room; sitting at the table with Don and Pablo.

"You came just in time. I was just sharing a few of my personal stories," the Don exclaimed to them both.

"How are you doing Daisy? Seems like we haven't talked in ages," he then professed. Daisy's ivory cheeks blushed in the dimly lit room, acknowledging him in a smile that warmed his heart.

As they shuffled the dominoes on the table the Don leaned forward and stared at the newest members of the group and exclaimed, "I want to talk to you about our cargo. I've been getting reports of bumps and bruises found on the men and women that leave here, so let me be clear. Be sure to tell your men to watch how they handle the new slaves," he exclaimed.

"Yes sir", Daisy said while looking into Don's eyes. As they divided the dominoes up each player took seven; leaving a pile with five in it. As the game progressed Nightmare watch his dad closely, knowing him as a world-renowned cheater at the board and card games that they played.

"So how do you plan on ensuring Don's wishes are met," Pablo inquired while raising his eyes to Nightmare.

"It has been considered and will be handled accordingly," Nightmare said while laying down a domino.

"But I want to know how," Pablo said while slamming down a domino on the table and sliding it to his position; "fifteen points".

"That's something I wanted to talk to you about. The new captive, Simone; I want to take her under my watch", Daisy exclaimed.

"I don't see a problem with that," the Don stated before anyone could question it a response to Nightmare's gaze.

"That's assuming you don't beat her like you do the rest of the captives", Pablo added.

"Pablo I've done a lot for the Family. I would never do anything to hurt it, or diminish its reputation", Nightmare said with frustration. The Don watched them closely, seeing the hatred for one another in each of their eyes.

The Don began to wonder, *perhaps this is backed by envy*

"What have you done for this Family, nothing compared to me, "Nightmare insisted while raising his voice and putting down another domino; "that's ten points."

"Until you have buried a man alive to prove a point, keep your mouth shut," Nightmare snapped.

"Ten points," Daisy stated while laying down a game piece on the table.

"You only did that because I wasn't there. I handle all of the dirty work, and have done more diplomatically than you ever will!" Pablo yelled.

As the game went on tensions rose higher, and the air was as thick as peanut butter when Pablo withdrew his pistol and placed it on the playing table stating, "I don't need a gun to take you down," then withdrew his switchblade and springing it open while staring into Nightmare's eyes. Nightmare sat back in his seat and opened his suit jacket to show the sheath containing his blade. It was at this point when Don intervened.

"I raised you two like my own. But perhaps you two have some unresolved issues, and I want them worked out by the time we return here," the Don exclaimed. After turning to his left the Don glared at, "Nightmare I may not have been there when you were born, but I was running the Family in Mexico and sending money to the United States so you could have clean diapers to wear. He then turned to his right and gazed at Pablo's brown eyes and stated, "I took care of you after your mom and dad were murdered by the Contreraz Family, and I will not have two of my children destroy one another over this petty animosity entrenched between you both." With wise words spoken from the man in charge as they withdrew their weapons and commenced the game, masking their true feelings as a sign of respect.

Chapter Fourteen

May 16, 2044. 3:00 P.M.
The City, Guerra, TX.

Simone stared at the dusty floor as her schizophrenia ripped her apart, she heard her thoughts and it was driving her insane. The voices in her head showed no mercy as they ate away at her sanity, little by little whittling little fibers of her naturalistic rationality. It seemed like a game of cat and mouse and it surely had caught up to her; although it had gotten worse before it had been almost a month since she had taken her medication and she was slipping back into a pool of mental instability. It wasn't long before she began to whisper to the voices no one else heard. Like rolling thunder from the clouds above the voices in her head screamed repeatedly in a low tone, "Its Sunday. It's morning. Good morning to you."

"Please stop," she muttered to herself while placing her hands over her ears.

"Stop, but Simone we are just getting started," the voice sounded repetitively between her soft whimpers.

The voices then began to make noises unlike before, it was as if miniature sadistic people were in her skull, bashing pots and pans against the rim of her skull in a repetitive fashion before giving off a low growl that felt as if it swept from one side of her head to the other, before commencing to beat like a drummer who hammered a bass drum like it was his grand finale. Simone inhaled deeply and began to mutter to herself again.

"There's no place like home, do you want to go home?" it asked her. "I feel like flying tonight, it would be a sweet delight," it screamed without giving her a chance to respond.

"You know, I forgot to tell you, Elijah is never coming back, and you're out of your league here. You should just kill yourself", it squeaked. She breathed deeply and pressed the palms of her hands against the flesh of her ears and squinched her eyes.

"Cat scratch, they scratch. Get the bugs from under your hide," it yelled at maximum volume.

"Do it," it exclaimed before making the beating sounds again.

It was then when Simone's will broke, she had completely lost her mind. After hearing the voices day in and day out, and not to mention that she entertained them with a conversation. She was devastated and disenfranchised, it was as if she had been hit with a ballistic missile; caught up in a web of lies and truth that screamed at her each day. It was more pessimistic fragmentation, with spurts of what little she knew of was going on. It had gotten so bad that she couldn't recall certain things that she once knew, but could regurgitate the garbage squashing around in her head.

"San Briana," it exclaimed, "That's his name."

Simone dug her nails into her scalp while giving off a wail of agitation. The scene was followed by her soft whimpers, as her actions attracted Jessica's attention; causing her to sit up and place her hands over her pregnant stomach.

"Is everything OK?" she asked with concern as the voice in Simone's head went silent.

After giving a hard swallow she responded, "They won't stop, I can't take this anymore," she cried as the voices then whispered; "The trumpets going to blow your house down, and eat her baby too."

"Don't you say that," Simone cried aloud.

"Say what, Simone, what's wrong with you?", Jessica inquired. All of a sudden Simone had a hallucination that a man standing before he reached his hand into her face and began to pull on her eye while saying; "In am King San Brianna". But it wasn't until she reached for his hand that she snapped out of it and it disappeared. Simone then saw the concern on Jessica's face.

"Someone please help!" Jessica screamed as she beat against the wooden wall with a balled fist, attempting to make as much noise as possible. Then like a snap of the fingers, Daisy entered the room; and Simone cried with moist eyes as her condition conjured more made up stories to tell.

Daisy cocked her pistol and pointed it at Jessica and exclaimed, "make one more noise and there's going to be a dead body in this room." She glared at the gun, afraid to even speak. Jessica then exhaled heavily and exclaimed, "something isn't right with her."

Daisy chuckled to herself and glared at Jessica, "I guess you didn't understand me; so let me remind you," she said while holstering her gun and picking up a baseball bat propped against the wall. Striking Jessica in the stomach with brutal force; it clinked off of the ground as she dropped the metal bat against the hard floor.

"Nooo!" Simone screamed before unveiling a river of tears!

"Get up," she yelled as Jessica gasped for breath. She spat on the woman grueling in pain before turning back to Simone.

"Now, where were we?" she inquired to Simone and continuing, "Oh yeah, I remember." She then turned her head back to Jessica before returning a smile at Simone.

"I know you think that was a bit extreme, but just know it can always get worse," she whispered in her ear while bent down before Jessica as she sat on the ground in distress.

"Come on, time for a change of scenery," she barked while grabbing Simone by her arm, peeling her off of the ground like a velcro strap. Simone gazed back at Jessica just before the door slammed shut behind them.

"You and I are going to get close, just you wait and see", Daisy exclaimed. They strolled down the hall and out of the back door to a small shed in the back of the house. When they entered the door she let go of Simone's arm and stretched out her arms and said, "welcome to my quarters".

"She's a fixer-upper but it's better than sharing a bunk with one of the grunts", she professed while walking towards a red blanket spread across the light grey cement floor.

"Have a seat", Daisy said while stretching out her hand to the other side of the blanket.

"Oh my goodness, look at me I almost forgot," she exclaimed while pulling out a pair of handcuffs and scheduling one of her arms to a pipe.

"Don't get any bright ideas," she exclaimed to Simone after setting the keys on a nightstand near the bed. Simone gazed at the assortment of food spread out across the blanket before her condition commenced to wreak havoc from within. "Oh silly me, I forgot the wine," Daisy exclaimed after wrapping a napkin around her neck.

"I'll be back in a second," she exclaimed while getting up and leaving the room. Although broken in spirit and crippled by the voices that plagued her, she still had some fight left in her.

"Run," the voices in her head panted as she exhaled heavily. The air was as thick as molasses, and her hands were perspiring; she knew that if she was going to escape now was the time. She stretched herself, reaching towards the nightstand with the other hand but she could not reach the keys. It was time for a different strategy, but she was on a limited time.

"Maybe you should bite your arm off," the voices exclaimed.

"No, that won't work," she exclaimed to herself.

"Why not, are you not hungry?" it asked as her heartbeat heavily in her chest, unsure of exactly how much time she had left. "What about if you scratch through the wall," it professed. She tugged on the handcuff scheduled around her wrist until her skin blushed red.

"How about using your foot," the voices exclaimed, sparking an idea that she hadn't yet considered. She pulled off her shoe and yanked the cuffs as tight as she could against the pipe. After stretching her leg to its limits she scooped them off of the nightstand with her left foot; picking them up with her toes off of the cement. In a matter of seconds, Simone was free, but it wasn't until the handcuff came off that she heard Daisy's voice growing near. She searched around the room until she found a red brick, Daisy opened the door to see that Simone was gone. She then stepped from behind the door and struck Daisy in the back of the head with the brick, and dashed out of the shed towards the woods. Although she only had one shoe, she moved as if they didn't matter.

"San Brianna is coming to get you", it exclaimed as she dashed past a tree; "I just felt like you should know", the voices exclaimed.

"San Briana", she said as she slowed to take a break, and unknowingly she was consumed by her condition.

Chapter Fifteen

May 20, 2044. 11:00 A.M. Kingwood, TX.

I t was the sight they had saw for the last few miles as Elijah and Gayla walked past abandoned cars. There had been a wreck on the freeway, but no police cars nor people were in sight. Elijah turned to look in a car with its windows down; a dead man was in the passenger seat with a fly poised on his eye. The sight made Elijah's sigh before he accepted his reality.

"This is life now, be thankful we're not like him," Gayla exclaimed.

"It just sucks that this had to happen," he exclaimed while continuing his walk with Gayla.

"Why do you think they declared war on their own country," he finished.

"Men do things for lots of reasons we will never understand. Money, power, fame or maybe just for the love of it; only God knows," she professed back.

"The Zodia killed my best friend," Elijah exclaimed while staring down at the earth before exclaiming, "he was like a steaming plate of your favorite food; filled with laughter and inebriation."

"And to this day, I have no idea if the whole no cell phone service had anything to do with any of this; but that's probably why I'll never see my fiance," Elijah exclaimed.

"Really?," Gayla said before inquiring, "So you were going to get married."

Elijah sighed before saying, "Yeah, I miss it a little, having everyone around; but she was a mess and I found myself asking myself why am I doing this when I'm unhappy. That's doing the same thing every day and coming home to a nightmare. We stopped having sex, granted we weren't married, but our sexual chemistry before our problems was amazing," Elijah said while reflecting.

Gayla laughed before exclaiming, "OK then. But you know, there are two sides to every story. I'm sure she would have some things to say about you too."

"What's the difference between an adult cat and a kitten?" Elijah poised.

"Well, one is younger than the other," Gayla exclaimed.

"True, but kittens have to learn to cover their poop, grown cats just do it, and baby girl I'm a big kitty."

"I prefer to be transparent, I follow what I love. That's how I prefer to live life," Gayla said.

"What if what you love isn't good for you," Elijah asked before continuing, "If it were taking you straight down with it. Would you still follow it if it was what you loved."

"Well, when you say it like that it just sounds so grim. Holy crap dude, I know our world has gone down to the swamp, but you gotta get yourself together", she screamed. She then reached in her belt and pulled out a big knife, "here I sharpened it yesterday. You should shave," She exclaimed.

With a dumbfounded expression he asked, "how am I supposed to see myself; I don't have a mirror," he professed while running his fingers through his small curls on his head, and then down through his scruffy beard.

"See that fountain up ahead, we should stop there and load up on water before we start again," she exclaimed while pointing up ahead. Elijah stopped dead in his tracks, looking at the knife in his hand before placing it in his belt and continuing.

"Have you ever looked at the miracles Jesus performed?" Elijah inquired. "When I was a kid, my dad used to tell me about the first one he performed. Turning water into wine," Gayla exclaimed.

"Wine would be amazing right now, I feel like I haven't had a buzz in forever", Elijah professed.

Gayla chuckled to herself before continuing, "Yeah, I have to agree with you a fountain of wine would be nice right about now". "Jesus told them to fill the ceremonial washing jars with water, then told them to take it to the master of ceremonies," Gayla exclaimed.

"Yeah, I remember reading that in John chapter two, it was the best wine of the night," Elijah said before continuing, "I know we should be obedient to God, but I bet they had to wonder what the heck is this guy up to. But all in all, it is always rewarding to be obedient to the will of the Lord, whether we feel we see what the plan is or if we are just oblivious to the entire scheme," Elijah exclaimed.

"It all goes back to trusting in God," Gayla professed before exclaiming, "That ties in with the second miracle Jesus performed in Galilee."

"That one is a bit foggy, which one was that again?" Elijah inquired.

"Jesus healed the official's son at Capernaum, but there is more to it than just one, two, three, poof; there goes the flu. Jesus said in John 4:48, Will you never believe in me unless you see miraculous signs and wonders?"

"I realize not all of us are born with the gift of faith; but that's what we are expected to have. We have to believe without seeing, but this man trusted Jesus and was met by his servants to hear the good news; his son was cured," Gayla finished.

"If you notice when it talks about this miracle in John chapter four, he addressed Jesus as Lord though he was an official; he humbled himself to Christ in his time of need," she said.

"I think it's kind of cool that he did it from a distance", Elijah exclaimed before stating, "It just goes to show you that your never out of God's reach, no matter how far we may think are from him". As they neared the fountain, the wind blew a refreshing mist into their faces. It refreshed them from the beating sun and scorching heat, the particles of the murky water painted a picture of revitalization as if they had found the fountain of youth.

"We should boil the water before we drink it, but this is a perfect time to store as much of it as we can," Gayla exclaimed. Elijah bent down to look into the greenish-brown water, staring at the reflection that refracted towards him. He scratched his hair covered chin, it was rough and scruffy like the end of a wire brush. He reached into his belt and pulled out a knife and began to cut off his facial hair with extreme precision.

"You know what I've always thought was kind of scary?" Gayla poised. "What's that?" Elijah responded. "Jesus cast out a demon from a man in Capernaum in Mark chapter one, but it's also mentioned in Luke chapter four; it's just the fact that stuff like that happens, you know. Movies generate voluminous funds from portraying demon's terrorizing people and influencing their actions, but in this case it was real," Gayla exclaimed.

"Jesus was teaching with authority and the people ate it up; but the unclean spirit called Jesus the "Holy One of God", Elijah yelped.

"He commanded it to be quiet and to come out of that man before he began convulsing. It amazes me at how strong the God we serve is, even the spiritual world obeys his commands, whether they are with God or if they were swayed to the opposition by the evil one", Gayla said.

"Yeah, by far the Gospel's are the scariest book of the Bible in my opinion. It's only because it gives us a clear depiction of who God is through his Son. When you look at the things Jesus said and did it shines a light on the epitome of morality, character, and humbleness. But just the fact that the opposition respects the commands of God makes me cringe, someone that powerful will be doing our judgment. I honestly pray that I never have to see those eyes of his flare with fire, or even have my ears perceive anger tindered by my actions; I feel like that would be the scariest movie of all", Elijah professed.

Gayla withdrew a metal bottle and began to fill it with water. She then said, "That's just the beginning though after Jesus healed Peter's mother-in-law, he cast out several demons and cured a multitude of people. But he didn't allow the demons to speak because they knew who he was."

"What book is that in?", Elijah inquired.

"You mean books?", Gayla exclaimed with a soft giggle to herself, followed by a warm smile and words as sweet as honey, "It's in Matthew chapter eight, Mark chapter one, and Luke chapter four".

"I guess what the scary movies don't tell you is that you don't have to be afraid of a demon if you have signed your fate with Christ", Elijah insisted.

"Do you think there are any fish in there?", Elijah exclaimed while pulling the knife from his face and pointing it at the murky water.

"I just feel like you didn't think that through very well", Gayla said.

"Oh, so because it has a fountain, does it mean that it can't have fish in it?", Elijah hollered. "What if there is a coy pond in there," he finished.

"So let me guess you're just going to sneak up on the little fishies and throw a knife at the water", Gayla aforementioned.

"You know that's not a bad idea, you must be a natural-born hunter", Elijah exclaimed. Gayla put her hand on her forehead at the sight of Elijah's rationality. That ecstasy must have killed off a lot of brain cells, but he is cute though, she thought to herself.

"Look I'll let you do that, who knows; you may catch something," she exclaimed with hope.

"After Jesus preached on shore of the Sea of Galilee, he got into Peter's boat when they were washing their nets and told him to go deeper and let down their nets. They had been out on the water all night and didn't catch a thing; but do you know what they did? They trusted him and went out there, caught a bunch of fish; so much that it filled two boats with fish. They nearly on the verge of sinking. Kind of an inspirational story right about now if I do say so myself. But I think you may be right, I'm just starting to get hungry again. We need to check the city for supplies," Elijah exclaimed.

"Your right, I think the last time I ate was the day before yesterday," Gayla exclaimed.

"Yeah, I think that's about right," Elijah exclaimed, "It would probably be wise to find a way to heat that water. But I mean, we could always pray over it."

"Honestly, I prefer we do both. We don't know what's growing in that water," Gayla retorted.

"You all ready to go," Elijah inquired to Gayla.

"Yeah, let's take a look around the city and see what we can find," Gayla exclaimed. Elijah exhaled a murmured sigh as he pushed himself up from a squatting position and began to walk with his companion.

"You sound like you are getting old," she said.

"It feels like it," he exclaimed; "I miss sleeping in my bed so much, the hard earth is for the dogs."

"Well I guess it's good to be thankful you can still feel your legs," Gayla expressed while looking at Elijah.

"You know that reminds me, Jesus healed a paralyzed man in Matthew chapter nine, Mark chapter five, and in Luke chapter two," Elijah said.

"Your right, some of the teachers of religious law were there and questioned Jesus authority when he told the paralyzed man, "Be encouraged my child, your sins are forgiven".

"But he proved to them that the Son of Man had authority on earth to forgive sins, and he showed the world by telling him, "Stand up, pick up your mat, and go home," Gayla exclaimed.

"You can find it in Matthew chapter nine, in Luke chapter five and Mark chapter two," Elijah exclaimed.

After a brief pause, she said, "Yeah, That's one of my favorites," she professed; "It's almost as good as when he cleansed a man of Leprosy and him \went and spread the word about the good news."

"Why is that one your favorite?" Elijah inquired.

"Lord I'm sorry that this is funny to me, but I guess he just couldn't keep the good news to himself," she chuckled.

"But you do know he also healed a centurion's slave without even touching the slave's body. The best doctor to walk the face of the earth was the Son of Man by far. That's like fixing a car without getting your hands dirty. You can find it in Luke chapter seven, and Matthew chapter eight," Elijah said.

"Your either really into this conversation or this is a bible bowl," Gayla exclaimed.

"No, not really; I'm sorry if it seemed that way. Ever since I sealed my fate with Christ that night I've been reading the Gospels like we drink water," he said; "I fell in love with how amazing Jesus is; you don't mind geeking out for Jesus with me do you?"

"Not at all, I guess we have something in common then, he is amazing," she professed.

"He was kind of a rebel", Gayla said before he included, "Or the Pharisees just placed religious law over the Son of Man. They wanted to kill him. Before he healed the man's hand the Pharisees asked Jesus, Does the law permit a person to work by healing on the Sabbath? He answered them by saying, If you had sheep that fell into a well on the Sabbath, wouldn't you work to pull it out? Of course, you would. And how much more valuable is a person than a sheep! Yes, the law permits a person to do good on the Sabbath," she said.

"He then told the man to hold out his hand and it was restored like the other. The Pharisees plotted to kill Jesus after his deed", she said while taking in a deep breath from all of the words she spilled into the air.

"Where's that at, I like to check that out later", Elijah inquired.

"Matthew chapter twelve, Luke chapter six and Mark chapter three," she said with a smile.

"I think my favorite miracle Jesus performed was when he raised the widow's son from the dead in Luke chapter seven. It was in Nain and a large crowd was following them. The Bible says that Jesus was overflowing with compassion and he told the woman, Don't cry. He touched the coffin and said, Young man, I tell you to get up. Then he sat up and began to talk," Elijah exclaimed.

"That was a widow's only son", he said; "she had no one else".

"I see where you are coming from. When Jesus calmed the storm in Matthew chapter eight, Mark chapter four, and Luke chapter eight; he showed that he had authority over the storms in life just like with the widow's son. But in this event even nature obeyed his command," Gayla said.

"How many miracles is that now?" Elijah inquired.

"Thirteen", she said; "But in total, he performed thirty-seven before his death."

"Moment of truth, if you could have any trait-like Jesus for one day what would it be?," Geyla inquired.

"To be able to love everyone, and care for the world around me. I feel like at times I can be a bit heartless, emotionless, and uncaring of who gets hurt or who are affected by my decisions. I see my heart as black to be completely honest but after reading Luke chapter six; I should be doing a lot of thinking," Elijah said.

"Your heart isn't black if Jesus is in it", Gayla professed.

Elijah chuckled to himself before stating, "If that's the case then there is a small seed in the center where he lives at and a piece of dead matter that beats slowly around it. It's guarded by acid and spears. ``

"I mean you had a fiance, how can you say something like that?" Gayla asked.

"I don't think I know what love feels like," he exclaimed as he briskly walked beyond the birds nestled in the trees etched along edges of the road. "I couldn't have loved her, by the way, I treated her, but we used to have a lot of good moments; those are really good memories", he said.

"I mean I had faults too, but she changed on me, it's really hard to explain. After her breakdown she just wasn't the same anymore, I remember I would come home and would hear her crying about the scars from her wounds she inflicted on herself, they soon began to keloid, and the crazy part was no matter what I did she was never happy. Everything shut down piece by piece; I think she was depressed. But I'm almost certain it was because she didn't die that day, and I always wondered was I wrong for stopping her?" he professed.

"Man, that's deep," Gayla retorted.

"Yeah, maybe that's where my void is, I long for something and seek happiness from substances. I do drugs and drink to get a buzz, and once that goes away I go to sleep," he exclaimed before continuing; "the things I would do for a blunt right now".

"I use to smoke hemp when I was younger," she said; "have you tried counseling".

"Never, I'm just not the type to open up too much about myself," he said.

"Not even to your fiance, I mean you haven't known me long and your hard-boiled shell is already cracking," she exclaimed.

"You sound like you're itching to see what's underneath it," he exclaimed while pointing at a gas station in the distance.

"I hope it still has some food inside," Gayla exclaimed.

"It looks like there was a lot of traffic here, there's a lot of cars around it. I wonder if any of them work; I doubt we will find any gas but we can siphon the tanks," Elijah said.

"You can siphon the tanks, I am not getting gas in my mouth," Gayla insisted while giving Elijah a dead stare while he walked briskly. Broken glass crunched beneath their feet from a busted car window, Elijah pulled out the pistol from his belt loop and passed it to Gayla; "You go ahead and go inside, I'm going to check the cars first."

With that she pulled out the clip and popped the bullet out of the chamber like popcorn flying out of a kettle, catching it in mid-air before staring at two others she held in her hand and exclaimed, "three bullets." She then began to sneak into the entrance.

"Let's see what Elijah will get for Christmas," he professed. He opened up a red car's door and searched the car's inner compartments.

"Come on, daddy needs something good," he exclaimed. Upon opening the glove compartment box he found a gram of hemp stuffed beside a balled-up envelope and a pair of keys.

"Bingo," he shouted. He reached his hand inside of it and removed the hemp and the keys. Sitting on the bare cement in front of pump number seven and leaning against the open car door; he sniffed the bag of weed with a huge grin on his face. Then it hit him; his baser urges evoked a thought that made his expression pause. If I can get a cigar from the store, I can roll up a blunt; and Eli can tote one before the day is over, he thought. Suddenly he sprung to his feet and dashed into the store to see Gayla sitting on the floor eating honey bun.

"Did you check to see if the place is clean?" he inquired.

"No, I'm kind of busy right now; if you can't tell," she said between chews. Elijah gazed at her amazed by her imperfection and natural beauty.

"Are those, sour smackers?" Elijah asked while pointing at the candy in front of her.

Gayla stopped chewing her food and with a mouthful of chewed pastry she replied, "yeah, you can go get your own they are on the other ile." Elijah then walked one isle to the right and saw them on a shelf next to other candies. He started for behind the counter and to his surprise, he found a man passed out by a case worth of empty beer bottles.

"Gayla, come here," Elijah whispered. She swallowed the last chew of the delicious honey bun, grabbed the pistol from the floor and raised to her feet, following Elijah behind the countertop. When she saw the man jumped back two inches, "I guess I should have searched the place as you told me," she exclaimed as Elijah looked at her and crossed his arms.

"Give me the pistol," Elijah insisted. She placed it in his hand with his other carrying the bible carried in the other and squatted down next to the man. After standing up instantaneously, she pushed the man with the brim of her foot; sending him from lying face forward on the floor until he flopped on his side in a mid snore. Warm drool etched from the corners of his mouth in a downward fashion, it hung from his the bottom of his chin like mistletoe atop of the kitchen door at a Christmas feast.

She kicked him onto his back only to see the same old scene; he was in a deep slumber.

"Think we should just let him sleep?," Gayla asked; "I mean he isn't a threat if he is sleep."

"I have an idea," Elijah exclaimed while lowering the gun and walking over to a counter in the corner of the store, he left the pistol on the counter as he grabbed the coffee pot, filled with a room temperature chestnut brown brew and carried it over to where he once stood.

"Odd time for a coffee break," Gayla exclaimed while examining him.

"No, it's a perfect time," Elijah exclaimed while pouring it onto the man's face; sending him jumping up in a heap of confusion.

"Elijah that was uncalled for," she said before turning to the man; "I'm glad your up". Elijah then left Gayla to get the pistol and replace the empty pot; only to return and point the gun at the man.

"Are you armed?" Gayla inquired to him.

"Is that coffee", the man asked in a grim tone.

"Sure is, you looked like you needed a boost to kick start your day", Elijah exclaimed.

"Are you armed", Gayla inquired in a stern tone once again. The man then turned his head to the side to face her, he licked his coffee-stained lips and replied; "no".

"Stand up, I have to check you to be sure," she exclaimed. He stood to his feet, kicking empty beer bottles across the floor as he staggered to his feet. Gayla started at his wet shirt, she went down his arms and legs; patting him down as if he was a suspected bomber to a team of airport security guards.

"Ok, he's clean," she exclaimed as she walked over where she previously sat and began to commence here meal.

"Take your shoes off," she demanded while pointing at his moccasins. As he slipped off his shoes Elijah inquired to the man, "What do you go by."

"My name is Gladius," he said.

"Gladius do you smoke hemp?" Elijah asked.

"Sure do!" he exclaimed with excitement. Elijah paused for a second and thought to himself for a second; "Here you go, go knock yourself out," he exclaimed while passing the man the gram of weed. He instantly snatched a pack of cigars from the back wall.

"Thanks", he said while walking to the bathroom. The door slammed behind him as he began to indulge. Elijah then grabbed a lighter and a pack of cigarettes before walking over to the candy aisle and grabbed a pack of sour smackers before sitting next to Gayla.

"You know these have to be my favorite candy," Gayla exclaimed while ripping open another package.

"Yeah, they are pretty good," he exclaimed.

"Gladius is smoking in the bathroom," he said.

"He had hemp or you found some?" she inquired.

"The later," he replied.

"Wow," she exclaimed with a smile.

"We are in a state of civil war and you still manage to find hemp," she said.

"Its like magnetic poles attracted to each other, I use to think we belonged together," he said.

"You can go join him if you want," she said.

"No, I thought it was time for a change. I did get some cigarettes before I came over here though," he said. Gayla smiled and went back to eating her candy as Elijah watched her devour the candy pieces.

"You got something you want to say?" she asked.

"What was your childhood like?" Elijah inquired as the smell of hemp filled the air, aromatizing the entire store from the bathroom.

"It was good, I lived with my dad for most of my life. My parents got divorced after I turned eighteen," she said.

"I'm sorry to hear that," he exclaimed while opening his candy and eating the bite-size pieces.

"No, it's ok, she wasn't there for most of my life, then was in and out on other parts. I don't know where either of them is now, and to be honest I don't care if they show up," she exclaimed. Elijah cocked his head to the side at her harshness and with a hard swallow of candy.

"It's coming from here!" someone outside screamed. Suddenly the door burst open and five armed men and women entered the room.

"Well, well, well, what do we have here?" one of the men walked up and said as Elijah and Gayla hid behind the row of pastries. He walked over to the bathroom passing their row with a whip in his hand.

"We have to do something," Gayla whispered.

"We cant we only have three bullets," Elijah professed in a soft tone; "just stay quiet." The man stood in front of the bathroom door with a smile on his face. He raised his hand to knock on the door before taking in a deep breath.

His knuckles beat against the door, "One second," Gladius called out. He opened the door to be flogged with a whip. Gladius fell onto the bathroom floor, he reached for the bathroom toilet to brace himself to a standing position. The man then flogged him in the back of the head. The whip wrapped around the top of his skull, tearing the skin at the top of his forehead. The gash bled profusely as Gladius breathed heavily on his back leaning against the toilet as blood dripped down his forehead.

"We are the Zodia," the man said.

"What month are you born in?" he inquired.

"Ok, you are a slow learner," he professed. He then struck him in the chest with the whip, tearing a hole into his shirt and leaving a whelp on the skin underneath.

"When I ask you a question I expect an answer," he said.

"May first," he said.

"A Taurus," he exclaimed back. "And what is your name?" he inquired.

"Gladius," he responded in pain.

"Your name is of Latin origin", the aggressor exclaimed; "I like that. You're going to come back with us. You need to do a little community service". He then left and two other men entered and grabbed him off the floor, carrying him out of the store.

"Elijah, what do we do?" Gayla inquired.

"There was nothing we could do," he retorted.

"But, we can't just let them take him, only God knows what will happen to him," she exasperated. Elijah grabbed her by the shoulders and gently shook her, "We have three bullets"; he said softly.

"What don't you understand about that, there were five of them," Elijah exclaimed.

"We need to move and keep scouting, maybe even find a car," he said. As he grabbed her hand they exited from the front door and ducked beneath the stalled cars. The passed by a sight that broke Gayla's heart, they were loading Gladius into the back of a truck; before taking off. All of a sudden Gayla paused.

"Do you see that," she shunted while pointing her finger at a huge banner with the number twelve on it. It was hanging from a limb on a tree, nearly touching the ground.

"Do you think that we are in their territory," Elijah exclaimed.

"There twelve Zodiac signs, so I think you are on the right path," she said.

"Come on, we need to get a move on," he said while grabbing her hand, trotting lightly across the cement.

Chapter Sixteen

May 20th, 2044. 6:00 P.M. Outside the Shady Oaks Housing Complex, Kingwood, TX.

Gladius sat in the back of the truck next to an armed Zodia guard as he wondered if he would be taken and what would happen to him.

"You sit tight, we have got to make a few rounds," the armed man said. He wore a red headband and a blue jean vest, his brown face was speckled with dirt; as if it hadn't been washed in days. His bulging fingers wrapped around the black trigger of an assault rifle, as he leaned back against the rear window while sitting on top of the toolbox perched against the back of the truck bed. The blood from the gash was now smeared across Gladius's face, his bones shook with fear.

The closest thing I've felt to that incident was a belt buckle to the skull by mamma's left hand, he thought. Suddenly the truck began to slow down to a halt. It was then that more men and women were brought out and loaded into the back of the truck. They gazed at the gash on Gladius's face as he trembled.

"Are you going to be ok?" one of them asked.

"Hey, no talking," the armed man screamed; forcing the speaker to jump back against the inner rim of the truck bed. Gladius examined him, he looked just a little over thirteen. He's just a boy, he thought before examining the others.

"There are three women, two men, and a boy. Were all going to die here," he gently whispered to himself. Although he thought his words would go unheard, he wondered why the person next to him looked at him with astonished expressions. The truck then began to slow a third time, when it stopped a man approached the reach of the truck holding a man by the back of his neck.

"I only found one today," the man said to the armed Zodia guard while throwing him in the back of the car.

"Hey, it's like a fishing man; more will show up," the armed man said. The new captive was an African American man with dreadlocks, he looked about twenty-seven; still in his youth. He sat in the only available spot, it looked like the inverse of the Island of Man's flag; with everyone's legs meeting in the middle all over the blood dripping onto the truck bed from Gladius's head. The blood streamed away to a pool in the center of their constraints. Gladius' attention was attracted to one of the women softly sniffling mucus back into her nose as tears dripped down her cheeks; it seemed to almost blend in with the sound of rushing wind from the truck's linear velocity. It was then that Gladius's eyes began to tear as well. Then all of a sudden the truck pulled into the "Shady Oaks" housing complex. They then entered the main plaza parking lot and came to a halt.

The truck backfired just before it was cut off. "Holy crap, Andy you have got to get that truck fixed," the man who whipped Gladius said as he exited the passenger seat of the truck.

"Well ladies and gentlemen welcome home," he said while smiling and letting the whip drag the floor while placing the other hand in his belt loop. "My name is Africa. Would any of you be interested in joining the great Zodia today and worship the stars," he said with a smile; only to be opposed by silence.

"Get out of the van," he then exclaimed angrily in response to the captive's silence. His face showed his unhappiness with how fast they were moving, so he swung the whip towards the back of the truck. "Move faster!" he screamed. This startled them all, as they started to scuffle as fast as they could out of the truck. He walked over to them slowly, examining them all one by one.

He ran his fingers through one of the woman's hairs on her head and exclaimed, "It's makeover time!" he exclaimed.

"Ladies and gentlemen, please follow me. You know this isn't going to be so bad," he said as they entered the main leasing office. There were three chairs with men holding hair clippers, with a pile of hair laying on the floor.

"Well all of you guys don't rush up there at one time," he exclaimed.

"Now, now; I know this a lot thrown at you. So let me put this as simple as I can, you belong to the Zodia now and what I say goes. As one of the women entered the chair the man with the whip exclaimed," We have an excellent doctor here, he will patch you up should you so much as get a scratch on your fingernail. Now don't get me wrong, I want you all to live; you guys are going to be making Neon Moon for the fiends. I must illiterate," he said with a smile; "malnutrition is not a doctor's visit excuse to get out of work."

"You will wake up at dawn each morning and make drugs, you may or may not get a meal; then you will go to sleep. Simple as that," he said while clasping his hands together and smiling at them once again.

As one person exited the chair another entered and the piles of hair on the floor grew substantially. Once all their heads were buzzed down until you could see their scalp the man with the whip said, "Now there is a condition, we have to be able to know your sign," he said while pushing open the door and walking over to a shed with a fire in front.

"My bleeding example of what could happen to you to is name Gladius. He is a Taurus," he exclaimed.

"Bring out the bull!" he shouted while giving a quick flex his muscles underneath his turquoise jacket.

"Gladius, come here ol' buddy ol' pal", he said while singling him to come closer with his index finger. But Gladius stood still, shaking in his shoes as they brought out an iron brand of a bull.

"Gladius, I thought you would catch on by now. I'm a little impatient; get your butt over here now," he said in a stern voice while dropping the whip down, hanging from his hand to the ground again while he put the brand in the fire with the other. Gladius inched over towards him, step by step the corners of his mouth curled, and the stream of tears grew larger the closer he grew to his upcoming fate.

"Now I'm only going to show you guys how this is done one time," he said to some Zodia men and women watching; "so pay attention."

"Take off your shirt and get on your knees," he said in Gladius's face. After he took it off and got onto the ground on his knees as the slave driver said, "hands on the ground too."

"Good, just like that," he said while walking over to Gladius's side.

One of the men with the slave driver grabbed the brand out of the fire as the man with the whip said, "Now all of you will go through this. I'm sorry kid, it's just protocol," he exclaimed while looking at the fear in the young boy's eyes. The man then took the whip with one hand and exchanged him the brand with the other.

"Ok now, just stay still," he said while pressing down the brand into his latissimus dorsi; forcing him to grit his teeth while the other captives looked away at the sight. Steam came from his skin as it sizzled through his epidermis, sending the smell of burnt skin into the air.

As pulled it out of his back and handed it to one of his men and smiled, "who's next?," he asked as Gladius still lay with his hands and knees to the earth.

Chapter Seventeen

As Elijah and Gayla neared the Dollar Only Store, they noticed the doors were already open. It had been vandalized; sacked for its milk and cookies. They were alert and perceptive with every step that they drew closer to the front doors. Elijah scanned the scene to be sure the coast was clear. After they entered, they propped the door open the door with a basket to allow more light to enter the store.

"We need to find anything we can use, candles, matches, lighter fluid; the works," he exclaimed. As they then stormed through the aisles looking for anything of use. Gayla passed by a teddy bear with a missing button at the ocular position and Elijah started down an aisle with a soap spill in the middle of the floor. When his shoe glided across the soiled floor he lost his balance, grabbing on to the shelf next to him; knocking it over in the process. It's empty shelves clanked against the tile floor as Gayla called out, "Are you ok?".

"Yeah, I'm good," Elijah yelled after two deep breaths; "it didn't land on top of me." After he pushed himself up, they snatched what little of value was left and meet in the front of the store in a matter of minutes.

"What do you have," Elijah said to Gayla as he took two of the trash bags off of their bag holster.

"Lighter fluid, a can of Wolfie Beans, a pot and two candles," Gayla exclaimed.

"What about you?" she asked.

"I found some rope, a pair of underwear, scissors and a hot glue stick," he said. While tying the rope around the trash bags to make a satchel. He then repeated the same process with two more bags and stuffed all of their acquired contents into them, even his bible; but he left the knife in his belt loop.

"There are some gallon jugs of spoiled milk in the freezer, we can empty them and fill them up with water," Gayla exclaimed. But given Elijah's expression, she crossed her arms at the sight.

"Won't that make the water stink, that milk has to be spoiled. The power has been out for a while now," he said.

"Well do you have a better idea?" Gayla hissed.

"I do. I'm going to make a frog trap out some of those old soda bottles and the stuff I've found," he exclaimed.

"Frog's and beans for dinner sounds good to me," Gayla said.

"I'll meet back up with you at the pond, I want to look around a little more," Elijah said. Elijah tried to hand her the pistol but she refused it.

"I can handle myself," she exclaimed; "I'll meet you back at the pond," she said while wrapping her arms around him; catching Elijah by surprise.

"Take care of yourself" she whispered in his ear in a soft warming tone; forcing Elijah to smile and perform the same gesture of affection. He slid his hands to the middle of her back, gently stroking the area with his hands. She flexed at his touch, gripping her fingers around his side. As she pulled away their eyes met, and it was then that her heart melted; she had fallen for the man who was engaged. Perhaps it was because they had been together all this time. They had been surviving and making a way for themselves, or maybe it was because of their mutual love for the Son of Man. Either or, she was in deep, and as their fingers interlocked as she pulled apart Elijah wondered; will I see this woman again, he thought to himself.

"I will," he exclaimed as she turned to walk off. As the Afrocentric Queen walked away, Elijah exclaimed; "Mmhm, I've gotta risk it for a biscuit."

Gayla was now standing in front of the cooler, emptying the milk juggs as Elijah walked to the back of the store to look for a water hose.

"You can take my satchel if you want, just put the rope over one shoulder," he said before sitting it down and walking out of the door. The grass on the side of the store was tall and Elijah hiked through it, staring at the bottom of the wall in hopes of finding a water hose. Then presto, he saw it. It was as if he heard the angels sing when he saw the brown water hose sitting on the ground. He withdrew his knife from his belt loop and kneeled beside it. A colony of ants had constructed a camp over part of the hose that he did not intend to use. He grabbed the end of it and cut through the hose with the knife, stirring up the bed of ants in the process. He held the short piece of hose as if it were a jewel, "Now we just need a car," he exclaimed as he walked to the front of the store. When he turned the corner he was surprised to see that Gayla had left, and his satchel was gone and two empty gallon jugs were sitting right in front of him. He emptied three bottles of soda from the powerless refrigerator and took the two-gallon jugs before walking through the parking lot, there were three idle cars still in the lot. All of them were locked but one, and that is the one Elijah selected; it was a gray Cameo. Not too stylish, but it was better than walking around in a place like this. It had white-walled tires and silver hubcaps. What Elijah knew for certain was that this was Zodia turf, and he had no aspiration to see where they had taken Gladius. He held the hose up to his mouth after placing it in one of the other car's gas tanks. Sucking gas into his mouth and quickly withdrawing the hose, Elijah single-handedly drained the tank into the gallon jug. After performing the same task again in the other vehicle he gagged as some of it went down his throat. It burned his insides as the fuel drained into the jug. He coughed and choked on the fresh air entering his lungs, giving two hard swallows before regaining his composure and standing to his feet while staring at a puddle of spit that had dribbled from his lips. He grabbed the two jugs of gasoline and headed towards the grey Cameo and emptying both jugs into the gas tank.

"Great now we have to get you going," he said aloud. He proceeded to open the door of the car, pulling out his knife and shaved down the wires and ultimately hot wired the car. As he heard the engine roar it sounded like music to his ears, he hopped in and began to take a stroll through the city to see what he could find. It was then that he noticed the radio was missing from the dashboard.

"Well we have 1/2 a tank," he exclaimed before his eyes caught on to a sign that said; "Ammo depot! 5 miles".

"Sweet," Elijah exclaimed while lowering the window and sticking his arm out of it.

Holding one hand on the steering wheel he drove on the empty street. The intersection lights were dead and black, noticing the fading sun as he turned on the headlights; navigating through the curvature of the road. After he pulled into the parking lot and disconnected the wires, killing the car. He was sad to see that it had already been looted; "there is only one car outside," he exclaimed while pushing open the door.

An "Open" sign hung from the inner window, it made Elijah smirk. Once inside he saw a man with a family, the wife noticed Elijah first; tugging on her husband's sleeve to get his attention. Once the man noticed Elijah he raised an AK-47 in Elijah's direction.

"Wow there; easy. I don't mean you any harm but I am armed," Elijah said followed by a brief pause before the man lowered his gun."My name is Elijah," he said before asking, "What is your name?"

"Gregory Bliss. This is my wife Tina, and my two children Caleb and Abby," he exclaimed as if he were exhibiting his team. "We are headed to Galveston,"

Gregory exclaimed in a shaky tone; "We heard there are a group of people trying to build a shelter for people afflicted by the war. I think they will be separate from the government."

"Where are you headed?" the man inquired.

"Northeast. You guys wouldn't happen to know if there is anything usable here?" Elijah inquired.

"That is a 9 millimeter," the man exclaimed while reaching into a duffle bag and pulling out a box of shells.

"I won't give you a gun, but I will give you these," Gregory said while extending the box of shells to him. "I hope you understand," Gregory exclaimed while picking back up his rifle; "I found them first". Elijah took them from his hand before he said; "I worked with the school back in Houston. I was at Empire Aoks I.S.D. for about three years before the war broke out."

Elijah's eyes widened and after a brief pause he grabbed the man's jacket and asked him, "Do you know a little girl named Sequoia."

"Hey, man calm down. I don't know your little girl," he exclaimed. Elijah let go of him in a spurt of emotion, wiping the tears from his eyes and accepting that he might never see her again.

"The president's plan sounded perfect on paper, but the Zodia were organized and everywhere. At 7:00 P.M. the whole system got shut down. Children got lost track of when the faculty wanted to go home to their families. It's no telling where your daughter is now man", Gregory said picking up the duffle bag and heading for the door. As his family went ahead of him to the car parked outside, he stopped at the door and said to Elijah, "I'm sorry about your daughter. Be safe".

The door clung against its frame as it slammed shut leaving Elijah in total darkness. He wept softly amid blackness, sheltered by its coldness as he outpoured emotion. Elijah then grabbed the box of shells off the floor and headed towards the exit. Pushing open the metal door into the night and starting towards the grey Cameo. The wind blew against him briskly, smudging the tears running down his cheeks. As he opened the car door and began to start it once again, another tear fell onto the cement from his contour. He gathered himself for a second before shifting the engine into drive and wiping away the aqueduct that streamed from the corners of his brown eyes. He contemplated for what seemed like hours, with one hand on the steering wheel and the other out of the window. The cool night breeze brushed into the window and his face, it soothed the skin of his head as he rubbed his curly hair.

"God, I don't know if she is still out there or if she is even still alive. But if my daughter is out there somewhere, can you bring her to me," he concluded; "Amen." Elijah then came around the corner with two hands turning the wheel. He pulled up to the pond and disconnect the wires; gently pushing the door closed as he approached the pond in search of Gayla with the soda bottles in hand. As he scanned from left to right he didn't see her, but when he turned to the left he noticed a faint light coming from a grove of trees. He gave a heavy sigh and a smirk crept across his light brown face. Walking towards the dim light in the darkness Elijah hummed a soft tune he sung to his daughter when she was young, it was called "Bluebird"; and it happened to be his daughter's favorite hymn before she fell asleep. The corners of his mouth began to curl before he swallowed it as he neared the grove of trees. Elijah smelled the scent of burning wood. Just as he entered the brush of trees at the fringe of the pond he saw Gayla sitting beside the fire, warming herself in the night air.

"Glad to see you made it back ok," Elijah exclaimed while walking over to hug her.

"Did you find anything?" Gayla inquired while wrapping her arms around Elijah.

"Not much, just some bullets and a car," Elijah exclaimed.

"Oh my goodness, thank you Father!" she praised aloud.

"Yea, we need to use the gas to get as far away from here as possible," Elijah said; "I didn't see any more banners, but you can never be too sure with the Zodia. It's just too close for comfort if you ask me," he finished.

"I completely understand, and I'm 100% with you", Gayla tagged in. Elijah then sat beside Gayla, he withdrew the scissors and hot glue from the satchel and began to configure a frog trap; cutting one hole into one bottle and cutting the others about halfway through their length.

"You were serious about those frogs," Gayla exclaimed with a smile; forcing Elijah to smirk as she laid her head on him. He leaned forward with Gayla's head on his shoulder, heating the hot glue stick in the fire until it was ready to use. Elijah smeared it across the cut bottles, assembling it into the eighth wonder of the world. Gayla watched him closely, trying to figure out what chance did he have at catching anything at all. It fascinated her and drafted her attention.

"See, it just took a little ingenuity and a few supplies," he exclaimed while holding up his contraption. Elijah rose to his feet and united one of the trash bags from the satchel before walking over to a tree and breaking off a limb, sticking it inside of the neck of the trap as he headed to the pond's outskirts after lighting one of the candles they had acquired. With the candle in one hand and the trap in the other and a trash bag by his side, Elijah began the great hunt. For what seemed like hours he paced back and forth in search of game, but his efforts were not futile. Although the first frog he encountered got away, he encountered three more and caught them all. Sticking them one by one into the trash bad, they croaked and screamed with the others in the free world as they sloshed from side to side in the bag while Elijah walked back to meet Gayla.

"Heat the beans, it's time for dinner!" he exclaimed with excitement as Gayla looked up at him. She then reached into the satchel and pulled out the beans, she grabbed the pot which was over a hotbed of coals under a hot pot of water. Gayla poured the water back into the plastic gallon jug, it left a trail of steam. Elijah handed her the knife and she carved open the can of beans.

"I wish we had some ice to cool the water down with," Gayla exclaimed.

"That should have killed some of the pathogens. Let's just pray about it and we can take it from there," Elijah exclaimed. She grabbed her hands as Elijah dropped the bag, causing one of the frogs to croak loudly.

"Father God, we come to you asking you to forgive us of our sins; we ask that you use this water to refresh our body. In your name we trust forever, Amen," he finished. Gayla pulled back her hand as her curiosity of what Elijah caught and how he caught it perplexed her.

"What did you get," she exclaimed as she could no longer contain herself; her stomach then growled loudly and ended with a bubbling noise. It caused Elijah to assume she was hungry.

"Are those bullfrogs or toads?" Gayla inquired.

"I'm not sure, but I'm going to eat them," he professed.

"How are you going to, you know?" she asked. Elijah lifted one finger to his lip and pondered for a second. He then withdrew the stick from the trap and placed the bag on the ground, kneeling to it and placing wrapping his fist around the opening of the bag. Elijah breathed deeply twice before freezing like stone with the stick in the air slowly ebbing.

"Oh for goodness sakes, I'll do it," Gayla said as she pulled the stick out of Elijah's hand and beat the frogs to death; causing Elijah to turn his head to the side and cringe. She hacked and hacked as if she was cleaving meat. When the deed was done she looked at Elijah and exclaimed, "You've never gone hunting before, have you?" she asked.

"I was always more of a catch and release type guy," he responded. Pulling the frogs out of the blood-stained bag she gutted all three while continuing her conversation with him, "I've never been fishing, I can't swim very well," she said.

"If the water was deeper I'd offer to show you," Elijah exclaimed; making Gayla's dark skin tighten as she burst into a smile.

"I'm going to take a wipe off later with some of the water," she said; "I need to clean up a little." Elijah reached into the satchel and pulled out the men's briefs, "You know, you can have them. The ones you have on can't be too fresh, `` he exclaimed. In shock, her bottom lip dropped.

"I'll have you know I sat in sugar when you weren't looking. I will take them through. Thanks, I guess," she responded in a soft tone while placing the frogs in the skillet with the beans; then turning to take the undergarments. She cooked both the beans and amphibians, frogs sat in the pot with an empty abdominal cavity, surrounded by the vegetables as she placed it into the bed of coals in the small flame. As time flew by with sweet wisp of conversation, and Elijah and Gayla ate and cuddled, before parting ways to bathe and returning to spend the night on the ground in each other's arms.

Chapter Eighteen

May 31st, 2044 3:00 P.M. Shepherd TX.

Between the treetops, a raindrop fell from a grey cloud. It landed on the dark green pine needles as thunder growled from the overhanging sky. Elijah stepped beneath the pine and white oak trees, with the pistol raised to the ear. Gayla was following him from behind; holding the tips of Elijah's fingers while placing one hand around a small tree to brace herself of a grassy mound of earth. The car ran out of gas about 30 minutes ago.

"You know you are starting to hold that like you know what you're doing," Gayla said while flashing a small smile at Elijah.

"I saw someone hold it like this in a magazine. But to be completely honest I've never fired one before", Elijah responded.

"Really? Don't you want to take her for a spin?", Gayla exclaimed while licking her bottom lip, sucking on it for a brief second after swallowing a sly smile.

"I hardly think this is the time or place. Plus it's about to rain," Elijah professed as raindrops fell around them.

"That's life for you. You may not always get optimal conditions to defend yourself!" Gayla yelped while pitching in her lower lip and turning her head to the side; putting her arms on her hips as if trying to convince him with a special look she reserved for the perfect time. Elijah flipping the gun over in his hand and glaring at its glistening appearance amid the humidity and sprinkles from above. Gayla then approached Elijah from the rear and placed her hands around the base of the gun, locking Elijah's finger on the trigger while aiming into the woods.

"Take a deep breath, hold it, and pull the trigger," she whispered in his ear softly. Her afro lay down in her face, and damp her chest pressed against Elijah's wet shirt.

"Stare down the sight", she processed in a gentle tone of voice before continuing; "and pull the trigger."

"BANG!" the shot echoed around them. Suddenly, a man screamed and a barrage of gunshots from an automatic shotgun sounded within their vicinity. Elijah and Gayla dropped to the Earth and covered their heads, but the gunshot the commenced. After ten shots the gunfire ceased and Gayla began to crawl on her knees to find its source and it seemed almost as if they are intent on releasing a full clip as the shots went into full swing again.

"What are you doing?" Elijah whispered. But Gayla shushed him and continued leaving Elijah in an awkward disposition of whether to follow his gut and stay put or to go against his instincts and follow her.

"I can't believe this," Elijah muttered in a near-death tone while rising from the ground to follow her on hand

and knee. By the time he reached the nearest tree, he saw Gayla's big hazelnut eyes grow even rounder. She fell onto her backside, perching herself upon the ground with her two hands. He heard the switching of a clip from an automatic shotgun mounted onto the Centurion Armour, laying over a Caucasian man's heavily muscled chest. He braced his feet to shoot again, but just before the situation reached extremes Elijah tackled him landing with his head near the muzzle of the gun. The shot rang in Elijah's ears as he fell shell shocked onto the ground beside him. The clip flew out of the gun as another loaded into the barrel. Elijah swallowed hard after looking back to see that Gayla was not hit. He watched in slow motion, as the shell fell onto the ground below. When his eyes shot back to the bearded white man, Gayla snatched the light blue looking glass attached to his headband that was bound by strips of rubber. Elijah fell onto the floor and gazed at the empty shell on the ground. Then he got up from the ground, with his pinstriped shirt spray painted in speckles of Mother Earth. He walked up with power beneath his steps and fire in his eyes, as if he was fighting to stay alive. He swung at Gayla with his light grey armored hand, it accented off of his white spandex shirt beneath his plaid overtone. By his second step, she had rushed to her feet and struck him with her foot to his face; knocking him onto the ground. She rushed to him and mashed the disengage button on the side of the black headband he wore. The barrel folded inwards as she began to rip off his soundproof earbuds and pursued with the contraption wrapped around his cerebellum. He was powerless and in pain. She grabbed the back of his armor and threw him into a nearby tree, busting his freckled nose in the process. Gayla pounded his face with a clubbed fist, as Elijah was just coming out of shell shock. The man's green hat was nearly beat off of his head when Elijah rolled onto his side holding his arm as if he just bruised it in the ordeal. Gayla reached her hands through the opened plaid shirt and gripped the sides of his spandex compression shirt beneath; shaking his head into the ground while Elijah screamed at him.

He picked up the pistol and walked over to the man with the intent of harm, but Gayla lurched her body over the bearded man. "Don't! There's no need to," she exclaimed as Elijah witnessed the man passed out and busted up.

He then lowered the gun and stared at the man's yellow teeth and bloody face; "Do you think he is one of them?" Elijah inquired.

"No way to be sure unless we interrogate him," Gayla professed. After removing the Centurion Armour Suit from his chest Elijah hobbled in pain through the woods with one arm around the man and Gayla following with the man propped up on her shoulder. A team effort to find a suitable location to constrain the victim.

"You know on the bright side, at least you didn't get held at gunpoint this time," Gayla chuckled to herself. Elijah gazed at her with a side-eye, giving a heavy sigh while failing to see the humor in the situation.

"How does Centurion Armor work?" he inquired.

"Blinking and eye movement controls were it shoots," she retorted before continuing, "Please don't put that on, it dangerous".

"I do kind of want it to give it a swing", he exclaimed between deep sighs of pain from his arm which began to pulse from within.

His arm was on fire, the only bright side was that his bruised ribs had healed. It was not long before they stumbled onto a black trailer with a tarnished silver metal roof. Its lawn is best described as light patches of green grass interspersed by stretches of bare earth. The inside of the trailer was a wreck, containing broken down couches, oodles of packaging, and an empty beer can galore. Elijah kicked the trash away from the cushioned chair while Gayla unplugged a fluorescent orange extension cord from the ground and tied it around the victim, constraining his arms and legs on the sofa. Elijah then plopped onto the loveseat, holding his pulsing arm and gritting his teeth as he felt the sting of the wound as he reclined his back against the couch's backrest. He slung the satchel onto the floor as Gayla sat down next to him.

"Thank you for what you did back there", Gayla professed while staring into Elijah's eyes and kissing him softly on the lips. He wrapped his arm around the back of her head as his tongue slid into her mouth, adding a sense of passion in their first kiss. Her eyes opened as she felt him suck the air from her lungs, and instantly she felt chills down her back. It was almost as if the man was nonexistent as she climbed atop of Elijah and wrapped her arms around his neck, and returning to his attempt at French kissing the person who had just saved her life. She locked her legs around his sides as he sat up to reach her as she leaned back. He then ran his hand through her wet hair in a beautiful display of black love. It was more passionate than your favorite soap operas, a fairy tale encounter that was truly magical; a kiss fit for a queen sitting on the throne. Elijah slid his fingers down her back to her round backside while trying to be smooth. The lust between them burned like a forest fire as she slid her hands across his shaven face. He lifted her shirt, exposed her bra. Her armpits had a little hair but none of that mattered to Elijah, his inner dog was coming out once again as he tore into her, gripping her sides and sliding his hand down her belt. Upon seeing him struggle to perform the task with one hand Gayla smiled and unbuckled her belt for him. She gorged herself in his essence with every kiss and touch he acted towards. Looking him dead into his eyes as her hips ground on him in her unbuckled jeans to the sound of the rain hitting the tin roof. The time they had spent together shown in each stroke she caressed the sides of his face. "Your kisses were sweeter than almond milk, and her scent is as sweet as Gardenias" he pressed as she leaned herself against him. A chill shot down her spine as his teeth slightly sunk into his bottom lip, creating a splendor unlike any other. She exhaled heavily as she pulled away from him slightly and stared deep into his dark brown eyes, and for a brief second, it was almost as if time froze. As he stretched out his arm and caressed the skin on her neck It looked as if the walls would be shaking, but the moment was interrupted by the scuffling of rappers of doomsday rations.

"That is just perfect", Elijah exclaimed as Gayla giggled softly before kissing him one more time, unmounting him, buckling up her belt, and turning towards the captive.

"I reckon you two can tie me up in my own house for how that looked back there, but at least respect Bella; that's the best coach I have ever had," the man said in a dramatic tone of voice.

"You don't look thin, and judging by the looks of this place id say your eating well. Where is the food?" she inquired while leaning towards him. He spits blood onto the floor and beaten stare at Gayla.

"If I tell you will you untie me?" he inquired.

Elijah peered at Gayla for a few seconds before she looked down at the ground and said; "Ok. But if you try to harm us again, I will kill you," she professed. Elijah then smacked his lips at the fact that he tried to and she retorted in the manner she did.

"No, Don't even start!" she snapped. She cut the knotted extension cord with a pair of wire cutters she found on the coffee table, freeing the man as Elijah picked up the Centurion Armour and proceeded to put it on.

"You be careful with her, she's custom," he exclaimed walking by them both to the filthy bathroom in the back of the trailer. Elijah fastened the headband around his head, pulling the light blue eyepiece over his eye in mid-stride. He pressed the armament and walked to the bathroom. Gayla grabbed the satchel and soon followed behind him. The clogged toilets aroma made Elijah gag on-air and Gayla covered her nose after they both followed him to see a bathtub full of doomsday rations. The sink was brown and covered with what looked like mildew, with a rotting floor beneath it.

"I don't get out much, the house needs some work; but I've just been trying to survive," he exclaimed in a thick southern accent; raising on his heels one time and landing back on the soles of his feet. As he tilted his head to the side, he pursed his bottom lip as if in deep thought.

The air was still and musty in the bathroom as the two watched the red-bearded man. The clock on the wall was the only sound being made, ticking stiffly amid grime.,He hasn't taken batteries out of everything. I wonder if there are more, Elijah thought to himself. Gayla's nose twitched at the hint of urea; "I'm sorry, but your bathroom is disgusting," she exclaimed.

"Well excuse me," he responded.

"I didn't clean today because it looked like a good day to go hunting," he said. Gayla crossed her arms as she stared at him with a disposition filled with disbelief.

"It looks like you haven't done any cleaning at all for a while," Gayla exclaimed.

"Surviving is hard," the man responded quickly. After a few brief moments of silence; "I think you're just making excuses," Elijah professed.

"Well aren't you two something, you shoot at me, you guys tie me up, then insult me in my own house. This is just downright disgraceful," he said while spitting more blood onto the floor.

"Elijah can we just take the food and go?" Gayla inquired while turning towards Elijah.

"Well wait a minute. You have more here don't you," Elijah asked while pointing his finger at the man.

"Gosh dang it, Allah they do me so wrong," the man exclaimed.

"Are you Muslim?" Elijah asked the man.

"Most certainly. Are you?" he poised with inquisitiveness.

"No, were Christian," Gayla stated bluntly.

"It's all the same at the end of the day," the man said while sitting on the rim of the sink.

"I am amazed you're able to keep that white shirt clean with the way you live," Gayla said while staring at him sit on the edge of the mildewy sink.

"Mama always told me to be sure to unplug everything from the wall sockets before you leave and keep your clothes clean," he expressed while spitting onto the floor again.

"Please stop doing that," Gayla hacked while putting her hand on her forehead, choking on the putrid imagery of seeing the man spit onto the floor again.

"Doing what?" the man asked. He coughed deep into his chest and began to hock the largest lugi known to mankind.

"Do not do that!" Gayla screamed at him while throwing up her arms by her face, Elijah turned his head away with one hand on his shoulder. The man stretched out his neck like a goose and suck it into his shoulders like a turtle receding into his shell, swallowing the lugi down his throat.

"Oh, my goodness. I'm going to be sick," she exclaimed.

"That was uncalled for in front of people you have never met before," Elijah said.

"Ah, man that one was granulated. I hope you two don't mind if I make myself at home," as he began to take off his pants revealing tie-dye underwear; "don't judge me".

"I call these my retro puppy's," he exclaimed while putting his hands on his hips.

"Ok, now you're making this weird," Elijah said while stretching his hand out towards him show an example.

"I thought you two would get it by now. I don't care about what you think of me, especially when I'm my humble abode," he said while stretching out his arms.

"Do you have any batteries?" Elijah inquired.

"You two disgust me by how you want to rob me of everything I own. This is all I have and I'm not giving you all of it," he professed boldly in his southern tone.

"Per Se we worked out a deal with you. We only get some of everything you have in exchange for something you want," Geyla hinted, giving Elijah an unnoticed wink of the eye. "I have an even better offer if you can beat me in a debate and convince me of anything; I'll give you all I have. I always liked debates", he professed boldly.

"Ok, then we pick the topic," Gayla said as she began to think of what it would be.

"Hold on, you said back there that Christianity and the Islamic faith are the same things. I can show you that they aren't!" Elijah contested on what the topic should be.

"Well let me tell you, I believe Jesus was real but not that he was not the Son of God. So explain why would God send his son to die," he asked?

"He had to die for the sins of the world," Gayla exasperated while staring at the wind blow the rain outside the window.

"But he was just a prophet, a man. He suffered hunger, thirst, and just sat there and let him kill him. A son of a God just let them kill him? Come on now, I think I know better than that," he hissed.

"First off, Son of God and child of God are two different distinctions. A child didn't have full rights in Roman custom, but a son does" Gayla exclaimed. "Galatians 4: 4-6 says, But when the right time came, God sent his Son, born of a woman, subject to the law. God sent him to buy freedom for us who were slaves to the law so that he could adopt us as his very own children. And because we are his children, God has sent the Spirit of his Son into our hearts, prompting us to call out, Abba, Father", Elijah added.

The man taunted with a flash of a yellow smile.

"Sensing the tension in the musty air Elijah reached into the trash bag tied into his satchel and pulled out the small square book that changed his life. He peered at the pages through the light blue monocle strapped to his eye.

"Let me start by saying, your argument is complete bull crap," Elijah said while wiping the rain off of its leather.

"Christians believe that Jesus was the Son of God, the Messiah; who died for our sins so that we may have eternal life. To look at something as big as the afterlife and say that something that big is to be overlooked like a piece of balled up paper; or the empty ration packages you have on the floor is utter disgraceful," he exclaimed, finishing with a slow inhale of foul air.

"Dude, what is your name," Gayla inquired.

"My name is Khalil," the redhead man said while scratching his butt through his underwear.

"Ok so so check this out, Khalil," Romans 3:25-26 says, "For God presented Jesus as a sacrifice for sin. People are made right with God when they believe that Jesus sacrificed his life, shedding his blood. This sacrifice shows that God was being fair when he held back and did not punish those who sinned in times past, for he was looking ahead and including them in what he would do in this present time. God did this to demonstrate his righteousness, for he is fair and just, and he makes sinners right in his sight when they believe in Jesus," Elijah exclaimed before Gayla said while nodding her head and giving a hard swallow. "He is more than a prophet to us."

"I'm still not convinced," he professed.

"The Bible refers to Jesus as the lamb, he was innocent; never committing one sin and the only one fit to die for me. A true exemplar of perfection," he exclaimed in a shaky voice.

"In Genesis God said, Let us make human beings in our image, to be like us. They will reign over the fish in the sea, the birds in the sky, the livestock, all the wild animals on the earth, and the small animals that scurry along the ground," Gayla pointed out before finishing.

"Us is the keyword I wanted you to see", Gayla said.

"Someone else was there from the beginning. Christ is Alpha and Omega because divinity never dies," Elijah expressed while turning around and walking into the living room and began to wipe the tears seeping from his ducts. Suddenly a shotgun barrel shot a hole in the trailer floor. The short-range through the halls, and accented from a scream from Elijah.

"Now look what you've done," Gayla hissed before continuing, "can we get our share already".

The man put one hand on his chin and thought for a while, before stating, "I'm still not convinced. So there is no share for you here," Elijah overheard him exclaim.

Elijah then looked down and pressed the disarm button and whispered in prayer, "Father God, I pray you to show this man who your true son is; the light of my world," he exclaimed while sitting in the living room.

"Now he's shooting in my house," he huffed. "Anyways, I haven't left this property in a month in a half. Let's go see the neighborhoods, we will split what we find. I don't suppose you two will let me hold a gun on the way, will you?" he asked.

"Jesus I know you paid the ultimate price for me, Father forgive me of my lust with Gayla," Elijah whispered as tears began to rise in his eyes and stream down his cheeks. Elijah wiped the tears from his eyes as he heard Gayla exclaimed.

"I'm sorry for shooting at you," he exclaimed. Khalil sucked in his emotions as the man headed out of the front door to lead the way. The shotgun turret made a short whining sound as he armed it and was ready for use. As they walked through the tall grass they passed yellow flowers being pelted by rain. Elijah gazed at the condensation forming at the rim of the shooter's monocle.

"We will go to Mary Todd's house first. I haven't seen my neighbor in a while," Kahlil exclaimed with excitement.

"She is my first cousin. Try not to stare at her skin, she doesn't like it. Her parents were first cousins, ``he said with a tooth-filled smile. As they left Khalil's front yard and crossed the street they stepped into a field with even taller grass.

"I see I'm not the only one trying to survive", Khalil exclaimed while looking at the height of the grass but Gayla just stared at him for an exaggerated second. They strolled past broken down cars and fallen trees and stepped onto the front porch. The wind blew into the front door as Elijah shot the hinges off of its frame and it fell to the floor. Gayla stormed into the house from the rain like Seal Team 3, with one finger on the trigger and looking for signs of danger. Rain poured into the entrance of the front door, smearing the clear outline of their footprints. With the pistol lowered, Gayla crept through the house like a field mouse, looking for anything that could help.

"Mary Todd are you here!" Khalil called out while stepping into the living room!

"Shh," Elijah sounded while holding up one finger over his lips. They suddenly heard a rustling sound, accented by the clinging of empty cans onto the floor. Elijah crept through the house towards the commotion, proceeding with defensive intensive cautiousness. "Marry I know you heard me call you! Why are you just sitting on the couch," Khalil called out while walking up to the body sitting on the couch with their back facing them.

"Oh my goodness, this man is something else," Elijah whispered to himself. After Gayla walked over to the man, she noticed the body of a dead woman, "She doesn't stink and she is still warm, this just happened," Gayla exclaimed.

"Well I guess I might as well," Khalil said while searching the body.

"Do you not have any respect for the dead," she inquired.

"What!? She doesn't need her stuff anymore," he exclaimed.

"Look she has a scratch-off ticket" he stated while picking it up from her pants pocket and holding it into the window's light. The sore sight of fortune seemed to take his breath away as he saw, "YOU WIN 750,000 smack in its middle."

"I won", he screamed with excitement; "I freaking won!

"You mean she won," she said. Khalil gave her the side-eye as he smacked his lips before saying; "I'm going to be rich."

As Elijah crept past the bathroom on alert as he neared the corner that the noise originated he heard Gayla call out as she resumed scavenging; "Yea, now you just have to stay alive to claim it". Then without warning a fair woman with rosy cheeks dashed out of the bathroom, startling Elijah as he turned to see her; and forcing the turret to fire into her stomach. She flew back onto the ground and shook as blood gushed from her insides. Gayla and Khalil rushed towards Elijah and the woman.

"What the heck, did you do!" Khalil shouted.

"Everything happened so fast," Elijah professed.

"She's not going to make it," Gayla exclaimed while kneeling to her before Khalil exclaimed. The woman shook on the ground as she wrapped one bloody hand from around her stomach to around Gayla's neck.

"Shoot me," she whispered to Gayla; making her eyes widen at the thought.

"Shoot me, please", the white woman exclaimed in pain.

With that she knelt on one knee and pulled out the pistol and placed it in the woman's mouth, her eyes grew twice the size of Gayla's as she stared in her eyes. The shot echoed in the room, the sight of her head in her brains made Khalil jump and made Elijah walk to the living room, ripping off the armor and throwing in on the ground. Gayla sighed heavily before raising to both feet with the gun in her right hand, it hung by her side as the thunder roared and rain poured onto the metal roof.

Chapter Nineteen

June 1st, 2044. 6:00 P.M. Dallas, TX.

In a state of comatose, Anastasia lay immobile in a hospital bed, hearing the outside world that portrayed visual imagery.

"She's been in it so long," A giant black mouse with a tan face and mole on its right cheek wore green worn-out overalls. It tugged on the straps while walking up to a white duck with etching neon blue feathers and a black beak. In the duck's left hand was a purple trident. It glistened in the light that hung overhead, swinging back and forth. The duck quaked if it were giving a speech stomping on a red and white magic carpet with silver embroidery, its ends flipped up and down as the duck marched. Anastasia bounced on the ground and unsettled her tiara which rests on top of her head.

The mouse was about 8 feet tall with gloved hands and sharp white canine fangs, then the whites of its eyes suddenly changed to maroon as it pulled out a bottle of Crazy Kay's hot sauce and began to shake it on top of the radiant blue and white duck while the duck exclaimed; "I know but we have to keep trying". It was then as if her world altered as everything turned 180°, but this didn't stop the mouse as he licked his lips; salivating over the bird. It drizzled on the bird's head and down its neck, wetting the white breast feathers on its chest. His eyes showed true evil but the duck did not notice a thing and it continued to parade in a circle on the ceiling with the trident in hand; it's tail feathers waged with each step as a rush of little people rushed pashed Anastasia from out of nowhere.

"Get out of the way", one of them yelled in a high pitched voice while another exclaimed; "Brody!, move your oversized anatomy". One of them then ran smack into her as she sat in the ceiling, knocking her onto her back.

"Hey, stay away from there," her voice called out but her lips did not move; to the outside world, she was still as calm water as she sat up on the ceiling in her mind.

"The longer this draws out the less of a chance that we will see any progress," the mouse exclaimed as he ate the little people and the duck and chewed them up in front of Anastasia with it all pressed against one cheek. The mouse put its hands on its stomach as it gulped the load down as she watched. The lump slid down its throat and dropped into its belly with a bounce. Then sucking in air, it pulled the magic carpet into its mouth. It put up a fight, attempting to grip the floor and getaway, but skit ended in it being slurped in with the mouse's tongue while looking at Anastasia next. She felt the hairs raise on her ivory arms and she sat on the ground while turning the tiara on right and running her fingers through her red hair.

"Do you see that?" the mouse inquired while spitting out a rainbow spit droplet containing gradient color in her eyes, it arched a hair just before plopped into her pupil before it splattered on her long eyelashes as she blinked as if it were an uncontrollable protracted illness.

"She's coming back," she heard the duck's voice exclaim from inside the mouse's stomach as flames consumed the evil mouse; but she was perplexed as she rubbed her eyes in her head but everything was bright and glowed with radiant color as she blinked her eyes into consciousness. She felt the table tilt as she was slowly lowered her back down flat from the upright position.

"Greetings Anastasia, I am Doctor Black," a white man in a white coat and brown shoes exclaimed while standing next to a brown woman in turquoise scrubs. This is Nurse Lisa, she will be tending to you; we can't leave you alone. You have been in a coma for about 3 months now. I didn't think you were going to make it," he professed. Anastasia gazed around the small room. The bathroom door was open, leaving a shadow speared by the light around the seams of its radius. As the Doctor left the room the nurse walked over to the side of the bed in her lime green shoes with grey laces.

"I'm so glad you're awake now," she exclaimed.

"I guess I have a lot of explaining to do, you were life-flighted to Dallas shortly after the first attack. They would have sent you to Houston but the city fell shortly after the initial attack. The Doctors got the bleeding to stop, but you were already in a coma. They had to perform a blood transfusion to save you. Be thankful you're with us though. A little fewer freedoms than before but look at the perks; air-condition, food, employment, the works; and just look at that view," she exclaimed while looking out of the glass wall dome that was over the hospital. The building was shaped like a golf ball on a tee, with a glass ball on top and a stone pillar beneath it.

"It's much better than being those constellation worshiping savages. Ha, who's going to bathe tonight! They don't even have power, they just pray to the stars and kill people, `` she said as she went to a cupboard and began to work with Anastasia.

"Do you remember any of the blasts?" the nurse inquired.

"I remember being there with someone, but I don't remember who he was," she exclaimed.

"Oh, that's unfortunate, I like to hear the patients stories, it makes the job worth whiled to me," she professed while pulling out the needle and preparing the new one she exclaimed; "I have to put you on your preferential diet."

"So who's winning the war?" Anastasia inquired.

"Propaganda may tell you otherwise, but the government still owns a lot of turfs," she exclaimed while unpacking a clean needle and preparing it, then inserted into her arm.

"They even have an app where you can see all of the U.S territories; quite fascinating actually," she exclaimed while pulling out her phone and selecting the app.

"I'll have to check it out," she exclaimed while looking back at the bathroom. Suddenly something rushed by the dash of light in the doorway of the bathroom, causing Anastasia to jump. The door slightly creaked in at the tone of a mouse, and Anastasia was the only one to notice. It unsettled her stomach as she stared into the bathroom door, gripping the sides of her bedsheets with her fingers.

"Are you ok?" the nurse asked. After taking a deep breath Anastasia exclaimed, "Yeah, I'm fine. I just thought I saw something," she said.

"Ok, well I'm going to move you to a different room, please lay back," she professed as another nurse entered. As she lay back he unlocked the wheels from the cart and pushed it from Anastasia's head with the nurse Lisa took the iv in hand. The wheels clicked from a misaligned wheel on the bed as they turned around the corner, entering the main hall. Anastasia's eyes wander everywhere, but she stopped when her eyes caught a glimpse of a chilling sight. While the nurses moved her down the hall she saw a pair of eyes pop out of the blinds, spying on her every move. They slowly slide to the right as she was pushed away in fear, too afraid to move or speak.

Finally, she could no longer take it anymore, after a matter of seconds that felt like years she said; "There's someone in there." The male nurse stopped pushing her and went back into the room, only to leave and turn out the light. "It's empty," he exclaimed while resuming to push her down to the other room.

Chapter Twenty

Elijah sat on the benchtop under the night sky. The moon was like a swollen crescent, surrounded by gallant galactic graceful bodies. He stared at the big dipper while he sat in the dark, smoking one of his cigarettes. He tasted the skin chilling chattels of tobacco he loved so much; it was his first cigarette in a long time, his face felt tingly as he inhaled again; he tasted its flavor in the roof of his mouth after he exhaled a cloud of smoke into the night, leaning back and propping himself up on one arm. He slightly pushed air from the air sacs in his lungs as he resituated himself. He then heard the front door of Mary Todd's house open and close as he turned to see Gayla walking towards him. He looked at the sky once again as she sat next to him on the benchtop.

"Hey I bet I can cheer you up," she exclaimed.

"I'm lower than the belly of a snake," he professed before continuing in an irate tone of voice, "I took a life, but you can go ahead and try!"

"You know what that reminds me of something, but first I think we should pray. We need to ask for forgiveness for judging Khalil back there and you killed someone, we both need to repent Elijah," she said.

"Your right," he exclaimed while taking her hands in the dark.

"Father we come to you with humble hearts and sound minds. Please forgive us for judging the man we encountered in this town," he professed before pausing and pulling out his bible from the satchel which lay on the benchtop beside them.

Gayla opened her eyes as she watched him flip the pages to Luke 6:37 and say, "Do not judge others, and you will not be judged. Do not condemn others, or it will all come back against you. Forgive others, and you will be forgiven."

"Father we are sorry, who are we to judge anyone on this earth. Please forgive us.", Elijah exclaimed. He started to flip through the pages as Gayla examined him.

"Elijah", she budded in.

"Let me have a try," she exclaimed after catching his attention, she then reached a gentle hand towards the book; unclasping it from his hand.

She flipped through its folios to John 8, "Jesus returned to the Mount of Olives, but early the next morning he was back again at the Temple. A crowd soon gathered, and he sat down and taught them. As he was speaking, the teachers of religious law and the Pharisees brought a woman who had been caught in the act of adultery. They put her in front of the crowd. Teacher, they said to Jesus, "this woman was caught in the act of adultery. The law of Moses says to stone her. What do you say? They were trying to trap him into saying something they could use against him, but Jesus stooped down and wrote in the dust with his finger. They kept demanding an answer, so he stood up again and said, all right, but let the one who has never sinned throw the first stone! Then he stooped down again and wrote in the dust. When the accusers heard this, they slipped away one by one, beginning with the oldest, until only Jesus was left in the middle of the crowd with the woman. Then Jesus stood up again and said to the woman, "Where are your accusers? Didn't even one of them condemn you? No, Lord, she said. And Jesus said, Neither do I. Go and sin no more," She finished before passing the bible back to Elijah.

He then went through the thin leaves like a jackrabbit to James 4:11-12, "Don't speak evil against each other, dear brothers and sisters. If you criticize and judge each other, then you are criticizing and judging God's law. But your job is to obey the law, not to judge whether it applies to you. God alone, who gave the law, is the Judge. He alone has the power to save or to destroy. So what right do you have to judge your neighbor?" he exclaimed.

He then flipped to Genesis 9:5-6 and cleared his throat, "And I will require the blood of anyone who takes another person's life. If a wild animal kills a person, it must die. And anyone who murders a fellow human must die. If anyone takes a human life, that person's life will also be taken by human hands. For God made human beings in his own image", Elijah paused and pulled the book down in fear.

"Have mercy on us both," Gayla said after making a small expression while closing her eyes again and ebbing with the closing statement; "Amen."

"See, now don't you feel better?" she asked.

"I'm not sure," he exclaimed; "that last verse was a little scary."

"Trust and know you are forgiven my brother," she professed while placing a hand on his shoulder.

"Maybe you're right. We should get moving, the sun is going down," Elijah exclaimed as he hopped off the benchtop and put on the satchel. Gayla sighed heavily at how hard Elijah was taking the fact that he pulled the rosy-cheeked woman's card.

"I just feel bad you know," he exclaimed while pulling out another cigarette and placing it in his lips and lighting it.

"You're not the first person to ever make a mistake, do you remember the Fall?", Gayla inquired.

"Yes I do, the shrewdest of them all; the serpent deceived Adam and Eve in the Garden of Eden," Elijah exclaimed.

"Exactly, imagine how they felt," Gayla professed, "God still loved them despite their actions".

"Do you know what the word shrewd means?" Gayla asked as they began to walk into the dying sun.

"Please enlighten me," Elijah retorted. "Having sharp powers of judgment", Gayla said, "I once thought it meant intelligent."

"That's interesting," Elijah exclaimed as they got onto the center of the road.

"Is it," she chuckled.

"Yeah, I mean it wasn't exactly correct but I understand how you could get that confused," he said; "I've never liked snakes though."

"Me either," Elijah laughed.

"They move so quickly as they slither across the ground, it gives me the creeps," he professed.

"What would you do if you saw anaconda?" Gayla inquired.

"Dude are you serious, I'd die from a heart attack before it ate me. The house we use to live in had a big ditch in front of it. The other kids in the neighborhood would make a snake trap in the ditch and cover it with a tarp. A day or two later they would stick their hand in and grab one of their tails, and flick it like a whip to snap its neck," he laughed.

"Wow, it sounds like you guys needed more toys growing up," Gayla exclaimed with a laugh.

"I never did it. Remember, I'm afraid of snakes but I did watch them. I even remember when little jimmy got bit by a water moccasin, but that was because he was running around barefoot after hurricane Tralon hit," he exclaimed.

"I use to work at Club Atlantis and it was nearly underwater," he laughed while taking the cigarette from his lips.

"Snakes in the city?" she chuckled while looking up at the sky while peering at the nimbostratus clouds.

"My grandparents stayed in the country," he exclaimed; "But I lived and worked in Houston."

"I liked working at Club Atlantis, but I don't think it was where I belonged," Elijah exclaimed; "there was more dirt in that club than on the bottom of a nudist foot."

"When you say dirt, you mean you guys did some screwed up stuff?" She inquired.

"Yeah, but the cops even knew about it," he exclaimed while staring at a giant billboard sign on the side of the road. Elijah then stared at Gayla and scanned her down slowly to her hand, without her even giving it a bit of attention as she exhaled deeply, making her breast raise and lower as she breathed out. He reached for her hand without hesitation, as if were a shark going in for the kill; though on the inside he was filled with nervousness and a serious case of butterflies in his stomach. When their hands met and fingers interlocked it was if the shark's eyes rolled back as a smile flashed across his face. It was beautiful, her fingernails were clean and he was a little dirty. He took his other hand flicked out the cigarette from his lips into the weeds.

"You need to stop that," she exclaimed, "It's a bad habit."

"First off, no smoker wants to hear that," he laughed.

"Do you drink?" he asked.

"Occasionally," she responded.

"Well imagine per se, you had a nice full glass of Chardonnay. It's as cold as the ice cubes inside and it's been a long day baby girl. I mean, you worked hard," he said while looking at her.

"Mhm", she smiled back while swinging their hands back and forth.

"But just as you place it to your lips and take a sip I look you dead in your eyes inches away from your face and say, I bet your liver is going to be screaming tonight," he exclaimed in a transition in tone of voice.

Gayla burst out laughing before saying, "I guess I get your point then."

"Elijah, I want to be honest with you, I think your an amazing person. I mean, I've met a lot of guys out there and no two people are the same; but you are truly one of a kind," She said. Elijah smirked while looking at her in mid-stride.

"You're not so bad yourself," he replied.

Gayla then stopped dead in her tracks and asked Elijah, "Do you hear that?". Elijah then stopped walking as he slowly slid his head to the side at the sadistic sound of a woman screaming for her life.

"Come on!" she snapped while grabbing Elijah's hand, tugging it with her in the direction of the pandemonium. They ran behind a red brick building beside an alley. Down the tube of the alley stood three armed Zodia members with their shirts cut off at the middle of their stomach. In front of them sat a woman who was tied to the chair beside a can of gasoline.

"Please stop!" the woman screamed as she begged for her life. One of the Zodia goons extended his arm and placed a baseball bat beneath her chin, using it to pick up her head.

"I'm not going to ask you again. Will you join the Zodia, pray to the stars and become apart of our family; trusting in our beloved horoscopes?" the man asked. The woman snorted in spit and air and spit it at the man, sending him in a frenzy. The veins in his neck began to bulge and his white skin began to flush red, he was like a pink salmon with a red headdress of hair on one side.

"Jason, give me your matches," he announced as he picked up the can of gas before a brown man with dreads passed him a small box of matches.

"No, please don't do this to me," she pleaded as her feet kicked the cement alleyway.

"Elijah we have to do something this time," Gayla hissed at Elijah in a soft tone.

"I know," he said while pulling out the pistol. The man then poured the gas on top of her head while she screamed for dear life, gas entered her oral and nasal cavities as she struggled to move, turning her head away from the pouring shower of gasoline. Once the can was empty he shook it over her head before throwing it at her and watching her cry.

"You're going to regret that decision," he said while pulling out the matches, causing her eyes to double their size as she stared at him and prayed.

Elijah gripped the pistol tighter and placed one hand on the wall while aiming. Then all of a sudden a swarm of bullets flew into the alleyway, hitting the two other Zodia henchman and leaving the other staggering with a bullet gauged into his neck. He coughed up blood that landing on the cement ground beneath them. His fall was slow and painful, first dropping onto one knee, then both; before falling on his face.

"Don't move a muscle," A deep voice called out behind Elijah and Gayla. As Gayla froze Elijah turned around to see an armed black man in camo. However, amidst the excitement, he did not notice he was an American Soldier. He lurched at the soldier knocking him onto the ground, causing him to fire his gun.

"Run," he screamed to Gayla as she pushed herself and after hearing his words charged off into the woods while more soldiers approached Elijah's big fight. The two men tussled in circles, rolling around in the dirt trying to choke each other into unconsciousness. The other soldiers then jumped in and began to kick Elijah in the ribs and legs, he was outnumbered in an unfair fight.

"That's enough," a voice called from behind him after a few minutes; "Get him up". The group circled Elijah then opened up and a short stocky dark-skinned man walked up to him.

"Are you one of them," a man said while taking a cigar from his mouth. Elijah looked up at the man, seeing his reflection in his black shades.

"No," Elijah coughed while attempting to breathe in pain.

"Take him to the cell, you boys know what to do," he exclaimed while walking off as the men grabbed Elijah and carried him off.

Meanwhile

As Gayla ran through the woods she eventually lost track of where she was and how long she had been running, or even if she was being chased. She stopped running and placed the palms of her hands on her knees, as she inhaled deeply. After a few breaths, she looked up at the sky and saw a cloud of smoke coming into the sky from nearby and began to follow it. The woods were spacious with occasional oak tree sagging down dark green pine needles. She places her hand on its crisp bark as she walked by. Thoughts of Elijah swirled in her head as she made her way towards the smoke.

She bit her knuckle with a chest full of nerves before calling out, "Father I'm sorry for worrying, but I pray you to keep Elijah safe; and even that you will return him to me. Please bring us back together, Amen," she said to God.

She was now approaching the brush where the smoke came from. She pulled it back to see an old man with a cowboy hat on splitting wood by a fire with an ax. He grabbed one log and placed it on top of the stump next to him and swung the ax once again, splitting the log in two. But it wasn't until Gayla stepped on a stick, causing him to look up at the noise and see Gayla in the brush. As he walked over to her with the ax in hand, she fell onto the ground while backing up and to her surprise, he lowered the ax and stretched out a hand to help pick her up. She stared at while taking a deep breath before reaching for it and was pulled up from the woodland floor bed.

"Your not one of them, I can tell," the old white man exclaimed; "My name is Crunchy."

"Mine is Gayla," she exclaimed while staring at him hold the ax.

"Are there more people or is it just you?" she inquired.

"My lady, you are at the Alta Vista Ranch, there is a community of us," he retorted. She gazed at the wrinkles in his white face, she examined his sweaty bald head as he pulled off his cowboy hat, revealing his receding hairline.

"Follow me," he said while leading Gayla to a metal wall that surrounded a compound.

"You guys built all of this," she exclaimed as a guard standing on top of the wall opened the gate. She looked at the buzzing community, there were stalls set up in the compound center that was cluttered with people scuttling about.

"We work on a barter system," he professed while walking past the stalls to a building in the back of the compound. They passed by a small tan boy kicking around a lime green ball. She looked to the left and saw a Pasteur filled with livestock being tended to men on horses.

When they entered the building in the back of the compound she thought to herself, "This is amazing". Her eyes then shot to a woman with her back turned sitting in a wheeled chair.

"Calvin I thought I told you to go find something to do," she exclaimed before slowly turned around revealing her face, "Oh, I do apologize, I thought you were someone else."

"Crunchy so who have you brought to me?", she asked before starting, "She certainly doesn't look familiar."

"This is Gayla, I found her at the edge of the wilderness. Gayla this is Patrice, she is in charge here," Crunchy exclaimed.

"Wilderness?" Gayla inquired.

"That's what we call the world outside these walls," Patrice professed.

"Well Gayla, Welcome to the Alta Vista Ranch, I'd like to give you a tour. At the least show you were the clinic is," the woman said.

"Great, because that wood isn't going to split itself; I'll keep in touch Gayla. I hope you decide to stay with us, `` he exclaimed as they all left the room and the three of them split up into a duo.

"Calvin is my son, you will see him running around here somewhere," Practice exclaimed a while walking towards a nearby building. She pushed open the door with Gayla following closely behind. In the room, a man was standing in front of an assortment of a flask on the desk in front of him.

"This is Dr. Earl Sherman," Patrice exclaimed while extending her hand.

"You get a scratch, infection, or bruise, come to him. Of course, you will have to trade for services," she said with a smile.

"Nice to meet you," the old slim caucasian doctor said. His lab coat was a little dirty and his glasses had clear round lenses that perched on his nose.

"This is my lab assistant Timothy," Dr. Sherman exclaimed while pointing to a smiling boy staring at a boiling flask in the corner of the room.

"He is a little slow, but he has such a strong infatuation with chemistry. It's quite beautiful actually," he exclaimed.

"Well I must get back to my work," he then professed.

As they left the building Patrice then looked at Gayla and said, "We have a few rules. First off no weapons, and you get a portion of what you work for trade and some for yourself," she exclaimed.

"If you're going to stay, we will need to find a job for you. Crunchy can handle that. In the meantime, I'll split some of my supplies with you. But if you leave, I understand," she said while looking into her eyes.

"I've been out there so long, of course, I'll stay," she exclaimed with a smile.

"I think you're going to do well here, welcome aboard," she said while extending her hand and shaking Gayla's hand.

Chapter Twenty-one

June 22nd, 2044. 10:00 A.M. Dallas, TX.

As Anastasia sat in bed, she stared at the grey walls of the room thinking of what she thought she had seen. The vein filled eyes still gave her the creeps as Nurse Lisa attend to her.

"We're going to work out your legs today, I'm going to get the wheelchair and help you down to the physical therapy department. The Dr. recommended that you do it at least four times a week," she said while leaving the room. Anastasia stared at the muted TV, it showed cartoons, her childhood favorite. She then turned her head to the side and stared out of the glass window, but just as she was calmed by the beautiful scenery the nurse entered the room with a pink envelope.

"You got a piece of mail," she exclaimed while handing it to her. Anastasia sniffed what smelled like expensive cologne draped over its capsule.

"It sure smells nice, I wonder who it's from," the nurse exclaimed before continuing what she was doing. Anastasia put one finger in the corner of the letter and ripped it across the top, opening it up and revealing a piece of paper folded hot dog style.

AND THE LETTER READ.....

My dearest Anastasia,

Your skin and essence are comparable to the splendor and smoothness of fine wine. Your skin is ivory white like the keys on a piano. Oh, how I wish to caress your flesh. Although you do not know me, I want you to know that I love you. I've spent hours watching you sleep, it started with a few hours; then that turned to days. We would just sit there and talk for hours. Even though you didn't respond I still enjoyed your company. You look so beautiful when you sleep. Your hair is like a rope, I just want to tie you up with it. I love you, I want to see you again.

P.S

I hope you won't be mad with me, but I would suck your toes sometimes while you were unconscious; thinking of it makes me want to spend more time with you. I'll keep in touch. Anastasia then put the letter down in fear.

"I'm going to tell the Dr. about your paranoia, he may be able to give you something for it," the nurse exclaimed while looking at her inlay in bed.

"Come on, let's go down there," she exclaimed before putting the letter on the table beside the bed and removing Anastasia from the bed, placing her in the wheelchair.

"I think you should read that letter, I don't feel safe here," she exclaimed. The nurse then picked up the letter and read it. After a moment she exclaimed.

"Oh my goodness, I think you have a stalker. I'm going to give the letter to the police." She placed the letter in her back pocket and pushed Anastasia out of the room only to be bumped into by a janitor pushing a mop bucket as the nurse backed out of the room.

"I'm sorry, I don't think I have my head on straight", the Janitor exclaimed while looking at them both before continuing to push the mop bucket.

"It's ok, I should have been more careful," the nurse exclaimed while continuing to maneuver her wheelchair to the physical therapy department. Once they turned the corner they went through a pair of double doors, entering what looked like a training complex, there were weights, a pool, a rock wall, and high tech cardio machines.

"You will be working with a man named Fabio today", she said, "I'm going to get in touch with the police department immediately".

She felt for the letter but it was not there, "I must have dropped it," she said, "I'll go back and check". As she walked back out of the double doors, Fabio approached her.

"It's going to be a pleasure working with you today, were going to start with some stretching then transition into some light-bearing exercises," he exclaimed.

"Sounds like fun," she responded.

"Have you ever done physical therapy before?" the man asked.

"No," Anastasia exclaimed while staring into the man's eyes. Then all of a sudden the nurse reentered and said: "I didn't see a thing back there, I even checked in the room."

"Look I don't want you to worry," she said while placing one hand on her shoulder, "Were going to get to the bottom of this".

Chapter Twenty-two

June 25th, 2044. 5:00 P.M. The Alta Vista Ranch. Shepherd, TX.

Gayla exited the gate of the Alta Vista Ranch, walking towards the place where she met Crunchy near the stump. Her hips switched from left to right as she walked down the side of the wall, she stuck out one arm towards the wall; running her fingers across the screws and bolts holding the wall up. She then took down her arm and placed her hands in her pockets as she approached the stump was Crunchy was sitting beneath a tree in a wooden chair with his ankles crossed.

"Do you spend most of your time out here", Gayla asked the old man.

He situated his hat on his head before folding his arms across his blue overalls and saying, "Yeah, it's nice and peaceful out here. Crunchy uncrossed his booted feet and began to stand up, putting his hands on his knees to brace himself as he raised.

"So looks like the order of business today is to find you a place to work here, now If I may madam; I'd like to make a suggestion. People need to eat, food and water have the highest value here. More specifically, meat," he exclaimed while signaling Gayla to follow him.

"So I thought I take you fishing, and if you like it; then I guess we have found out where you fit in," he exclaimed with a smile.

"I've never been fishing before," she said.

"No need to worry, I'll explain everything," he said as he hobbled through the woods. The earth beneath them was illuminated by patches of light that passed through the treetops.

"Shepherd is a beautiful place, most of the town was national forest before the war began," he exclaimed before Crunchy led her to an oval-shaped pond containing brown water. On the bank of the pond lay a florescent pink canoe with its keel in the air, two neon orange life jackets, a black oar, and a styrofoam cooler.

"This would be a nice place to go on a date," Gayla exclaimed.

"My lady, I'm much too old for you," Crunchy confessed with a laugh.

"No, someone already has my heart. But I don't know where he is or what has become of him. I only hope God protects him," she exclaimed.

"Well trust your prayers are heard," Crunchy said to her while flipping over the canoe.

"I've heard that before," she giggled while walking over to two fishing rods propped up against the tree by a small white container, reflecting on her words to Elijah.

She ran her finger along the string to the hook, which was tethered to the pole by the kook's barb.

"Will you please bring that stuff over here," Crunchy asked Gayla while putting the boat into the water and placing the cooler inside of it. She grabbed the two poles and the container and eased her way into the canoe with a yellow life jacket on. They fastened on their life jackets as the sunlight danced across the water; the only shaded area was in the corner near a tire swing that hung by the bank.

"Ok, so first things first," Crunchy exclaimed before continuing, but Gayla began to tune him out. The more she thought about Elijah, the more she missed him. She then began to twiddle her fingers while looking down at her hands, causing Crunchy to stop in a mid-sentence; noticing she wasn't paying attention to him.

"What was that young man's name," he inquired while rowing through the water.

"Elijah," she retorted.

"He sure is a lucky man to have such a beautiful woman like you to be this concerned about him in a time like this," he exclaimed while switched sides to row on.

"I'm not all that, and he has a fiance out there somewhere, so I just feel like I'm wasting my time. But when we are together I feel like I'm flying through the clouds," she said.

"I can see God in him despite his imperfections," she exclaimed. "I think I'm in over my head. I mean I don't even know where he is," she finished.

"Sounds like quite a sticky situation," Crunchy exclaimed.

"I don't want to think about it," she professed; "Lets just fish."

"Ok, then let's get started," he exclaimed while grabbing one of the hooks and unhooking the barb.

"Open that white container", he said while examining the rod. Gayla opened the container to see a mound of black dirt filled with fat worms.

"Will you please put one on the hook for me?" he inquired.

"I'm not touching those," she retorted while passing him the worms. Crunchy smacked his lips before reaching in and grabbing a really fat one, it wiggled from side to side in between his dirty fingers while dirt dribbled off the worm back into the container.

"Just so you know, you're going to put your worm on your hook," he exclaimed while sliding it onto the hook and attaching a weight. He then sat up in the canoe and cast the rod out into the water.

"Here hold this rod, I'll get you a weight," he exclaimed while passing her the rod. But just as fate would have it a fish nibbled at the hook twice before grabbing it and trying to swim in the opposite direction.

"Hey, I think we got one," Gayla called out in excitement as the string tightened.

"Reel it in," Crunchy screamed before taking the rod from her, "No, your doing it all wrong, you bring them in like this". A smile crept across Gayla's face as the fish drew closer and closer.

"Here, finish him off I need to get the cooler ready", he said while passing her the rod again, grabbing the cooler with the other hand. He dipped it into the brown water, preparing temporary storage for the soon to be caught fish. By this time the fish was ready to be pulled up and Crunchy turned around with the cooler between his legs, he reached for the edge of the string and pulled the fish up; it flipped in the air as it struggled to breathe. With a firm grip on its mouth, he stuck his hand inside its mouth and pulled out the hook. He then looked at his companion and stuck his fingers in the gills and said, "Put it in the cooler." But as the fish transferred hands it flipped and wiggled, startling Gayla and causing her to stand and scream; throwing her arms up in the air like she was being held at gunpoint. The commotion caused the canoe to rock to one side sending Gayla overboard with the fish in hand and almost throwing Crunchy out as well, but after her displacement, the canoe resettled on the water's surface. He then dropped the fishing rod and stared at the water looking for her.

"Gayla are you ok," he called out; "Can you swim?"

But there was no sign of her, not even a bubble surfaced from beneath the water. Then from out of nowhere, Gayla burst up to the surface with her afro laying in her face. "There you go," Crunchy exclaimed with a smile; "Do you still have the fish?"

"'Take me to shore now!" She screamed. Crunchy wiped the smile off his face, situated his hat and reached out his hand to help her in. After she crawled in breathing as if she had run a full marathon, Crunchy rowed them back to the shore.

"Maybe fishing isn't for you," he professed, "But I have another idea".

"What's that?" she responded between breaths while looking up at Crunchy.

"Hunting," he said with a smile.

Chapter Twenty-three

June 26th, 2044. 5:00 P.M. Agua Nueva, TX.

Simone sat on the ground in the middle of open pasture. She breathed deeply as she ran her fingers through her hair as she whispered to the voices in her head.

"He's coming. Where is he," she murmured; "Oh no, please don't be upset with me."

"Why are you asking questions?" the voice in head sounded in a low tone.

"Don't you know your king is looking for you?" it asked.

"What's his name?" Simone whispered back. The voice then grew louder, sounding as if it were swelling from one side to the other.

"Ok, I'll tell you," it exclaimed; "But if you look behind you, you will see him". Simone lurched around so fast the dirt in the pasture unsettled from her excitement, but she saw no one there.

"Hey you lied to me," she exclaimed to the voice.

"Did I, well would I be lying if I told you his name was San Briana," the voice screamed.

"San Briana," she repeated while running her fingers through her hair again, pulling it from its roots.

"Yes my dear," it said; "he is coming for you."

"You have seen him before," it repeated three times in a row.

"I have," she retorted in the empty pasture after the voice had finished.

"Yes," it ticked repeatedly.

"Remember the man you saw," the voice exclaimed as she flipped through mental pages to the hallucination she had before she escaped.

"San Briana," she whispered while smearing the sweat on her face with her dirty hands before raising to her feet.

"Where are you going," a voice called out to her.

"I'm going to find him," she professed while turning in a circle, unsure of were she was or which way to search for the man that didn't exist.

"Go north, ill escort you," it exclaimed.

"Which way is north," she retorted with frustration. The voice in her head began to make a snorting noise that pricks Simone's nerves, provoking her to start screaming in the empty pasture.

"Which way is north!" She screamed louder before having a breakdown, memories of her rape then began to surge within her head; making her feel dirty once again.

"Ok, now look; I don't want you to get your feathers all ruffled up over nothing so this is what I'll do," it exclaimed.

"I'll let you talk to him, here he goes," it said.

"Simone," the voice called out with little alteration of sound.

"San Briana is that you!" she screamed.

"Yes, Simone I'm coming for you", the voice in her head exclaimed as she began to walk.

"Where should I meet you," she called out.

"Look for me where the wind blows, I have to go now; take care", the voice exclaimed before it made a whirring sound as low as thunder.

"Guess whos back!" the voice screamed.

"No, bring him back!" she screamed; "I want to talk to him."

"It's not fair," she exclaimed while having a breakdown, tears streamed down her light brown cheeks.

"That's not fair," is repeated twice in a low tone.

"You make me sick!", it screamed before she could get a word out. The voice in her head made a hacking sound before it spat a mythically in her head; forcing more sobs to erupt.

"It's not fair", she said repeatedly while wiping her eyes, consumed by her condition and slipping further into the pool of insanity.

Chapter Twenty-four

June 30th, 2044. 6:00 A.M. Shady
Oaks, Kingwood, TX.

Gladius lay on the floor in one of the houses of the Shady Oaks housing complex, the Zodia had turned the entire community into a drug lab. Run by slaves like Gladius to make the precious Neon Moon. He had been there for almost two months, the harsh conditions caused some that came with him to perish, the others were shipped off. He had one friend and her name was Raven. He thought about them all as he lay in a slump. The Zodia had ransacked the houses the slaves stayed in. There was a gaping hole in almost every wall, the toilets were removed, and there would be up to twenty slaves living in one house. His stomach grumbled as he rolled onto his side, facing the dusty feet of another slave. They were treated like animals and were dropping like flies. But the more that dropped, the more came in, but only of the Taurus, Aquarius, and Sagittarius Zodiac signs were allowed to work at this camp; the rest worked in other facilities throughout Zodia territory. Every day, sun up to sun down he made drugs for people he never saw; the only things he knew about the fiends were myths and legends. Some of the newbies brought in sometimes have stories of how terrifying the fiends are. Now they help make more of them, truly ironic to say the least, he thought to himself. He then rolled onto his back staring at the powerless ceiling fan. He ran his finger across the scar left behind from the gash left by the whip, a painful reminder of what Africa was capable of. Then all of a sudden the door burst open and a Zodia member enter the room banging on pots to wake everyone up, as they did every morning. Gladius sighed to himself and raised from the ground, starting with stretch and ending with a yawn; he walked out of the door to see Africa standing outside of his quarters.

"Good morning Gladius," he exclaimed with a smile; holding the whip coiled up in one hand.

"Good morning sir," Gladius exclaimed.

"Sir", Africa chuckled. He then put his arm around Gladius as they walked to the drug lab.

"Do you see the butt on that woman," he whispered in Gladius's ear while Africa stared at Raven. Gladius did not know what to think, he didn't want something to happen to his friend because of his actions, and never really looked at Raven in that way.

"Well, are you going to respond?" he asked after displeasure in Gladius's silence. Gladius' mouth felt dry as if he swallowed a mouthful of cinnamon.

"Uh," He started before he was cut off.

"Everyone stop!" he called out as everyone ceased to move. Africa got into Gladius's face, allowing him to smell his putrid breath.

"Is there something your not telling me, you know secrets don't make friends," Africa said.

"Are we not friends?" he inquired. But Gladius remained silent.

He then grabbed him and yelled, "Well?".

"We are," Gladius said in fear of the fire in his eyes.

"Good. You know what I think. I think you like a fellow slave; and we all know how I feel about that, it's forbidden," he said while backing up and letting the whip swing to the ground. He walked behind Raven and grabbed her butt in front of Gladius while whispering something in her ear. She closed her eyes in displeasure but was as still as stone.

"You all carry on, Gladius come here please," he yelled and just like that the crowd continued to go to the drug lab. It left him and Africa in the middle of the street.

"I suggest you stop keeping secrets Gladius," he exclaimed with a laugh in Gladius's ear; "Or I'll give her to the fiends and make you watch, just to see the look on your face. Now get out of my face." Gladius then followed the crowd with sadness in his heart, he feared for his friend; and it hurt to see her be violated in front of everyone.

"I'm sorry about that," Gladius said to Raven.

She sniffed in a tear before exclaiming, "it's ok."

They both stripped to their underwear and then put on turquoise rubber gloves and a yellow face mask and approached the lab bench. Everyone's brand showed on there latissimus dorsi and in the lab, everyone was exposed in their undergarments. Gladius began mixing the compounds on the table while trying to be slick with a conversation because they were not allowed to talk to each other.

"He thinks I like you", Gladius whispered as she began to mix chemicals as well but did not respond.

"That doesn't worry you?" Gladius whispered.

"I'm trying to stay out of trouble, please be quiet for both our sake," she whispered back. With the silence came wandering ears. Gladius listened to the talking guard's conversation by the door.

"Want to see something funny?" one of then exclaimed while breaking the piece of bread into two pieces and throwing one piece on the dusty floor. The slaves immediately abandoned work and ran to it like a group of stray cats; fighting over the crumbs that once was half a slice of bread.

"This is sick," Raven whispered in reaction to the sight.

"I haven't eaten since Friday, but I'm not an animal," Gladius exclaimed in an upset somewhat death tone.

"Ok now, get back to work", one of the guards exclaimed while pulling one of the slaves off the other and throwing him towards the table.

"I don't want to upset Africa, but it seems like that man has a strange infatuation with me.

"He wants to see me suffer before I die, and I know that", he professed while heating the mixture while starting another batch.

"I think your thinking too much and that can get you in trouble here, Gladius I don't want to lose you, just keep your head down," she said softly while stirring her batch of drugs.

"What did you do before the war?" Gladius asked Raven quietly.

"I was a painter. What about you," she retorted.

"I was a car salesman," he mumbled.

"I wish you could sell me a car so I could get out of here", she giggled to herself before clearing her throat and going back to work; starting her second batch as she put the first over a fire.

"What would you use as currency?" Gladius inquired with curiosity .

"Love and affection," she retorted softly.

"Affection doesn't put food in my stomach," he chuckled to himself.

"So if you had a car and you wouldn't sell it to me, would you take me with you?" she asked.

"Um, what is the best way to ask this. Please tell me, what is the purpose of your companionship again?" he inquired while turning his head and smiling, though his mouth was covered up by the mask.

"I can't believe you just said that," she responded.

"I'm just pulling your leg, calm down," he said softly as he went back to stirring the mixture once again. But amid conversation, he accidentally knocked over a bottle of chemicals; attracting everyone's attention as the glass bottle broke on the floor.

"What is the meaning of this?" the guard stammered while walking over to Gladius.

"It was an accident," Raven exclaimed.

"Quiet slave girl, I was not talking to you. Well, what do you have to say for yourself?" he exclaimed while turning to the both respectively. But Gladius's mouth felt as if it were full of cinnamon again before they grabbed him; dragging him out of the lab and across the front yard to the place Africa resided. Fear shot through the slave the spilled the Neon Moon, but as they took him he prayed that Raven be spared; he knew that he messed up but did not want others to be punished for his mistake. As they opened the door they slowed there speed, allowing Gladius to begin walking instead of being dragged. Then the door to his chamber opened. Elegant furs and fancy photos hung on the walls with a canopy bed to be the cherry on top. Africa was sitting in a cushioned chair facing the large pane window. He then stood up and faced them and said, "to what do we order the pleasure of this visit." He walked over to his whip and grabbed it, it sat coiled in his hand.

"This slave spilled the Neon Moon," one of the Zodia guards exclaimed while throwing him towards Africa.

"Gladius, who were you near?" he inquired. Gladius found it hard to breathe, his pupils dilated, and his rate of respiration increased as he felt true fear.

"Kedrick who was he near?" he inquired to one of the Zodia thugs.

"She is an Aquarius. I believe her name is Raven," he exclaimed.

After a brief moment of pausing, he exclaimed, "You have got to be kidding me Gladius."

"I see you're scared as crap, I mean you look like you could poop yourself right now," he exclaimed with a smile.

"I like that. It means we have an understanding. But don't get me wrong, I like you so I won't kill you, you being the keyword my friend. Now I think as fair punishment you and your friend should spend a week in the black hole. Get him out of here and put them away", Africa exclaimed while swishing his hand as if he were banishing them from his sight. He then was dragged outside, around the corner to a house with boarded-up windows. They opened the door and tossed him in, but as he was being thrown in the looked back and saw Raven being dragged the same way, then just like; his view was taken away by the closing of the door. He crawled over next to the wall, curled up in a ball; and wept softly.

Beautiful Flowers

Chapter Twenty-five

July 1st, 2044. 12:00 P.M. Livingston, TX.

As Elijah lay encapsulated in an octagon-shaped cell in a small bed with white sheets, he watched a fly buzz its way from one side to another while thinking about Gayla and her possible well being. He had been locked away in blue coveralls for about twenty-two days and although he was being fed daily, he missed the outside world but doubted he would get a chance to experience it for a long time.

Attacking a soldier is a serious offense, Elijah thought to himself; They will never let me out of here. The fly then flew back into Elijah's view, it landed on the bedpost and scuttled around on the end of the bed frame before Elijah shooed it away with his foot; forcing it to take flight again. He sighed of boredom as he rolled onto his side while listening to the fly's buzzing wings until it landed on something else in the cell. He lay there staring at the scratches and writings on the wall. The markings hung on the wall like family photos of the previous guest of the cell. Each one carved with varying precision with unknown objects.

"I wonder, maybe some of these were made by the prisoner's fingernails," Elijah exclaimed. Elijah ran his hand across the places were names, pictures, and some of everything had been engraved into the grey paint. He ran his fingernail into the paint as if attempting to add to the mural, but it simply would not do the trick; not one centimeter of paint was displaced from the wall. All of a sudden his eyes lit up with excitement as an idea sparked in his mind. He flipped over like a cat on its spine and hopped out of bed, getting on the floor and checking the bedpost for screws or nuts.

"Ah-ha," he sounded as he felt a nut fastened to the headboard. He tried to grip it, but it slipped around in the palm of his hand. Sitting up and putting his hands on his knees, he examined what was going wrong in this failed attempt. Elijah snatched off the white bedsheet, dragging it onto the floor with him pas he used it to get a better grip on the bolt. He held his breath and twisted with such a grip a bulbous vein showed in his temple, though his efforts were not atrophied; he commenced in breathing deeply once it had broken loose, unscrewing it completely from the bed. He rested his head on the now loose metal bed frame and laughed to himself. Elijah pushed himself up from the ground and hopped back in bed with the nut in hand, he scratched at the wall like a chicken looking for a worm, starting on the left side of an open patch on the wall then switching to the other side of space. He drew in his time of bona fide boredom, making a flower here and a beetle there, with a butterfly landing on a rose. Through the flowers looked semi-melted and distorted and the insects looked cartoonish, with jagged oversized eyes and an unrealistic pattern on the butterfly's wings, but to say the least, it was abstract. To let the truth be told, it was the most fun he had since his incarceration. He smiled as he withdrew himself to admire his masterpiece.

"Hmm, its missing something," he exclaimed while holding the hand with the nut in it to his chin.

"I'll add a verse, he professed.

"John 3:16," he said to himself; but as he went back to scratch on the wall again the cell door unlocked and Elijah twisted around as he was doing nothing the entire time. Three soldiers then entered the room, but only two were armed.

"I'll pretend I didn't see that," one of the soldiers that held a gun exclaimed as they entered the room.

"We're taking you to do your polygraph. My superiors tell me your background check came back clean, except that you fought a member of the armed forces," the unarmed soldier exclaimed as they all left the cell and walked down the hall, escorted by the two armed men.

"But they seemed to believe you were startled and are willing to Pardon your offense if you are willing to join the Army," the unarmed soldier exclaimed while stopping and pressing the button for the elevator as Elijah stood between the two armed soldiers.

"Join the army?" Elijah asked while turning over his shoulder to look at the giant window in the middle of the ceiling; the sun's bright rays reminded him of freedom.

"I'll do it." he exclaimed.

"Well hold on there," the soldier professed as the elevator went; "Ding."

"You still have to pass your polygraph, we have to be sure you're not one of the enemies." he professed as they all entered the elevator and the door closed. The unarmed soldier pushed a button on the panel of the interior of the elevator and the elevator began to go down like a falling apple. One of the soldiers put his hand over his mouth as he coughed in the silence, hold the rifle in one hand. Elijah rolled his neck, it popped twice before he finished its rotation and the elevator stopped and the doors opened. The guards escorted them midway down the wall to a room with big glass windows on the right. A man sat in a chair next to a polygraph machine.

"Hello Elijah," the man exclaimed while standing up and shaking Elijah's hand; "I'm Corporal Bennet."

"Please, have a seat," he exclaimed as the others left the room and Corporal Bennet began hooking Elijah up to the machine. In no time Elijah was hooked up and the man cut on the machine, causing its line to start drawing on the page. After Corporal Bennet sat down again, he reached a nearby end table and grabbing a clipboard.

"Let's start simple. Just as a test run," the man exclaimed.

"What is your full name?" he inquired.

"Elijah Xavier See," he professed as the line continued to wave normally.

"Your eyes are what color?" the man inquired.

"Brown", Elijah responded as the needle acted the same.

"Ok, I think we are ready to go. I just have a few questions to ask you," Corporal Bennett exclaimed.

"Are a member, or have you hidden Zodia members at any point in time?" the man asked.

"Never," Elijah professed, Corporal Bennet paused for a second before writing something on his clipboard.

"Have you ever transported or taken the illegal drug Neon Moon?" the man asked Elijah.

"I have not," Elijah retorted as the line continued to behave normally.

"Have you encountered or know of a Zodia military unit called the fiend," he asked.

"I have no idea what you are talking about," Elijah exclaimed before blinking and staring at the man.

"Ok, I think we are done here; I'll tell my superiors you passed", he exclaimed.

"I'm sure you were informed of your two options, have you made up your mind yet?" the man asked.

"I'll join," Elijah exclaimed with a smile.

Chapter Twenty-six

Gayla stared down the arrow sight of a hunting bow with Crunchy instructing from the rear, some of the group of them had been practicing for two days and Gayla almost had it down packed but still struggled on occasion. While they trained on the range the compound buzzed with excitement; people walking here and there as if it were the most popular water park in the heat of summer.

"Hold your breath," Crunchy said as Gayla followed his command. There was a brief pause as he examined her hold the string back before Crunchy exclaimed; "Shoot your shots". Gayla's bow went from a semi triangular shaped to its resting position as the arrows whizzed down the open range, flying through the air and impaling into the outside of the target that represented a bull's eye.

"Dang it!" Gayla hissed while lowering the bow.

"Calvin well done," Crunchy exclaimed; causing a jealous to surge within Gayla. Seeing frustration in her composure, Crunchy walked over to her.

"Try again", he said while placing his hand on her shoulder.

"I've been trying this for two days and Calvin is hitting bulls eyes already," She exclaimed while pointing to Calvin's target.

"Galatians 6:4 says, Pay careful attention to your work, for then you will get the satisfaction of a job well done, and you won't need to compare yourself to anyone else," Crunchy said.

"I understand," she exclaimed while looking down, then reaching into her quiver and pulled out another arrow and began to load it into the hunting bow.

"I know I can do it," she professed while pulling back the string again. The group watched the scene as if they had individual bags of popcorn. Her mindset brought a smile to Crunchy's face.

"Come on baby girl," Crunchy whispered. Gayla tried to tune out her surroundings, ignoring the talking of people, the clucking of chickens, and the occasion trotting by of a horse. Closing one eye and focussing on her target before holding her breath and letting go of the arrow. It flew through the air like a ballistic missile, piercing the target in the center. She dropped the bow and threw her hands in the air and pulling the back down by her side.

"I did it," Gayla screamed.

"You sure did," Crunchy professed while wrapping his arms around her and her doing the same to him. Calvin looked around at the others before clapping his hands and the others doing the same. It was beautiful, the sun even peaked part of its circumference from behind a cloud as they celebrated. But outside the compound trouble was stirring. Two men in turquoise bandanas rode on a dirt bike, one of them held an AK-47. As the bike swerved from left to right the man on the back raised the gun and fired it at the wall, forcing everyone to drop to the earth. They unleashing nearly a full clip by the time they had gone by.

"Is anyone hit?" Crunchy inquired after the sound of the dirt bike dissipated. Patrice they rolled out of the office star struck and confused.

"What in the heck is going on here," she screamed while everyone slowly rose to her feet.

"I don't think anyone's hit," Crunchy professed while walking over to her, dusting off his overalls with his hat along the way.

I think someone wanted to make a point, Patrice pondered while rolling up to the gate, staring at the bullet holes in the metal wall.

She ran her finger on a bullet hole through one of the cut trees bracing it up. "But the question is, who could it be?" she inquired.

Chapter Twenty-seven

Crunchy walked to the housing quarters on the side of the compound, he strolled past the inside of the metal wall. It was braced with cut trees, with a wedge interlocking with a metal crossbar on that extended along the back of the wall, and an opposite pole sharpened like a spear to dig into the hole in the ground. The trees were of oak and pine, not too large; but enough to the job. Crunchy opened the door of one of the dorms in the housing sector and walked down the isle of bunk beds lining the edge of the room. He watched Gayla sleep like a baby for a hot second before waking her up. It brought a smile to his wrinkled ivory face as she rose from her sleep.

"Rise and shine sunshine," he exclaimed; "Time to hunt some game". She sat up and hung her feet off the bottom bunk, rubbing her eyes before stretching her arms into the air.

"What are we hunting with?" Gayla inquired.

"You will use a hunting bow, just like when you practiced," he exclaimed as she stood up and they walked out of the building.

"I can even show you how to fletch your arrows," Crunchy exclaimed.

"We have one hunting dog here, her name is Alexis," he exclaimed while crossing across the empty stalls of the compound market.

"The dog handler's name is Joe", he professed before continuing; "You two look about the same age."

"How old do I look?" Gayla inquired as she continued to follow Crunchy.

Just a day past beautiful," he exclaimed, forcing Gayla to creak out a smile before swallowing it and taking a second to admire a new friend.

"Joe should have the dog ready to go," Crunchy exclaimed while walking to a gated pen with a light brown man inside. He wore a headband that pushed up his short dreadlocks and square glasses perched on his nose.

"She's all ready to go," he exclaimed while pointing to black labrador. Gayla squatted down and scratched the dog on the head gathered the rest of the items from a nearby shed.

"She's a really good dog", Joe exclaimed; "I found her shortly after everything went down."

"She was by a fire station when I happened to stroll by," he professed.

"She sure is pretty," she exclaimed while stroking the dog's short black fur.

"Ok, let's go," Crunchy exclaimed while returning to Gayla and Joe.

"It was nice meeting you," Gayla exclaimed while reaching her hand out to she Joe's hand before they left with the dog; Crunchy holding a leash and Gayla holding the crossbow.

"Now pay attention, Alexis isn't all show. She is a hunting dog. Let her do the work for you and make sure your shot counts, `he exclaimed as they reached the front gate. Crunchy waved his hand, giving the signal for the guards to open the gate; once they had exited and the gate shut Crunchy took the leash of Alexis.

The Story Through The Eyes Of Alexis

As the leash unclipped she instantly began sniffing the ground, picking up various scents of different strength, until a bush by the woods made her stop in her tracks.

Her tail stopped wagging as she heard Gayla exclaim, "I think she has found something".

I know this scent, the labrador thought as it dashed into the woods; *is it a Rabbit?* But of the two of them, Crunchy had the hardest time keeping up.

"I'm right behind you," he called to Gayla as Alexis sniffed the trees, their roots, and even the rocks as she trotted along; following the scent.

I don't know what in the heck that could be, the labrador pondered as it hopped over a fallen tree with Gayla soon behind and Crunchy dragging in the rear. Alexus then slowed down as the scent disappeared, it perplexed her.

Where did the trail go, the dog wondered as she sniffed around in the area, *Find the trail*. But after about a minute of sniffing, she darted east, heading towards a denser brush filled area. Then she saw it, an armadillo. It flailed its teeth and turned towards it as Alexis barked frantically.

Wow, what in the heck is that thing, she wondered while perplexed and pouncing in the air and land on all fours.

"She found something!" Crunchy screamed at Gayla as she caught up with the labrador as and saw the cornered animal. Gayla pulled up the hunting bow and fired a shot just as it tried to make a break for it, the arrow pierced through its neck as it bled out on the woodland floor. Alexis approached the dead animal, she sniffed were the arrow had pierced its hide; but before she could lick it Crunchy pulled her by her collar.

"Good girl," he exclaimed while scratching her head, forcing her tail to wag amid excitement. Then, all of a sudden her ears shot up like rockets in the sky, she heard an unfamiliar voice and curiosity got the best of her. She broke loose from Crunchy's grip and shot like a dart through the woods once again.

"Alexis!" Gayla called out before chasing after her again.

"You get her, I'll get the game!" Crunchy screamed. The labrador gave out a low growl as it approached the origin of commotion, where the brush was thinning. Lowering herself to the ground as if it were about to pounce before it leaped for a man holding a pistol. Although initially she just wanted to play, the gunshot and it startled her; and she began to fight for her life. She bit onto the man's leg as he swung the stock of the pistol at her head, infuriating her even more. She wanted blood, letting go of his foot and lurching for his arm then neck as he attempted to swat her away with his hands;

but it was no use. She sunk her teeth in until she tasted his blood, letting go and licking his bleeding neck as the man slowly died.

In The Kingdom Of Heaven

The Father leaned forward as he sat on a golden throne adorned in jewels, he shone like a light brighter than the sun; staring through the floor at Alexis, Gayla, and Crunchy.

"This will not do", God exclaimed to one of the angels beneath him; "She has taken the life of a creation made in my image."

"Read me Exodus 21:28," God said to a young dark-skinned male angel with short curly hair.

"If an ox gores a man or woman to death, the ox must be stoned, and its flesh may not be eaten. In such a case, however, the owner will not be held liable," the young angel professed after unrolling a scroll.

"Shall I send the order Father?" a tall angel holding a trumpet asked.

"Yes, her actions will not go unpunished," God professed with temper in his voice.

Through The Eyes Of Gayla

As Gayla caught up to Alexis, she saw what she had done. She rushed to the man she checked for a pulse, but there was no life in his body. Alexis had severed his jugular vein and her mouth was covered in blood, it wet the labrador's black fur beneath its muzzle, causing the fur to clump together. Gayla grabbed the pistol from the man's hand and stuffed it beneath her shirt. She then turned around to see Crunchy holding the armadillo over one shoulder. He dropped it on the ground once he saw what the dog had done.

"Is he dead?" Crunchy inquired.

"Yes," Gayla retorted as Crunchy resituated his cowboy hat and looked at the dog.

"Do you know him?", Gayla inquired before Crunchy shook his head no.

"Well, we can't just leave him for the buzzards to eat" he exclaimed; "You get the food, I'll get him". He approached him from behind, grabbing him by his arms and sitting him up before flipping him over and picking up his dead weight, lumping him over his shoulder as Gayla snapped the leash on Alexis and tied the other end around her belt. They walked through the woods in silence, both Crunchy and Gayla bearing a separate load. Blood leaked from the armadillo as Gayla carried it back to the Alta Vista Ranch, leaving a distinct trail from where they had been.

"So you're going to bury him?" Gayla inquired.

"Our world may be a war zone, but that doesn't mean everything has to be barbaric," Crunchy exclaimed before continuing; "We have a burial ground in the back of the compound."

"My wife was buried there shortly after the war began, God rest her soul," Crunchy professed.

"How long were you married?" Gayla inquired.

"Fifty-two years," he said with a smile followed by a grunt as the dead man began to slip off of his shoulder; he paused for a second to redistribute the man's weight again.

"How did she pass away?" Gayla asked.

"Dr. Sherman claimed it to be from a heart attack, but our love sure was amazing," he said as birds chirped in the trees.

"We had a love like Song of Songs," he said before looking at her and asking; "Have you ever read it?"

"I can't say that I have," Gayla retorted while continuing to walk beside Crunchy.

"It's beautiful, it showed us what love is supposed to be like between a married man and a woman," he professed before continuing; "the story was almost as beautiful as she was".

"Ah, I remember her like it was yesterday," he said while fading into the crypts of nostalgia before being cut off by Gayla, "Something isn't right."

"The gate is open", Gayla exclaimed while pointing to it. As they entered the gate, a swarm of loaded trucks were in view, they parked by the market stalls. There were men and women adorned in turquoise bandanas, with some in shorts and others in pants that hung below their waistline.

"I'll take that," a man in a bandanna exclaimed as he came from behind the open gate and ripped the hunting bow from Gayla hands and pointed a pistol at her.

"Did y'all kill him?" the gang member inquired to Gayla before looking at the blood around the dog's mouth before asking; "Or was it her".

"It was the dog," Crunchy exclaimed while looking at the man with a semi fearful expression, sitting the dead man down onto the ground.

"Very well," He said before escorting them through the market, past all of the flagged goons and into Patrice's office, were a man in a suit jacket and blue jeans sat in her chair; with black cornrows that stopped at the bottom of his neck.

"Patrice, you didn't tell me there were more of you guys!" the man exclaimed in a loud voice before calming down; "My name is Juicy."

"I was just sharing with your leader about how nice this place is," Juicy said.

"I'm even let you guys keep it," he exclaimed before continuing; "But you will give us two-thirds of everything you make."

"That's outrageous," Crunchy exclaimed in fury. Juicy then arose from the chair getting in the old white man's face and saying, "Are you going to stop me?" Juicy looked at Gayla next and signaled one of his men to take the armadillo from Gayla.

"Thanks for the food, you must have known I was famished," he said. Juicy then startled the entire room by pushing Crunchy in his chest, forcing him to fall on the floor. Gayla rushed down to his aid, sitting him up as he lay astonished while resituating his hat.

"I think we are done here boys," Juicy said while getting ready to leave.

"Boss there is one other order of business we must attend to," the goon who escorted him said, "The dog took out one of our boys."

"Really," Juicy exclaimed while leaning down and looking into the dog's light brown eyes. It growled and showed its teeth before he gave the labrador a mug expression.

"You mangy mutt," he exclaimed while pulling out his pistol; "It almost saddens me to do this".

"BANG!" went the gunshot as the dog fell lifeless on the floor. The sight was atrocious, the dog's brains lay on the floor; the only positive artifact at this point was Juicy and his crew was leaving. Gayla helped Crunchy to his feet before she walked out of the building as the last car pulled out of the Alta Vista Ranch.

Chapter Twenty-eight

Elijah sat on the green bus, making his way to boot camp after he recently signed up to join the armed forces. All he had was his Bible, a pair of dog tags, a white shirt, and cargo pants provided by the army. But he was not the only one to have little, many on the grunts joined in rags with hopes of a better life. The army had begun allowing women to participate in combat due to an increased need for troops. The war had devastated most of the economy, and many were starting to doubt the president's capability of restoring order to one of the greatest nations on the face of the Earth. The civilians lived behind US-controlled borders, dwelling under the discomfort of martial law; and tensions we're rising. The biggest complaint was overbearing of control, the country had shifted by increasing government control, and the citizens were starting to get rowdy. All of a sudden a man hopped into Elijah's seat while the bus was still moving, Elijah took his gaze from looking out of the window to the man sitting next to him, turning away from his reflection of his freshly shaven face and head.

"Hey man, my name is Jewel. What's yours?" he asked Elijah as he stared at the star of David on Jewel's neck. He stuck his hand out to shake Elijah's hand and after looking at it for a few seconds he shook the man's hand.

"My name is Elijah," he professed while letting go of his hand.

"Man I can't wait to bring it to those Zodia freaks. I'm from up North, near Arlington," he exclaimed before continuing; "But the city wasn't like Houston".

"I heard Houston fell to the Zodia shorty after everything popped off," he said.

"It did, I was there," Elijah professed while looking down as the bus increased speed on the empty freeway.

"Man that's crazy," Jewel exclaimed; "glad to see you made it out." Elijah could tell the young man was in a little talkative as he opened his mouth again to start a conversation, "man there sure is some nice Dames on this bag of bolts". Elijah signed to himself as he stared out of the window again, thinking of Gayla's chocolate skin and gentle touch. It was at this time that the bus began to slow down near a fenced-in the complex. Elijah stared through the how's in the metal fence, watching men climb over obstacle courses In the distance   .

"Welcome home ladies and gentlemen," the bus driver exclaimed while pulling into the complex. Elijah then saw a man wearing a Stetson hat exit a building, and he watched the bus pull over to him. Elijah then turned his gaze to the front bus window, dirt had clustered the area above the windshield wipers; provided a limited area to peer through as his hands rest on top of the back of the seat in front of him. When the bus pulled up next to the building with the man outside the bus door opened and he walked on; gravitating all attention as the entire bus was a bundle of nerves; you could hear a pin drop if it were not for the engine idling in the background.

"Welcome to Fort Hadknot, I am Sergeant Wells!" he screamed in an irate tone of voice.

"Now get your hind pots off this bus and get in a single file!" The man then got off of the bus and stood on the outside the open door as the recruits grabbed their belongings and rushed off of the bus; standing in line before the Sargent. He paced down the line of enlistees, "You will be here for two months. You will not eat, sleep, nor wipe your butt without my permission."

"Is that understand private," he screamed while turning towards Jewel.

"Sir, yes sir," Jewel screamed at the top of his lungs before the Sergeant continued pacing down the line.

"Although I do not believe women should be allowed in combat, Uncle Sam believes otherwise. Therefore, I will treat you no differently. Is that understand private?" he yelled with passion while turning and facing a beautiful Hispanic woman.

"Sir yes sir Sergeant Wells," she yelled.

"What is your name Private," the Sargent exclaimed inches away from her nose as a woman with a ponytail came out of the building and stood at the end of the line.

"Katanna Sir!" she yelled in his face.

"Private Katanna it may be independence day, but be sure to remember you belong to me for the next two months, and I will run you until lactic acid comes out of the pimples on your bacne." Private Jewel giggled to himself until the Sergeant inquired.

"Who did that?" but not a mouth moved a muscle. Sargent paced away from the woman at the end of the silent line of recruits.

"Who thought it was funny, that's insulting, and I'll be dead before I let scumbags like you to insult me," he said while holding up one finger and giving a stern expression. "Well if no one wants to come forward, I'll have no choice but to punish all of you on the first day", he yelled.

"It was me, sir!" Jewel yelled, Sergeant Wells walked with authority, with both fists balled; Elijah followed him with his eyes as he walked by.

"What is your name kid!" he yelled in Jewel's face.

"I'm Private Jewel Sir" he retorted.

"Private!" he exclaimed with a disgusted look on his face before continuing; "Your new rank is Maggot."

"Now drop and give me fifty", he screamed in Jewel's face and like a sack of rocks, he dropped to the earth and began to do push-ups.

Sergeant Wells then placed his boot on his back while screaming; "What is your name?"

"Maggot Jewel", he responded under strain.

"What number is that Maggot Jewel?" the Sergeant yelled.

"Eight Sir", he screamed before having to repeat himself after Sergeant Wells exclaimed; "I can't hear you!"

"Eight Sir", he yelled back as loud as he could.

"Get up," he said while taking the boot off his back. As he breathed hard the Sergeant started pacing again and a woman entered the room and he professed, "My colleague here will take you ladies to your quarters."

"Gentlemen will you all follow me," he said before exclaiming while pointing to the woman on the side of the end of the line. Elijah carried his bible to the dorm that they would be staying in, there were bunk beds rowed along the sides of the wooden building, with white square tiles on the floor with the American flag plastered above the front door near the exit sign.

"You all are to meet me outside in 1400 hours," Sergeant Wells exclaimed as Elijah sat his bible down on a bottom bunk. Elijah then looked at the clock that ticked on a post in the center of the room which was used to help brace the ceiling up.

So we only get about twenty minutes," Elijah thought to himself as he got up and walked to the back of the dorm, past the water fountain to the restroom. There was no door, it was open as a field of flowers. He stepped on the teal tile and entered a stall of the same pigment as the flooring and locked the door. Elijah pulled down his pants and began to poop, giving off a sigh of relief as he excreted waste from his bum. But as the clock continued to tick Elijah lost track of time and found himself sitting on the toilet, daydreaming about what he would see in this new era of life. Perhaps fame or honor, at least that's the picture his mind painted of war from movies and TV shows he used to watch. Then all of a sudden he noticed how quiet the dorm had gotten.

"Guys, what time is it?" Elijah called out; but there was no response as the last bit of fecal matter dropped into the water beneath him. Elijah reached for the toilet paper and began to wipe himself with what felt like sandpaper. As he looked at the pooped stained toiletry he noticed blood was stained on the balled up soiled toilet paper.

"That's just great," Elijah exclaimed as he finished tending to himself. He then pulled up his pants, feeling a sting between his butt cheeks as they came together. Elijah pushed open the stall door and walked to the sink to wash his hand, pressing the soap dispenser and turning on the hot water; lathering his hands together before placing them under the faucet. He glanced at his clean-shaven face in a mirror mounted on the wall before the sink, shaking his hands in the bathroom sink before walking away and entering the dorm once again. But to his surprise, it was as empty as the stables of an abandoned farm.

"Oh crap," Elijah screamed while looking at the clock on the pillar, it was 2:05 P.M. and Elijah should have been outside about five minutes ago. He rushed outside to the building where they had been dropped off, bringing all of the cadets into view as the Sergeant's eyes shot to Elijah as he fell into line.

"Private what time did I ask you to report outside!" he screamed while walking to the end of the line was Elijah stood.

"1400 hours sir!" he yelled back.

"Then please explain to me why are you late," he hollered in Elijah's face.

"I was using the restroom sir," Elijah exclaimed while trying not to look in the Sergeant's eyes.

"You are a little maggot too," he yelled at Elijah.

"If one thing is for certain you will be punctual and you be ready for war", the Sergeant said.

"What is war?" the man screamed.

Elijah fumbled for words as he stuttered his speech before being cut off by the Sergeant,

"War is hell, I will do my best to make you ready."

The Sergeant then turned to the rest of the line and exclaimed, "Since your fellow soldier is a poop fountain with no words to explain himself you all will run one mile for every minute he was late."

"Attention", he screamed; "Move out."

The Sergeant hopped to the front of the moving line and exclaimed, "Follow my lead."

"Mamma says the Zodia is no good," he exclaimed as they repeated his words after him; "But killing those freaks gives me a wood."

As the chant continued as they jogged Elijah asked himself; "What on earth did I get myself into?"

Chapter Twenty-nine

July 23rd, 2044. 10:00 P.M. The Alta
Vista Ranch. Shepherd, TX.

G ayla walked out of the housing sector holding a red sack containing what little she had been given by Patrice. Most people lost a lot after the gang showed up, but life goes on, and Gayla wondered if she could sit still to wither and die. She then sucked on her bottom lip as her stomach grumbled. She opened the sack and peeked at its contents, merely the extra clothes she had been given. There was even a beautiful dress inside, it almost hurt Gayla to let it go, but she had to eat. As she walked to the market stalls she noticed a lot of commotion coming from further in the compound. As she strolled past the market the voices grew louder; she could smell the tension in the air as the voices raised the volume and the group of people begun screaming. It pricked her curiosity just a bit too much as she began jogging; turning the corner to see an angry mob chattering loudly in front of Patrice's office. Crunchy then exited the house, be sure to keep the door closed so no one could look in; once the door closed he turned around and began speaking to the crowd.

"Now I need you all to go back to work or go home. Patrice has this handled," Crunchy exclaimed while gently trying to push the ground back with his arms.

"What about our stuff," one of the members of the crowd yelled as another seconded with; "Yea, they took more than a three day's wages."

"What if they come back," an elderly woman yelled in the group; causing the whole crowd to go in an uproar again. Gayla looked at the fenced-in pasture to see Joe leaning on the fence watching the whole thing. Gayla walked towards him, examining him while the wind blew in her face as she made her way to him.

"How are you holding up," she called out as she stood next to him, joining him in watching Crunchy attempt to calm the crowd in the background.

"I'm sorry about your dog," Gayla exclaimed before Joe intervened; "Don't."

"Crunchy told me what she did," he exclaimed; "She had it coming." Gayla smirked at Joe, his taking of the situation was enlightening to her, to say the least. It was the only positivity insight.

"I have no idea what's going to become of this place," Joe exclaimed while continuing to stare at the mob.

"Are you afraid?" Gayla inquired.

"Who me?" he asked before sighing; "No".

"We can't fight them but we can't let them sap us dry like leeches on someone's back," he said while taking off his glasses and wiping them with his shirt before returning them to his face.

"I understand where you're coming from", Gayla exclaimed before asking; "So you are more of a pacifist?"

"I guess you could say that," he retorted.

"Deuteronomy 5:17 says you must not murder," he exclaimed; "I read the scriptures."

"I'm not bloodthirsty by any means when someone does you wrong to you turn the other cheek," he finished.

She stared in his eyes and asked, "So what do you suggest in a situation like this; if we don't fight the gang what do we do?"

"Leave, it's as simple as that," he retorted.

"And go were?",she inquired while raising from the fence.

"Are you going to start a garden in a backpack to take with you?" she chuckled.

"I believe the Father will provide for his flock".

"Matthew 6:31-34 says, So don't worry about these things, saying, What will we eat? What will we drink? What will we wear? These things dominate the thoughts of unbelievers, but your heavenly Father already knows all your needs. Seek the Kingdom of God above all else, and live righteously, and he will give you everything you need. So don't worry about tomorrow, for tomorrow will bring its worries. Today's trouble is enough for today," he finished.

Gayla paused for a second before saying, "I was just teasing you". Then the uproar in front of Patrice's office calmed as she exited the building. Gayla and Joe walked towards her to hear if anything would be said at all.

"Take me with you if you leave," she whispered while looking at him in mid-stride. Joe smiled as he pushed his glasses back up on his nose. As they neared Patrice you could see was under stress, she had bags under her eyes as if she had been crying through the night; getting little to no sleep at all. She sat like a zombie to the front of the crowd and professed, "I'm sorry that this has happened to all of us."

"I feel as if I have failed you as a leader, they have more guns, and they pose a threat to our survival," she exclaimed. Then her voice squeaked as she squeaked, "But we are not fighters, we are farmers, herders, and craftsman".

"If we fight them we will surely lose," she finished as the crowd grew angry.

"Where is your spine?" one of the members of the crowd screamed.

"I'm leaving," another member of the crowd yelled as another sounded; "Yea."

"Well I'm going to fight," a man in the group yelled. It was then that Joe intervenes, coming from the back of the pack like a dove in flight.

"Listen, If you fight them more will die. We don't have the guns to take them down, not to mention the moral implications of taking a life," he professed in a loud voice to the crowd.

"Go home, back to work, or leave. Can't you see your pestering is brought her down? We all felt it since they showed up, it's not her fault, and you have to be smart about your actions because they affect more than just you," he finished; leaving the crowd in pure silence as they began to disperse one by one. As they walked away

Patrice went back inside with a sluggish demeanor, and Calvin came out of the dying crowd.

"Thanks for helping my mom back there," he professed to Joe while looking down; "You should have heard some of the things they were saying".

"Don't let it get to you kid," he exclaimed while picking up his chin with his finger, forcing a smile to creak across his face.

As Calvin walked off Gayla approached Joe and exclaimed, "That was amazing."

"Not really," he retorted; "I'm just trying to help out."

"Well thank God you were here," she said while hugging him.

"Listen, the gangsters didn't take all of my stuff, they didn't find my secret stash. I'd like you to have dinner with me one day, `` he professed while looking her in her eyes.

Gayla looked down and blushed as Elijah flashed across her mind but she paused for a second.

"I'd like that," she responded with a smile before walking off towards the market stalls.

Chapter Thirty

Anastasia walked into the room on a walker, with a bent spine as if she was an old woman as she snailed her way to the bed. She was accompanied by Nurse Phillips. He was a brown man who wore black scrubs every day; he assisted her along the way to her bed.

"Almost there," he said while holding his hand on her back.

When they reached the bed he helped her sit with her legs hanging off the side of the bed and exclaimed while sitting on the end of the bed as people walked past the room's doorway, "The doctor says you should be able to leave in a few months."

"We have to check your pupillary reflexes and your blood pressure today," he professed while pulling out a banana and salt tablets out of the pocket of his scrubs; "But first, a snack."

Anastasia took the items from him and reached to the table next to her, to grab a glass of water; swallowing the pills with a gulp of water first before eating the banana in segmented pieces.

"How long have you been working here," she asked the nurse.

"About three months, I worked a lot with you when you were unconscious," he professed.

"Sometimes, I feel like I can recall the bombing," she professed as he washed his hands and put on gloves.

"It was at Beautiful Flowers, but I still don't remember who I was with. It irritates me that my memory is faded," She professed while swallowing the last bit of banana.

"Don't be irritated, you have been through a lot," he exclaimed while getting up and grabbing the instruments he needed.

"Ok here we go," He said as he shined the light into her eyes while looking through the gadgets scope; watching her pupils dilate normally.

"Can I be honest with you and you not think I'm crazy," she asked before he checked the other eye.

"Sure," he professed while pulling back from her face.

"I feel like someone is watching me," she exclaimed with an insecure tone of voice.

"I get moments were I feel like someone is looking at me," she said before continuing; "Nurse Lisa saw a letter someone here wrote to me."

"The things they said creeped me out," she said as she shook her head from side to side.

"Nurse Lisa told the police and their working with security to get to the bottom of the issue. But she lost the letter, they could have at least fingerprinted it," she exclaimed.

"Interesting, I had no idea," he professed while going to the wall which possessed a mounted sphygmomanometer; he strapped it around her arm. The sound of air pumping resonated throughout the room as he tightened the band around her arm.

"I'm scared here. I'm ready to leave," she exclaimed.

"You would be surprised how often I hear that," he retorted before exclaiming; "121/80".

"So, what's your point?" Anastasia inquired.

"The point is, you're going home soon. Try focusing on what you want to go when you get out. On that note, I have work to attend to; I hope your stalker issue will get taken care of and your safe here. But that's simply not my department," he professed while returning the instruments and starting to walk out of the room. Anastasia scoffed to herself at his words she just heard.

"So I'm just supposed to swallow that pill. You are so inconsiderate," she called out while folding her arms as he left her by herself. She looked around the room, upset and frustrated with Nurse Phillips's attitude as the Janitor walked in the room.

"Hello", he said while pulling out a bouquet of morning glories from behind his back.

"I had the day off today, so I thought I'd drop by. When I saw you that time, you looked like you could use a little cheering up," he exclaimed while giving off a strange vibe. He then walked to her nightstand and placed the bouquet, but as it slid onto the table his nerves got the best of him and resulted in the vase shattering into pieces glass on the floor.

"I'm sorry," he exclaimed in a skittish voice. Nurse Lisa then entered the room after hearing the glass hit the floor, making the man's eyes double in size before he walked quickly out of the room.

"That was weird", Anastasia professed. Then suddenly. Nurse Lisa stopped at stared at the broken glass.

"Who gave those to you?" she inquired.

"The man who ran out," she professed before inquiring; "Why do you ask?"

She then walked to the side of the bed and bent down to the floor, picking up a small camera amidst broken glass and flowers.

Chapter Thirty-one

August 10th, 2044. 10:30 P.M. Fort Hadknot, New Orleans, LA.

Elijah walked in line to a giant building in the back of the training complex, it was in the right-hand corner of the large fenced-in area; still on the gravel earth surface which was surrounded by a thick patch of grass. The Sergeant stood near the outside of the doorway, inspecting each recruit from the length of the women's ponytails to the tie on each male cadet's necks. Elijah strolled into the building as the light automatically turned on as the after the first cadet left the nearby wall. Immediately Elijah was amazed at what he saw.

"Cadetes, today we will be training indoors, you will all use the battle simulator, and I have a special treat for you later just before you all eat lunch. But I will do my best to drive you like cattle so you can survive through just about anything. The battle simulator will give us a better perspective on how quick your reflexes are, so they can tell me what I need to do," he yelled while pacing back and forth down the line of men and women.

"If you look to your left you will find dressing rooms, change your clothes and meet me back here. Were going to start with a little run, dismissed," he finished before passing them each a numbered key then he turned his back to then and walking towards a giant treadmill. It was at least ten yards long, containing a single wooden bar at the top and a long black belt for them to run on. Elijah strolled to the men's dressing room. Eyeing the Private Katana like a cat stalking prey.

"I'd let that one stay where it's at," Jewel exclaimed to Elijah before walking off and leaving him standing there; "She's as mean as a rattlesnake." Elijah began on his path again, passing beneath a red and white exit sign as he entered the dressing. There was an assortment of green lockers in the room, with a teal carpet in the center of the grey floor. By the wall was a large counter containing four sinks, they stood just below a large mirror which was on the side of the opening to the showers. Elijah walked to a bench near the lockers, staring at the number on his keys and approaching the appropriate locker. As Elijah sat down he began taking off his clothes, starting with his boots and working his way up; leaving him standing in his white briefs and a dog tag. He reached into the locker and pulled out a pair of green shorts that hung from the center of the locker, slipping one leg in at a time. He took a deep breath while staring at the compression shirt still in the locker. He grabbed it and slipped it on, pulling his dog tags out of it do that they lay on the outside of his shirt, next putting on the brown Running Man Shoes in the bottom of the locker. Before he knew it he was all set and left the dressing as did his colleges as they finished getting dressed. They stood on the outside of the treadmill, admiring it like a marvel.

"This is the Brejeneir 3000", he exclaimed while pointing to the treadmill after all the recruits were standing beside it.

"Ladies and gentlemen let me be clear, you will only make it through this through teamwork and oral communication. Motivate each other as you would on any other day, but if your butt falls off that treadmill you will have an extra opportunity for improvement. I don't care if your excuse is your legs stopped from trying to pull up someone else. Are we clear?" he finished loudly.

"Sir yes sir," the crowd of cadets screamed with excitement.

"Well what are you just standing there for, mount up," the Sargent yelled at them and like migrating birds they positioned themselves on the treadmill; with some etching on the wooden railing. Elijah began to move his legs, starting out walking but ending in a jog.

"I will incline this baby every ten minutes, you will also be exposed to the elements as well. But as I have advised before, do not fall off," he exclaimed as he stopped increasing the speed.

"Hut one two three!" the Sargent yelled before the cadets responded, "Living in the Army!"

"What is your creed," Sargent Wells exclaimed.

"Hunt them down and make them bleed", the cadets retorted.

"I said burr", the Sargent yelled while acting like it was cold inside before the cadets retorted. "Burr, It's cold in here, there must be some cadets in the atmosphere," he yelled.

"Oh How cold?" he continued to chant.

"Too cold," they retorted before the group repeated the same segment again.

"Maggot Jewel break it down," he exclaimed to Jewel, who was just starting to sweat on his forehead.

"I said," he drew out for a few seconds before continuing; "I got the sauciest syrup in the south."

"Let me talk about it," the group exclaimed.

"Oh, how cold?" the Sergeant chanted again.

"Too cold," they responded.

"How cold?" the sergeant chanted again.

"Too cold," they sounded again.

"Maggot Elijah breaks it down," the sergeant sounded.

"Well, I'm the man, with the eye. I have an aim so good, I'll shoot the nuts off a fly," Elijah exclaimed as the treadmill incline a few inches.

"Oh, how cold?" Sergeant wells exclaimed.

"Too cold," they retorted.

"How cold?" he chanted again.

"Too cold," the responded.

"Private Katanna breaks it down," the Sergeant yelled.

"Call Private Katanna, or Lady K. You know I grind the bones of my Zodia prey," she screamed.

"Oh How cold?" The Sergeant yelled.

"Too cold," they retorted.

"How cold", the sergeant screamed.

"Too cold", they retorted.

Then all of a sudden the Sargent stopped chanting and walked to the side of the treadmill, eyeballing one of the cadets that had sunk to the rear of the group.

"Private Chesters you look tired," he said to the chunky private.

"If you were a portion of food you would be a meat pie. Why are you a meat pie?", the Sargent exclaimed to him while inclining the treadmill again.

"I don't know sir," he yelled back while stretching out his stride and slowing down even more. It was clearly evident he wasn't going to make it. Elijah began to slow his pace, sinking to the back of the treadmill by Private Chesters and grabbing his hand as they ran side by side

. "Fall off," the Sargent yelled at him.

"Come on man, keep your eyes up; keep pushing," Elijah exclaimed in an attempt to motivate the hefty young man as sweat dribbled down from his chin and his jaw hung low.

"How about this, if you fall off I will run you even more," Sargent Wells teased.

Between gasp of breaths and whimpers he exclaimed while holding his side, "Man, I can't do this."

"Yes, you can," Elijah yelled at him while increasing his speed while still holding his hand, forcing him to speed up as well.

"Private Elijah, stand down. I want to see Fatty Mc. Fat-Fat fall on his bum," he yelled. But Elijah didn't listen and continued to tug the man by the arm to the top of the treadmill.

"Maggot Elijah that's an order", he screamed.

"Sir, I will not stand down. We never leave a man behind," he retorted as private Chester's legs swung loosely beneath him. He ran like a baby deer, fumbling his legs about as he was pushed harder than he had ever been pushed before.

"Maggot Elijah I like you, you have balls," he screamed.

"Now, per se, it rains", the Sargent exclaimed before they retorted; "Then let it pour". The Sergeant then turned a switch on the controller in his hand, unleashing a downpour of water from the ceiling. The water mixed in with the sweat running down Elijah's temples. Cooling his body but weighing him down with his freshly wet clothes. It stuck to his skin and got in his eyes, dripping down his chin in a stream as his jaw hung lower than a camel hoof. Private Chester then began to slip from his grip. He then turned on the vents poised over the treadmill, blowing the water harder towards then. The Sergeant then inclines the treadmill from the remote control once again; raising it to a 30° angle. It was then that the cadets started dropping like wildflowers in the winter. One by one sliding off of the end, only one raised to the challenge. Although private Chesters slipped from his hand, Elijah continued on gripping onto the rail to help himself stay up at the top.

"Well done Maggot Elijah", Sargent Wells exclaimed; "I am impressed."

"Don't get me wrong, I'm not going googly for you; but you stood out today," he exclaimed while turning off the treadmill and lowering it back to the floor. The belt slowed gradually as did Elijah's legs as well. They felt like noodles in hot water, dripping wet and weak with his shorts sticking to the skin of his thighs. Elijah hopped off of it after the speed had decreased substantially, one of the cadets then walked up behind him and patted him on his shoulder, but shortly He was joined by Maggot Jewel and Private Chester. Elijah gazed at Katanna who stood on the outskirts eyeing him with her arms crossed before turning away.

"Cadetes we still have more work to do. Please strap on the vest, put on the helmet and enter the battle simulators before me. If you die in the virtual world you will disappear, your controls will deactivate and your capsule will open," he said while standing beside the aligned contraptions. Elijah walked towards one of the capsules, it was made of shiny metal at the bottom with a navy blue glass cover that raised up when opened. He opened up the capsule and fastened on the compression vest, it was attached to an air compressor to fill with air when shot, simulating actual impact. He then buckled the helmet around his chin, the gear was heavy but it was probably attributed to the prior energy expense in the previous exercise. He climbed into the simulator pulling the glass cover over him as he sat inside. All of a sudden the machine began speaking through the headphones placed inside of the helmet.

"Engaging," a voice called out from the headphones in the helmet as the glass roof of the capsule turned into a screen, displaying what looked like a beach in the Caribbean. The capsule then rotated Elijah 90°, his feet hung beneath him and when he walked he moved on the screen. Elijah gripped the handles of the control mechanism, turning in a circle while admiring the beauty he saw. Crisp light blue waters on a tan sandy shore as he stood gazing from a boat in the shallow water.

The birds squawked in the distance as another commander popped up next to him holding a rifle, "It's crazy how real this feels." Elijah nodded his head as he hopped off, trotting through the water as the liquid entered the capsule up to Elijah's knees. He sloshed through the water with the other commanders, all going towards the beachhead like a herd of seals. When they all made it ashore, Sargent Wells appeared on a screen in the sky.

"Your mission is simple, defend your position and eliminate all threats on the island. The enemy will come to you," he finished as the screen blanked out, going back to the resemblance of a light blue sky with sparse clouds.

One of the cadets then tried to take charge, walking up to the front of the group and saying, "Ok guys we need to split up."

"Thomson, Gerrard, and Elijah you're with me," he exclaimed before being cut off by him being shot with a bullet in the back of the head. Blood flew every with bits of the skull before his body illuminated with a blue light and he disappeared from the virtual world. The shot forced Elijah to duck for cover, he sat with his back perched against a jeep parked on the beach as bullets whizzed by his head. He was soon joined by private Chesters, who was ducking being the same vehicle with one hand on holding on his helmet. As the bullets fly by private Chesters exclaimed, "I've heard of cadets dying in this thing before; the vest can crush your rib cage".

"You're focussed on the wrong thing private," Elijah retorted as he began firing at the simulations, killing two of them; but before they disappear their bodies illuminated with a red light. Everywhere across the battlefield blue and red lights were going off, and before long there were only a few cadets left. Private Chesters stood up and placed his Light Machine gun on the hood of the vehicle, unleashing a hailstorm of bullets at the enemy while screaming sadistically as if it were all real. After peaking around the corner of the jeep Elijah dodged forward behind a pile of rocks on the beachhead.

Then all of a sudden a helicopter flew around the corner as one of the troops screamed, "Get the RPG!" In no time the soldiers had it deployed and ready to use, whipping it up over one shoulder as if they were carrying it home. The bullets from the helicopter trailed directly towards Elijah, spraying across the battlefield from left to right as he ran until it was struck by a missile launched from the RPG. It whirled in a circle, spinning out of control before plopping into the sandy beach; sending bits of propeller flying everywhere. Elijah stared across the battlefield as he watched Katanna charge towards the enemy with an assault rifle in hand, shooting down enemy targets left and right. It inspired the men as it seemed the on pour would never end. Red lights lit up the edge of the beach as the enemy bodies disappear from the virtual world, they were dropping them like flies.

"Frag out," one of the cadets screamed before throwing a grenade at them. After a few seconds of gunfire, it exploded, sending dirt and three virtual enemies flying into the air. It was like the best war game ever created with the perfect comeback, but the lights dimmed low and the capsules deactivated as Katanna took down the last enemy troop; spraying him in the side of the head from afar angle. Suddenly they began to hear the clapping of Sargent Wells as he walked down the line of capsules, with each cadet either standing beside it or getting out.

"Well done ladies and gentlemen," he sounded as he stopped clapping.

"That took about twelve minutes, not the fastest; but your not to far off. Maybe some of you are killers after all," he exclaimed with a smile. But the sore sight of his grin was swallowed fast as he proceeded with business.

"Follow me. Single file," he shouted as he turned away and started walking away. The cadets rushed in line, they were worn out from the day's work but excited to see what was next. One of them rubbed his ribs, which were bruised from the vest compressing with air. He led them out of the building through the door they entered and he began to walk behind the building. As they neared the rear of the building the heard a chain dragging on the ground. As they turned the corner they saw a large tent over a pen with a man inside.

"Now there are more to the Zodia than they appear, they are fierce. So you need to know your enemy," he exclaimed while pointing to the man in the cage. He was chained to a post that was cemented in the ground in the center of the fenced-in area. As he noticed them, he sat up from the ground, rising to its feet and charging at them only to be pulled back like a dog on a leash.

"Is he dead?" Elijah inquired to the Sargent while asking a closer look.

"No, just really messed up. He was administered a drug given by the Zodia after completing one of their Zodiac rituals. He won't eat, and will eventually die. They just crave the fix," he finished as the man reached for them; showing his teeth and filled with rage.

"You mean Neon Moon?" one of the cadets inquired.

"Affirmative," the Sargent retorted as Katanna exclaimed while looking at him wither away; "this is disgusting".

"Dismissed, see you all in the mess hall," he finished as he walked away from them. The cadets slowly cleared out one by one, and Elijah used this opportunity to get a chance to talk to Katanna.

"Nice shot back there in the simulator," he exclaimed to her while walking over to her.

"Oh, that was nothing compared to the real thing but, thank you," she exclaimed while walking beside Elijah.

"Where are you from," he inquired to Katanna starring in her face. She was a beautiful Hispanic woman with a beauty mark on her left cheek. The hair of her ponytail stopped just above her neckline.

"Pflugerville," she retorted as she ran her fingers through her ponytail, pulling out the scrunchie holding it together; only to reput it back in to freshen herself up. The breeze blew her hair as she let it go, it shone like black silk in the sunlight.

"The fiends are kind of creepy," Elijah exclaimed while trying to scrape up bits for conversation.

"I agree," she chuckled to herself, "It's really sad though".

"But they chose that," Elijah hissed back.

"But if you look at the makeup of a cult it all wraps around manipulating the public to carry out rash extremes," Katanna said while using her hands.

"So you feel sorry for them?" Elijah inquired as they turned the corner.

"For the fiends, yes, but they can still eat a bullet on a bad day," She exclaimed as they walked into the mess hall.

"Well it was nice talking to you," Elijah exclaimed while walking over to Jewel; who was sitting at the end of a black table. As Elijah walked over to him a smile crept across Jewel's face. Elijah shook his head back and forth before exclaiming, "I was just making conversation."

"I'm surprised she didn't bite your nose off," Jewel hissed while looking up at her enter the bathroom door across the other side of the room.

"She isn't so bad, maybe I just have a natural touch with the ladies," he exclaimed with a smile.

"Well ladies man you sure risked it today with Sargent Wells, had you fell off that treadmill all hell would have broken loose and you still risk it for a fellow cadet," he said while putting down his fork and placing an arm around Elijah while looking at the other cadets sitting next to them.

"Man we shot great in the battle simulator today. I bet we could take Leather," Jewel professed as the whole table instantly got silent.

"Who's Leather?" Elijah inquired to Jewel after a few seconds of silence.

"He's a Zodia general," Private Chesters exclaimed to break the silence causing an African American cadet in front of him to look up at him.

"He does awful stuff," Jewel professed while sitting back down and commencing to eat.

"He wears a gas mask, black gardening gloves, blue overalls, and rain boots," he said with a mouthful of food.

"Yeah but clothes don't make you scary," Elijah retorted.

"He also carries a flamethrower and three tear gas grenades," Jewel said before continuing; "They say he holds the flame in your face to melt off the skin".

"Legend has it that he takes the skull after its been fire-polished, cleans it up, and chains it to his waist," he finished while taking in another mouthful.

"Is that so," Elijah retorted.

"They say he used to be with the US Army before the war. That's how he got his name because he was burned in battle. To make matters worse he took about ⅓ of the troops from his platoon with him," Private Chesters exclaimed as Elijah stared at his chubby cheeks.

"Point blank period, the guy is a hotshot", Jewel professed; "Just pray to the Father you never see him, okay." Elijah rolled his neck around in a circle, popping it in a few places along with the rotation.

"All right I need to get cleaned up," Elijah exclaimed as he rose to his feet and headed for the bathroom to freshen up.

Chapter Thirty-two

August 15th, 2044. 10:00 P.M. The
Alta Vista Ranch. Shepherd, TX.

Gayla leaned against a post in Crunchy's shack while he cooked himself dinner.

"So my lady, what do you have planned tonight," Crunchy inquired settling a pot over the stand positioned over the fire.

"A man is treating me to dinner tonight," she retorted with a smile.

"So you have a date," Crunchy asked while sitting back in his chair.

"I guess you could say that," she professed while crossing her arms and looking down while still leaning on a post.

"It's with Joe," she exclaimed while looking up at Crunchy. His eyes glowed like flashlights were abaft the lenses of his eyes.

He gave a hard swallow, "he sure is a nice fellow."

"Yeah, he's sweet; and I haven't seen or heard from Elijah in forever. I wonder if i can keep myself holding on," she exclaimed.

"What does your heart tell you?" Crunchy asked while leaning back forward, poking the fire with a stick he picked up from off of the ground.

"That's a good question," Gayla retorted while she pondered to herself.

"You seem a bit indecisive," Crunchy exclaimed after few seconds.

"My advice is live your life, and if fate brings your friend back then so be it; but don't live in a bubble," he exclaimed as she raised up from the post.

"I should get going," she professed while walking towards the door.

"Enjoy yourself baby girl," Crunchy said with a smile as she left the shack. She walked out of the building heading towards the front gate to enter the compound. When the man taking surveillance at the top of the gate saw her he signaled for the gate to be opened. She strolled past the market stalls and past Patrice's office to a gate on the side of the fenced-in area. As she headed toward the place were she and Crunchy had met Joe by the shed. But when she arrived there was a fire burning outside and the shed door was open. Her curiosity got the best of her as the neared the entrance to have a peek inside.

Inside the Shed

"I just don't understand", a spider exclaimed to a roach that was standing beside the spider's web.

"I mean after having a family, over a dozen freaking eggs!" he exclaimed dramatically, "And, she tries to eat me!"

"It's the circle of life Tim," the roach retorted while scuttling over a few steps.

"It's downright disrespectful," the spider professed as the argument dug deeper into the grit.

"I think you're thinking about this too much, I mean what do your friends say?" the roach inquired.

"They all had little ones, and for what; to become the next day's snack!" the spider screamed.

"Now where are they?" he inquired.

"In the epitome of some arachnid's stomach!" the spider screamed in an irate tone of voice.

"Tim, I think you're thinking about this too hard", the roach professed before being cut off by the spider; "How am I making this a big deal."

"You know, I think the problem here is that you can't relate", the spider exclaimed to the roach as the door creaked open and Gayla entered the shed.

"Maybe your right", the roach exclaimed; "But that's beside the point."

It was then that they began talking over each other, neither of them listening to each other nor paying attention to their surroundings and in a matter of time Gayla had snuck up on them and hushed the spider up as the stepped on the roach. As her shoe lifted into the air the roach screamed for it life as it slowly began to dwindle away. The spider sighed to himself as he walked higher up on his web, perching himself up beside a nearby wall.

Through Geyla's Eyes

"Gosh, darn it," Gayla exclaimed as she looked at the bottom of her shoe; seeing the crushed roach beneath it. She scraped it on the ground, rubbing the roaches mangled body onto the floor; tearing him in half in the process.

"Ew," she exclaimed as it came off and she continued exploring Joe's shack.

She analyzed the assortment of shelves and its contents, each stacked and positioned precisely.

He is very organized, then left the shelves alone and walked over to a bike leaning against a post inside. It was flagrant and beautiful. It was the color of a flamingo with shiny brass handlebars. She caressed the black leather seat to its crossbar and onto the handlebars as she walked by. There were silver pegs for pumping someone on the back, and black tassels on the handlebars that hung down to the top of the tire. Then a hole in the roof in the corner of the building caught her attention, it hung over three potted plants which were illuminated by the moonlight peeping through the hole in the ceiling. Her finger slid off the edge of the bike as the walked to the rear of the shed, maneuvering her way through the dark past darkened objects. It wasn't until she was right upon the potted plants that she figured out what it was.

"So he smokes hemp or weed?" she asked aloud to herself while looking at the plants sitting in the moonlight.

"It's for personal use, and yes it's hemp," Joe's voice called out from behind her. She spun around quickly and fumbled for words as she thought of how bad this looked.

It's just the first date and he already caught me peeking through his things, she thought.

"It's ok," he insisted; "Come on, I have everything set up outside." She then followed Joe out of the shed to the fire outside where they both sat on a blanket that was not there before. He reached into a basket that was beside him and pulled out three loaves of bread and two blocks of cheese, capping off the presentation with a bottle of wine.

"Pink Moscato for the lady," he professed while sitting down the bottle of wine.

Gayla chuckled to herself before asking, "How did you manage to get this?"

"I always keep a stash. Dr. Sherman taught me that," he professed.

"Anywho, they didn't find it the last time they came," he exclaimed.

"They should be coming back sometime soon," she said while looking down.

"Let's not think about that tonight," Joe exclaimed while walking over to a guitar propped against a tree and returning to his position beside her.

"Tonight is about having fun," he professed with a smile while strumming the strings of the guitar, starting the fringe of a popular acoustic song.

"How long have you been playing?" Gayla inquired.

"I have been playing for about seven years now," he retorted while continuing the strum the strings like a pro, cord after cord coming out as clear as water. Gayla broke the bread and stuffed it into her mouth, it was sweet like sugar cane on the fringe of her tongue.

"I hope it's still fresh," he professed.

"It's perfect," she retorted while picking up a bottle of wine.

"So the thing is, I don't have cups; but your germs can only build me immune system," he exclaimed with a smile. Gayla chuckled to herself and unstopped the cork and water falling it over her mouth.

"Mmm, that's good," she exclaimed.

"I'm glad you like it," he exclaimed while strumming the strings softer.

"So you don't have anyone you're talking to?" Gayla inquired while holding the bottle in her hand.

"No, not too many women here spark my interest," he professed.

"But if I must be honest, you sure have sparked my curiosity," he exclaimed.

Gayla giggled to herself, "That's sweet, but someone already has my heart."

"What's he like," he asked.

"He loves God," she professed while thinking about Elijah, "But he does have a fiance out there somewhere."

"Don't judge me," she said while putting the cork back in the bottle and picking up the cheese.

"Trust me, I'm not," he retorted.

"I like that," he said; "You like him because he loves God."

"Quite beautiful actually," he said while putting down the guitar after strumming the strings one final time a little harder than before. He reached for one of the blocks of cheese and broke a corner off.

"He sure is a lucky guy to have a girl like you," Joe said while stuffing his face.

"I keep hearing that, but I'm not all that. I'm a mess," she retorted with a laugh.

"I guess it's open to perception," he said while reaching for another piece of bread.

"You know what would be fun?" Gayla poised.

"What is that?" he responded.

"We should ride the bike in the shed. I haven't been on a bike in forever," she said with a smile.

"Sure thing," he exclaimed while rising to his feet. As he walked away she called his name, forcing him to turn around as she said, "You're a great friend." He gave a soft smirk before turning back to the shed and leaving her sitting on the blanket by the fire. She poured more wine into her mouth as she stared at a nearby tree, thinking of the man she had fallen for but hadn't seen in what felt like ages. Not knowing what became of him flustered her, but her heart clung to the feelings for him. As Joe walked out of the shed with the bike she closed the bottle, put it down and rose to her feet.

"I'll pedal," Joe insisted; "You shouldn't drink and drive."

Gayla chuckled to herself as she got on the back of the bike, standing on the pegs before he took off like a speeding bullet. Gayla placed her hands on his shoulders before relaxing and enjoying herself; spreading her arms out like a bird as they sped through the dark field.

Beautiful Flowers

Chapter Thirty-three

August 30th, 2044. 8:00 A.M. Kingwood, TX.

As the door to the black hole swung open, letting in light through the doorway. It shined in Gladius's face as he lay curled up against the wall.

"Good Morning, Gladius," Africa exclaimed as he made a signal to two of his men and they left him alone with Gladius.

"I brought you something," he said while pulling out a half of a sandwich wrapped in a napkin; "I know it has been a while since you had a meal."

"You know Gladius I'm like you," Africa professed; "I'm a Taurus". He then turned around and lifted up his shirt, exposing a brand of a bull on his upper shoulder. Gladius gazed at it as he devoured the sandwich, licking the mustard off of his dirty fingers as he turned around.

"Man you were really hungry. Well that should hold you a while," he exclaimed; "Come on you have work to do." He rose to his feet following Africa out the black hole for the first time in two months. The sunlight blinded him as he savored the flavor of the sandwich he was brought, sliding pieces of meat out of his unbrushed teeth with his tongue and swallowing them one by one. He then looked behind him as the door to Raven's black hole opened and they pulled her out.

"Now look," he professed while holding up one finger; "Next time you mess up I'll throw her in there instead."

"Do we have an understanding?" he exclaimed in a serious tone.

"Yes sir, we do," Gladius retorted before he was dismissed by Africa, and commenced to another grueling day in the drug lab with Raven.

As he near her he gave her a limp expression but before he spoke she said in a weak voice, "I don't want to hear it."

Chapter Thirty-four

September 30th, 2044. 8:00 A.M. Fort Hadknot in New Orleans, LA.

"Elijah wakes up", Jewel exclaimed while shaking Elijah out of his sleep in his bed.

"What?" Elijah exclaimed as he enters consciousness, arising with the gracefulness of a swan.

"Sargent Wells is coming," he exclaimed as Elijah rushed out of bed from the other side, hopping onto the floor and pursued getting dressed. Jewel then left him beside and pursued the same, buttoning his pants as he walked back to his ironed shirt. As Elijah put on his pants he cupped his hands over his mouth and blew his breath in his hand to smell his breath.

"Wow!" he exclaimed while jerking back. His eye then shot to the open chest at the end of his bunk; a yellow toothbrush lay inside. He reached in and grabbed it without haste, blitzing through the room of male cadets scurrying about getting dressed. Elijah's target was the bathroom with his toothbrush in his mouth, his tube of toothpaste in one of his shoes, while he carried them along with his shirt ironed and pressed. He dropped the items in the restroom sink. He turned on the hot water, spritzing it on his face in cupped handfuls before looking up at his reflection in the mirror. He then took off his shirt and changed into his normal dress attire before brushing his teeth. Foam spilled from the corners of his mouth as the toothbrush slid in and out of his mouth, it even dripped into the sink as he reached to the back to get his wisdom teeth. But the mess didn't last long as the running water washed it down and he washed out his mouth with hot water. Elijah then looked at himself one more time in the mirror, wiping his hand across his bald head and cleanly shaven face. He put his shoes on at the right time as he rushed out and put his contents in the chest, Sargent Wells walked in.

"A-Ten-Hut," He yelled as Elijah closed his chest and turned around to attention. Sargent Wells paced down the line of male recruits with a letter in his hand.

"Today it saddens me that I will be letting all of you go," he exclaimed.

"The military has deemed each of you worthy of bearing that cross," he said.

"So today I will be reading was you all will be going," he finished.

"Private Singletary," he screamed.

"Sir, yes sir," one of the cadets called out.

"3600 Infantry. I hope you brought a jacket it's going to be cold up north, congratulations.

"Maggot Elijah!" the Sargent shouted.

"Sir, yes sir," Elijah called back.

"1200 Infantry," he exclaimed; "You're going to Austin, may God have mercy on your soul."

As Elijah swallowed hard the Sargent yelled, "Maggot Jewel."

"Sir yes sir," Jewel retorted.

"1200 Infantry. I'm just glad we got all of the snickers out of you," he teased.

As he called the rest of the male cadet's divisions they would be apart of, Elijah glared at Jewel. They would be fighting side by side, but this wasn't in some virtual world this was real life. Jewel peeked a smirk at him after noticing his gaze, forcing Elijah to do the same.

"Ok, dismissed," The Sargent exclaimed as he finished the list and walked up and posted it on the wall on a bulletin board with a stick pin before leaving out of the room. Jewel was the first to run over to it.

"Elijah, Katanna is with us too," Jewel called out to Elijah. It brought a smile to his face as Jewel acted childish, making a skit that he was going to war with a lover.

"She is attractive," Elijah exclaimed.

Jewel burst out laughing, "Come on man, if HQ finds out something like that is going on you'll get sent away. We haven't even fought our first battle together yet a man. For me, just don't do it," Jewel professed.

"I'm not making any promises," Elijah exclaimed while crawling back into his bunk, staring at the coarse surface of the painted ceiling.

Chapter Thirty-five

September 30th, 2044. 3:00
P.M. Shepherd, TX.

A s Gayla crept through the woods with the hunting bow in hand, searching for a game of any sort.

This was so much easier with Alexis.

Still, nonetheless, she made each step with the uttermost precision. A gentle breeze blew her hair in the wind, as she took another step. The humidity was causing her body to sweat, staining her red bandanna maroon with sweat. It dripped down her dark-skinned thighs as she crept past a medium-sized pine tree. She scanned from left to right, looking for anything that could be the next meal. A bird chirped in the silent forest as a mosquito buzzed by her ear, she swatted it away; only for it to return. Then it happened, she smacked it against the muscles of her neck. Then something in the brush moved, she then held her breath and didn't move a muscle. She looked to her right that she saw a deer eyeing her down. After about ten seconds it went back to feasting on vegetation and Gayla commenced back to breathing once again. She pulled an arrow from her quiver and pulled the bowstring back with the arrow armed, all the while she was as quiet as a church mouse in mid-service. She stared down the sight and let the arrow go, it flew through the woods and pierced into the deer's neck; forcing it to fall onto the earth before trying to get up and falling over again. The deer gave up one final wail as it gave up and died. It was a great kill. She rushed over to it and pulled out her knife, slitting its throat to finish it off. Once her game had demised she picked the deer up and braced it across her back shoulders, making her way back to the Alta Vista Ranch. Its blood dripped on her shoulder as she carried the dead animal. She was filled with self-accomplishment, it was her second kill, and it was much bigger than the first. She wondered where she would gut the kill and how much she would get for trade, but more importantly were would she store it so Juicy and his goons couldn't get it. It wasn't long before she neared Crunchy's shack just outside the wall. Crunchy was sitting on the steps of the porch but stood after seeing her struggle, her legs had begun to get weak from the load.

"Well then, what do we have here," he professed while taking the game off her shoulders.

"I saw her out there grazing," she exclaimed with a smile.

"Looks like you got a doe," Crunchy processed while sitting the animal on the porch. He then walked inside the shack as Gayla inspected the animal, but when he came back outside he held a double-headed hook, with one hook at each pole; the tight end had a yellow rope hanging from it. Crunchy walked out to a tree limb and hung the hook on a limb, with the end with the rope hanging down.

"Help me hoist him up," he professed while whipping the deer's blood off of his arm. Gayla walked to the dead deer which lay on the front porch of Crunchy's shack, grabbing two legs as Crunchy grabbed the other two; carrying it to the tree and placing the hook through one foot while tying the rope around the ankle.

Gayla pulled out her knife and prepared to gut the deer as Crunchy inquired, "Do you remember the man Alexis killed?"

"Yeah, what about him," she retorted as she cut into its meat.

"Well I heard a gunshot", Crunchy exclaimed before continuing; "When I caught up to y'all I didn't see a gun."

"Oh really?" she asked sarcastically while trying to blow it off and change the subject; "Crunchy will you do me a favor."

"Gayla did you take that gun?" he asked.

"Crunchy," she exclaimed while pulling the knife out of the deer.

"No, Gayla you could get a lot of us in trouble if Juicy's men find that," he retorted.

"I know, I'm going to hide it now," she exclaimed while trying to pass the knife to Crunchy, but he refused it.

"Bring it to me, I won't have you getting yourself in more trouble than you can get out of. I care about you baby girl," he exclaimed while she put the knife in his hand.

"I won't give it to you, but I will hide it," she said while walking away, leaving Crunchy standing by the cut open deer. She wiped her hands on her pants as she entered the front gate of the buzzing compound. Three men on horses rode by her, staring at the deer's blood on her clothes, one of the men tipped his cowboy hat too her as his horse trotted by. She then made her way to the housing quarters, passing by a stall filled with fragrant flowers. Before long she was at the dorm, she rushed to her bunk and lifted the mattress, pulling out the pistol she got from the man Alexis killed. She then turned around and looked for a place to put it. Then a spot caught her eye, a piece of loose floorboard she eventually pulled up and placed the pistol inside.

"Gayla," Calvin's voice called out as she was about to seal up her loot.

"Hey," she exclaimed while turning around and dropping over the hole.

"I just want you to know, you're doing a great job with the bow," he professed before turning to leave.

"Thanks," Gayla retorted before he left her squatting down by the loose floorboard.

Chapter Thirty-six

October 15th, 2044. 4:00 P.M. Austin, TX.

As Elijah sat on the ground, with his rifle across his chest and his combat knife in its sheath; Jewel chewed on a candy bar from an MRE package. But the party was soon interrupted by activity at the base. They were then approached by a man in a military uniform approached them, putting on his hat as he made his way over to them.

"I'm Corporal Chambers, Are you one of the recruits?" he asked.

"Yes Sir, Private Elijah Charlie 1200 Infantry," Elijah exclaimed before looking at his companion and teasing, "This scab here is named Jewel."

"Private Elijah, We have Zodia activity in San Marcos. It's time to mount up, Private Elijah your driving," the man exclaimed as Elijah and Jewel rose to their feet. The three of them then began walking to the giant diesel trucks, whose truck beds were beginning to be filled with armed soldiers. Elijah climbed into the driver's seat of one of the running trucks. He sat in the front seat afraid and excited at the same time. His fingers began to shake as the Corporal entered the other side of the two seated vehicle.

"You're nervous," he exclaimed while looking at Elijah's finger twitch.

"You should be," he finished. Elijah then cleared his throat as someone slapped on the side of the truck bed.

"Time to roll out," the Corporal exclaimed as they pulled out of the base. The radio then began to off in the background, filling the trucks quiet ride with occasional chatter as they got off a small road. The Corporal then began whistling as he let the window down and hung one arm out.

"Let's put a little speed on it shall we," he exclaimed as they drove on the empty freeway. Elijah mashed the gas pedal until the speedometer read ninety miles per hour, they were the first truck of a line of six that stormed through the empty roads with fire in their eyes and a taste for blood.

Elijah stared into the side view mirror to see the other truck behind him tallying along before Elijah asked, "How many battles have you been in?"

"I lost count after six," the Corporal retorted.

"One thing I've learned though, you will never get used to losing men," he exclaimed.

"I can only imagine," Elijah exclaimed as he maneuvered around a bend in the road.

"Where are you from?" Elijah inquired.

"Mississippi," he exclaimed while exposing his southern accent.

"Do you have any family back home?" Elijah inquired while trying to make a conversation during the trip.

The man then reached into his back pocket and pulled out a wallet, flipping it open and removing a picture of a woman and three kids. "These are my little ones, and that's my wife," he exclaimed while looking at the picture of the family.

"That's beautiful," Elijah retorted.

"Ah, there not so bad," Corporal Chambers exclaimed while putting away the wallet.

"What about you," he asked while placing his arm back out the window again as the radio continued to chatter.

"Yes I do, but it's a complicated situation. I haven't seen my family since the war started," Elijah exclaimed.

"That's unfortunate," Corporal Chambers exclaimed; "But you're not the only one."

"I met a private in battle who was eighteen years old," he professed with a smile; "It was his first battle."

"He kind of reminded me of a younger me," he professed, "Anyways he had lost everything."

"His parents got killed by the Zodia before he joined, those sick biscuit eaters gave his sister to a fiend. I'm sure you can figure out how that went," he finished.

"What happened to him?" Elijah inquired.

"He got shot in the head, while we were talking in battle; his blood splattered on my face," he exclaimed.

"Man that's rough," Elijah exclaimed.

"Yeah, tell me about it. I got the man who did it though, so it brings me some closure; still, he was just a kid in my eyes," he said.

"Well, how old are you?" Elijah inquired.

"I'll be thirty-seven on Monday" he retorted.

"I'm going to get wasted," he said with a smile.

"Well I hope you enjoy yourself," he exclaimed with a smile.

All of a sudden a man ran into the road waving his arms in the air, but Elijah swerved the wheel to not hit him.

"Get out of the road!" Corporal Chambers yelled at the man as the other trucks performed the same maneuver.

"You see the smoke?" the Corporal asked while looking through binoculars out the window of the road ahead. The trucks came to a stop just outside the warzone.

"The man we are after is named Mercurious Khil", Corporal Chambers said while pulling out a photo of a dark-skinned bald man; "Otherwise known as Todd Freeman."

"His parents were members of the Zodia, he was practically born into it," he said as all the men unloaded the Corporal started giving orders; splitting the men up into groups. Jewel and Elijah trotted at the back of their group, running behind a burning house. Then all of a sudden Jewel stopped to tie his shoe as the other men ahead trotted along.

"What are you doing?" Elijah asked him while stopping as well, turning around and coming back to him as gunshots went off in the distance.

"My shoestring is loose," he said while placing his rifle on the ground and bending over, pulling the laces and tying them as Elijah turned his back to him. But sometime in between a buff Asian man wearing a sugar skull mask and carrying a crimson-stained blade, Elijah turned around and grabbed his knife from his belt and threw it at the man's neck. The man choked on his blood as he fell to the earth.

"Wow!" Jewel exclaimed while looking back; "Good looking out man".

"Let's go," Elijah exclaimed as he rushed along the path the others took, having to stop after a good distance because they lost the group.

"There they go," Jewel professed as he pointed to a burnt down house with troops huddled inside. They dashed across the street to the other side of the road to the burnt house. The men were all loading their ammo.

"If you want to keep your head, don't get lost again," Corporal Chambers said before rolling over on his stomach and firing six rounds from his rifle. Elijah peeked to the left to see one of the men praying with a sweaty grit filled face. But it wasn't long before all of the men fired at the building.

Clip after clip they expelled more ammo than at target practice, leaving the house with bullet holes before the Corporal exclaimed; "Hold your fire!" One of the men then shot the rifle one more time after the command, making the Corporal command again, "I said hold your fire!" He pressed the stock of the gun against his shoulder, turning back around to look at the shot up residence. Then all of a sudden the front door creaked open and the leg of a chair stuck out with a white flag.

"They are surrendering," the Corporal exclaimed as he raised to his feet. Mercurius Khil then exited the house holding the chair.

"Take me to your leader," the Zodia leader yelled with his hands in the air; "I surrender."

Chapter Thirty-seven

October 15th, 2044. 11:00 P.M. The
Alta Vista Ranch. Shepherd, TX.

I t was the end of the day and the merchants were
cleaning up and packing to leave for the housing
quarters. Calvin had been taken recently by the Juicy
and his thugs for attempting to shoot Juicy with Gayla's
confiscated pistol, but in the darkness other trouble was
brewing.

"See you later Mindy," the compound baker exclaimed
as he left her in the market by herself.

"See ya," she exclaimed as she put her items into a
cardboard box. She was a candle maker in this world, it
wasn't her passion but before the war, she worked in real
estate. She sighed to herself as she looked at the rest of the
items she had to pack up. Then all of a sudden she heard
something move in the dark.

"Is someone there?" she called out while grabbing
a lit candle off her market stall. She crept through the
night holding the vanilla-colored candle in her left hand,
cupping her hand around the flame to keep the gentle

wind from blowing it out. She tilted her head to the side as she inspected her surroundings, not seeing anyone in the nearby area. Feeling convinced it was just nerves getting the best of her she turned around to see a man in a pink bunny outfit with a white tummy holding a sickle. She then turned to run, looking over her shoulder; staring at the bunny's smiley face as he chased behind her. She then turned the corner like a jackrabbit, heading for the housing sector while running for her life. The bunny turned the corner after her and started gaining on her. But about fifteen yards from the door she tried to jump over a table and tripped, landing face-first into the dirt and barrel rolling on the ground as the bunny lurched over the knocked over a table and began to assault the Mindy. He hacked and hacked at her body until she stopped moving, leaving a crimson stain on the bunny suit as he dashed off into the night.

Chapter Thirty-eight

October 16th, 2044. 10:00 A.M. The Alta Vista Ranch. Shepherd, TX.

Gayla's eyes opened to the sound of commotion outside the housing sector. She could hear people communing outside the building as she placed her feet on the ground, standing to her feet and walking outside to see a crowd of people huddled in a circle. It wasn't until Gayla got closer that she saw what all of the fuss was about. In the center of the circle lay Mindy, mangled and bloody.

"Move out of the way," Dr. Sherman said while shoving the people aside, forcing them to generate rude remarks. He then squatted down to the woman who lay in a pool of her own blood. He inspected the woman closely before placing two fingers on her jugular.

"She's gone," he exclaimed before standing back up.

The crowd gasp and chattered amongst themselves as Gayla walked up to Dr. Sherman.

"Are you sure?" Gayla inquired while grabbing his shirt and looking back at the woman.

"Hey, who's the Dr. in this situation?" he asked while brushing her hands off him.

"Does Patrice know?" she inquired.

"I think we better tell her," Dr. Sherman exclaimed. As they both headed off leaving the crowd Geyla exclaimed; "I need to talk to her as well."

"Oh, joy," he professed in a sarcastic tone of voice.

"Things have been offaly strange here lately, a bunch of thugs show up and take a bunch of our goods; and now it seems we have a murderer on the loose," he said.

"He probably preyed on her, like an animal; it looked brutal," he cried in a soft tone.

"We have to find out who is doing this," he said as he pushed open the door of Patrice's office, holding it open for Gayla.

"I'm thinking of leaving because this is just too much. It's like chaos," She said before walking into the door and seeing Patrice propped up in her chair against the wall; she had her arms crossed and her hair lay in her ivory face. Gayla looked at the table and noticed a half-drunk bottle of scotch laying on the office desk.

"Mindy's dead," Gayla said to her while plopping down in a chair on the other side of her desk, turning semi sideways to still communicate with them.

"I know," she retorted in a grim tone.

"Everything is falling apart," she exclaimed before reaching for a glass filled with liquor and gulping down some.

"I've spent years building this place, and at its height; it falls apart with the sands of time with me," she exclaimed.

"They took Calvin, what do I have left," she finished.

"I wouldn't say that. I mean we don't know where he is or where he is but we can pray he is safe," Gayla retorted.

"We must at least conduct an investigation for the murdered woman," Dr. Sherman added in; "Justice demands it."

Patrice grabbed the glass of liquor again and before chugging it down she said, "I agree."

"Gayla I want you to figure it out," she professed.

"Why me!" she screamed while sitting up in the chair.

"Because I need someone right now. I'll pay you," she said.

"Fine, but if it happens again I'm leaving," she retorted. Patrice tilted her head to the side before pouring another glass and exclaiming; "Deal."

"There is one other thing I need to talk to you about," Gayla insisted while standing to her feet.

"What would that be," Patrice inquired.

"The gun Calvin had was mine," she exclaimed while looking down; "I'm sorry."

"Sorry doesn't bring him back," Patrice exclaimed in a cold tone of voice.

"You should do well to remember the rules of this place. The rules keep us safe," she stressed while taking a sip of the liquor her glass.

"But, now there is a killer loose," Gayla said in a smart tone; "So the rules don't mean much." Patrice then put down the glass, and with a face scrunched up like a bull dog she said; "Find the killer, and stop talking about it."

Chapter Thirty-nine

October 16th, 2044. 3:00 P.M. Shepherd, TX.

J uicy sat in front of Calvin in the living room of Juicy's condo, they had been together for a while now and Calvin still wasn't cracking. Juicy was determined to recruit the little rascal, whether he wanted to be involved in a gang or not. The whole apartment complex had been used by the gang ever since society went down the drain, occupying many of the rooms and forcing some to leave. They had a compound, guns, and power. Juicy pursed his lips and breathed deeply as he tried to tolerate Calvin's silence.

"We're going to jump you in today," Juicy exclaimed.

"You act tough, let's see how tough you really are," he said.

"What?" Calvin screamed.

"Oh, now you want to talk," Juicy retorted with a smile.

"What does that even mean?" Calvin inquired.

"It means after today your going to be one of us," he said.

"I don't want to be one of you guys! I want to go home!" he screamed.

"The only way your going home is if were dropping off your dead body or your collecting at the depots with us," he exclaimed.

"It's us or death, my little friend, there is no other option," he exclaimed.

"You'll even get your own gun," he said.

"I want to go home," he exclaimed again while starting to cry.

"Hey, stop all of that!" he then yelled at Calvin, making him sob even harder.

Juicy sighed and looked down before saying, "You know if you're quick about it it won't be that bad, I won't let the boys get too rough with you; we know your just a kid."

"That should be the other boys now," he exclaimed while getting up and walking to the door, letting in two bulky men, a fat man, and another who was pencil-thin. Calvin rose to his feet as the men surrounded around him one by one, creating a square around him as juicy walked up and got in Calvin's face. He reached in his pocket and pulled out three American silver dollars. Juicy held them in front of Calvin's face while staring into his eyes. Although Clavin's attention was he captivated by Juicy's gold tooth, he was greatly afraid at the time. His fingers twiddled as they stood in front of him.

"Three for the founders," he said.

"You will never forget that," he snapped.

"We use it for everything," Juicy exclaimed as the other men said in unison; "And we are everything as one body, one mind, one power".

"What about God?" Calvin asked.

"What about him?" Juicy retorted as the men laughed amongst themselves.

"Kid, they are going to beat your butt until you pick up the three coins and place them heads up," he said before the skinny man punched him in the stomach and he fell on the floor. Juicy then threw the coins in the air and they landed in various parts of the living room as he sat on the sofa and watch the men smack the kid around. They beat him to a pulp, drawing blood from his mouth in a beating that lasting about ten minutes. But as they fought him around the room, throwing him over here and kicking him over there he couldn't manage to pick the coins up, let alone put one on heads. In the beginning, he tried, grabbing one, only to lose it after a heavy blow; and after a few of those by the bulky men he was down for the count. It turned into him being mauled by savage animals.

Beaten and battered the teenager lay on his knees after Juicy yelled, "Sit him up!"

"Your a little tougher than I thought, but you didn't get them all on heads," he exclaimed in a cold tone.

"I'm not joining you!" Calvin screamed before spitting blood in his face. Juicy inhaled deeply, wiping the spit off of his cheek and smacking the young boy with the back of his hand, causing him to hit his head on the end table. Blood gushed from Calvin's head as Juicy squatted down next to the boy and pulled out his blood-stained handkerchief and dipped it in the boy's blood.

As he stood back up he exclaimed to the men who beat the boy up, "Clean this up." It then that Clavin was no more, one of the men then pulled out a pistol and shot the boy in the head; ending his life. After the men cleaned the place up and got the body out, they soon threw it in a van as they drove to the Alta Vista Ranch; dumping the body outside the gate while speeding away down the street. Once the guards had seen what had been thrown out of the van, they opened the gate and rushed out to Calvin's before seeing the bullet wound and realizing he was dead. It was a sad sight, a child taken by another street gang wreaking havoc in America. The guard then raised up from the body and carried the body to Patrice's office.

Chapter Forty

October 25th, 2044. 12:30 P.M. Austin, TX.

"I'm telling you guys, I wouldn't be here today if it wasn't for my brother Elijah," Jewel exclaimed to a group of people in the mess hall. Katanna being one of the people in attendance. She was already eyeing Elijah from afar, but his brave actions and can-do attitude made her hot and bothered for his attention.

"Well boys I'm out of here," Katanna exclaimed while standing up from the table, and heading off before exclaiming; "I have scout duty today."

"See you later," one of the recruits exclaimed as she walked outside, meeting Elijah and another African American private outside the mess hall. They then loaded into the jeep parked by a nearby building with Elijah having a radio strapped to his back, entering the front seat of the vehicle as Katanna entered the driver's seat. The engine hummed like a bird as they cranked it up and drove out of the military base, starting down the small road before getting on the highway and heading south.

Katanna drove like a speeding bullet once she got on the highway, but she was alert and perceptive as ever.

"We are supposed to get out at New Braunfels, and patrol the area," Katanna exclaimed while taking one hand off the wheel.

"Don't they have a water park there," Elijah inquired.

"You mean Water World?" The African American cadet inquired.

"Yeah, that's it. But we don't have time for a swim," Katanna said while adjusting the rear view mirror.

"Man, that use to be the place to be in the summer heat," the cadet in the back seat said as he placed his arms across the top of the back seat.

"I used to take my daughter there," Elijah exclaimed as the radio on his back buzzed in the background.

"You have kids?" Katanna asks with excitement.

"Well yeah, assuming she is alive out there somewhere," Elijah retorted.

"I don't have any family left," Katanna exclaimed in a cold tone of voice. It took Elijah a second to process the words she had said as he retorted, "Not even a sibling?"

"I had a sister," she exclaimed; "She stepped on a rusty nail and we had no medication in wilderness."

"I'm sorry to hear that Private", Elijah exclaimed.

"No, it's fine. At this point, everyone has lost someone," she professed.

"I heard that Private," the man in the back seat exclaimed while resituating himself.

"We'll get those cowards though, there's no way they can beat Uncle Sam," he continued.

"They're putting up a good fight," Elijah exclaimed while placing one arm out of the window.

"Did you hear about the battles in the midwest?" Elijah inquired.

"I did, the Zodia is pretty mean for pushing us back like that but I think it's just a phase. Luther probably gave them a speech before they all got loaded up on Neon Moon before the battle," he joked as the others laughed to themselves.

"For real though guys, I didn't expect a cult to fight that hard. To make matters worse they have good supply lines," Katanna said while maneuvering the steering wheel, changing lanes to avoid an abandoned car. Although the car ride was filled with laughs and good times it wasn't long before they had reached New Braunfels and exited the jeep. The place that they parked had an excellent view of the Water World Water Park. But they weren't concerned with the view as they started down the road on foot, getting off the highway and going into the neighborhood. The radio continued to buzz and the only other sound made by the Privates were their boots walking across the ground. Katanna wiped the sweat from under her combat helmet as Elijah pulled out a cantine and began to drink water from it.

But it wasn't long before the African American Private exclaimed, "I have to pee."

"I shouldn't have drunk that extra soda at the base," he finished.

Elijah chuckled to himself as he exclaimed, "Find a tree."

As the Private hopped across the front yard of a house with the front door open, peeing on a tree at the far corner of the yard. All of a sudden Elijah heard a low rumbling noise growing louder in the distance.

"Do you hear that?" Elijah inquired while putting one hand on Katanna's shoulder to stop her from moving. He grabbed the radio and called up his headquarters after Katanna heard it too and gazed into his eyes.

"HQ this is Private Elijah reporting", he called into the walkie talkie; "Do we have any allied armored units nearby?"

"Negative Private", the radio called back. Elijah's eyes then grew large as he and Katanna ran for the house with the open door.

"Private we have action, we have to get out of here," Elijah called out to the other man by the tree as a tank with Zodia members screaming on top of it rolled around the corner. One by one they dashed into the house before sawing, but the private who was by the tree was seen and the tank fire just as he jumped into the doorway, and although he was not his by the shell; he did have splinters of wood gauged into his leg. He screamed in pain before Katanna wrapped her hands around his mouth as dust fell to the floor from the blast.

"HQ we need emergency air support and medical aid," Elijah screamed into the radio as Katanna grabbed the wounded soldier, wrapping him over her shoulders and carrying the private out as Elijah followed behind, trying to get in touch with the supreme command.

Chapter Forty-one

October 31st, 2044. 10:00 A.M. The
Alta Vista Ranch. Shepherd, TX.

dward was one of the field hands at the Alta Vista
Ranch tended to the crops in the compound
garden with Will as the birds chirped in the
distance. Edward was an older man, in his upper forties
and as he was as socially awkward as he could be. Not
having many friends in the compound and practically
a social outcast. Edwards pushed himself up from the
ground next to a pile of weeds while pushing himself up
from the ground he said, "I'm going to go get a drink of
water."

"Ok," Will said back to him as he disappeared.

Will pulled at the weeds while secretly upset, he
always thought Edward was trying to skip out of work;
seeing him as a lazy slouch who cared nothing for his
labor. But nonetheless, he worked with him, harvesting
crops and pulling weeds in the garden to get there share
for keeps and a share for trade. Though while he wasn't
looking the pink bunny popped up into view behind him,

stalking Will from the woods with the sickle in hand. The man in the blood-stained bunny suit crept up behind Will as he stood to his feet, picking up the weeds he had pulled and taking them over to a pile he and Edward had built. But by the time he had realized he was being watched. it was too late, turning around from the pile to see the bunny slash him across the face as he wailed in pain before being sliced up like swiss cheese by the killer. However, all ears were not out of reach; as Gayla was strolling by she heard the man scream and followed the noises to the garden to see the bunny hacking Will to bits. She had been investigating for a while now and had no leads, but nowhere the killer was right before her. Gayla ran after the bloody bunny with the hunting bow in hand and quiver on her back, chasing him into the woods for what seemed like minutes before stopping and aiming an arrow for his leg. The arrow pierced the bunnies suit, sinking into the flesh beneath it; but this didn't stop the murder as he limped on his right leg out of sight. Gayla had lost him but ran back to Will to see him starting to expire. She placed his head in her lap as his bloody hand grabbed her wrist while he choked on his blood; trying to get words out but none escaped his lips before he let go of his life and died in her arms.

Chapter Forty-two

November 1st, 2044. 10:00 A.M. The Alta Vista Ranch. Shepherd, TX.

Gayla strolled to Patrice's office with her fist balled up and her things packed and loaded on two horses the group leaving with her traded for, along with the two bags of cornmeal and one bag of bread they bought as well, with glassware apparatuses and flask secured in boxes next to wooden tables by the other belongings they decided to bring. The group that decided to leave the Alta Vista Ranch with Gayla consisted of Crunchy, Joe, and Dr. Sherman, and although they were not sure where they would settle they had made up their minds that anything was better than here. They were a group of pacifists seeking a better life, safe from terror; a haven that shines like a beacon of light to those afflicted by the war or tired of governmental constriction. Gayla opened the door and entered Patrice's office, she was sitting in her chair next to a pistol and an empty bottle of scotch.

"I see you killed it," Gayla chuckled while pointing to the empty bottle.

"How are you holding up?" She inquired.

"I'm done, it's over," she exclaimed while looking at the empty bottle.

"Look I'm sorry about Calvin, I feel like it's my fault," Gayla professed.

"Don't" she interrupted, "I didn't protect him."

"I should have stopped them," she exclaimed while looking up at Gayla.

"But I let them take him, my son's death is on my hands," she cried.

"No, you couldn't do anything about it. They were armed," Gayla pleaded to try to cheer her up.

"I could have done something, but I didn't. Don't tell me that crap like I'm supposed to just eat it off your plate," she hissed.

"Ok," Gayla exclaimed as she gave up, throwing her hands up in the air in the process.

"I'm sure you're heard there was another murder, I almost had him. But I know you remember our deal," she exclaimed in a soft tone.

"Yes, I do," she whispered.

"Well I wish you the best," she said while looking up with a smile.

"Thanks," Gayla retorted.

"Who is all going with you?" she asked.

"Joe, Crunchy, and Dr. Sherman," she exclaimed while placing her hands in her pockets.

"Oh, it's a lot of you," she exclaimed in another soft tone.

"I wouldn't say all of that, we just want a better life," she retorted.

"I understand," she exclaimed sadly.

"Well you should be on your way," she said softly again.

"Oh, and lock the door from the inside before you leave," Patrice finished.

"Bye Patrice," Gayla said while locking the bottom lock on the door and closing it, begging to make her way to the wagon with the group ready to go. Then out of nowhere, a gunshot went off from inside Patrice's office, it forced Gayla to stop in her tracks and then turn to run to the door, but turning the handle was futile; it was locked shut.

Chapter Forty-three

November 5th, 2044. 7:00 A.M. Just outside the city of Houston, TX.

E lijah rode in the back of the truck as he whispered a prayer before going into battle. Bullets could be heard whizzing around in the distance. They had been informed that they should expect heavy Zodia resistance and showed up with plenty of ammo. It was then that the truck stopped, and Elijah exited off with the other soldiers.

"Charlie, on me," Corporal Chambers said as two men called out the alpha, bravo, sigma, and epsilon squadrons. The men and women Elijah's squadron rushed towards a burning building, propping up next to it and peeking around the corner; looking for the enemy. After seeing the coast was clear they dashed down the street in a single file, breathing heavy under the heavy gear as they kneeled behind a burning bus.

"I want troops in that building now doing overwatch," he professed while pointing to a building with a small fire on top.

As Jewel, Elijah, and two other Privates ran into the building the radio on Elijah's back started to buzz during battle as allies communicated to each other. Once inside, Elijah dashed up the stairs of the smoky building. The second floor was dark, the only light that enters came from the rectangular glass windows the room possessed. Elijah dashed from doorway to doorway, making sure each room was clear. But it wasn't until half of the rooms were checked that he heard a fiend nearby. Elijah then caught a glimpse of it upon hearing it scream like it was insane, dashing into one of the rooms to see a Zodia member inside; it appeared to be an old drug lab. He lurched to activate a bomb in a duffel bag before the fiend had tracked Elijah down. It had a mask with a long nose, under which it scratches the skin beneath it so hard blood dripped onto the floor. Elijah dashed behind the table in the back of the room as the fiend charged for the Zodia member but not before the bomb was activated.

"Oh crap," Elijah exclaimed while watching the fiend attack the man then looking at the timer tick from three minutes. Elijah dashed out of the room as the fiend had beaten the Zodia man unconscious, staring at a shiny metal plate that hung on the wall as it scratched beneath its mask.

But outside the room, Elijah did not stop running though he got on the radio; "We have two minutes in counting, to get out of here. There us a bomb in the building."

"Affirmative," a voice called back. He dashed for the window, jumping through it and falling into a trash bin bellow, which was filled with bags on bags of trash;

somewhat cushioning his fall as the building exploded and fell to rubble. The demolition caused a huge cloud of smoke to perk up in the air. As Elijah raised to his feet he heard Jewel call out his name.

"I'm back here," Elijah called back while hopping out of the trash bin. Jewel smiled big when he saw he was ok, running towards him and wrapping his arms around him in a heartfelt hug.

"Let's go," Elijah exclaimed.

"Wait, let's get that garage open," Jewel said while walking over to it and lifting the door; exposing a Zodia member on an armored truck who instantly turned around and fired the mounted 50 cal at Jewel. Elijah watched as another friend died at the hands of the Zodia, the gun nearly ripped the man apart. Elijah fired a shot and hit the man on the mounted truck in the head, knocking him off onto the ground. As Elijah walked up, inspecting to make sure the threats were gone and Jewel was alive, he heard something rustle in the garage. Then out of nowhere, Leather walked out with the flamethrower in hand. He ducked behind a wooden crate in the garage only for the flamethrowers flame to consume it and him to fall on his back.

"Father be with me, give me strength," Elijah said as he stared down the barrel of his aggressor's weapon of choice. But just as it looked as if all hope was lost, the flame thrower ran out of fuel. He then threw it down and pulled out a big combat knife and pulled off a tear gas grenade, dropping it onto the floor as he swung the knife at Elijah. He ducked and dodged as much as he could, but Elijah knew he had to make it a fair fight; and just like that he put all of his kibbles on the table. He reached for his gas mask as he swung the knife at his stomach, and though Elijah could barely see he managed to grab the tip of the mask and remove it without being hit; sending tear gas into Leather's eyes. With a hard right and a strong left Leather hit the floor as Elijah jumped on top of him and gouged his eyes out with his fingers.

As Leather screamed in pain, singling to the other troops. He pounded his head into the ground and left him looking like bruised fruit as Corporal Chambers pulled him off of him and said, "That's enough Private." As Elijah gave up and the other men seized Leather, Elijah brushed the Corporal's hands off of him and looked at Jewel before walking down to his corpse and breaking down crying.

After a moment he then felt the Corporal's cold hand on his shoulder from behind him.

"I told you, you'll never get used to it," he professed while taking his hand off of him and walking off.

Chapter Forty-four

November 6th, 2044. 12:00 P.M. Dallas, TX.

As Anastasia left the golf tee shaped hospital she left behind all memories of her stalker and left to a new life. The janitor had been busted a week later, being arrested and a restraining order placed on him. But now she was free, but still struggling to move about as she made her way down the street. Dallas was under military control and in the big Texas city, tensions were rising. She walked past a military policeman and a civilian arguing in public before the soldier pushed the man down and pursued to arrest him. Anastasia's eyes widened as she viewed the scene, looking back across the street as she saw the military men carry the man off out of sight. She passed by an electronics store with TVs in the window, with all the channels on the Presidential conference; showing David Alexander's face on the front of each screen though she could not hear his words. She then opened her purse, which she received upon leaving the hospital with the rest of her things; checking her coin purse inside to see five hundred dollars as she looked up and noticed a motel sign blinking in the distance. As she made her way to it with no family or place to go, she wondered what living in this new world would be like, what she would do, and become. After buying a room for four nights, she went to the room shaken by the military's presence in the area, it was truly martial law; with armed soldiers walking down the sidewalk of the hotel as she entered the hotel to get to the room she purchased. But not too long after she sat on the bed and cut on the tv there was a knock at the door. Curious as to who it could be, peeking through the peephole to see an elegantly dressed man with shades on. She opened the door to surprise him as he took his shades off and arched his back.

"Oh, I guess he left," he exclaimed.

But after seeing the dumbfounded look on her face he asked, "What's your name?"

"Anastasia," she retorted.

"Well, I am Sephan; and you look like an interesting person. Do you mind if I come in and talk to you?" he asked.

She knew he was a homosexual upon noticing how the man carried himself flagrantly, and she had no friends or family. So she opened the door and started her story from what she remembered, sitting on the bed as he paced around the room.

Chapter Forty-five

November 7th, 2044. 6:00 P.M. Houston, TX.

Elijah's platoon had been chasing the Zodia on foot for two days now, pushing them back to South Houston in the process. Then soldiers of Elijah's platoon were exhausted, many of them Elijah had once called friend, but now we're on a one way trip on a medevac flight out of the warzone. But surprisingly Elijah felt safer on the battlefield than in the wild, was the Zodia run rampant in a non-government controlled area. But here he had a heightened sense of alert as he walked past a burning church. Elijah wiped the grim from his face while he propped himself up against a car, before creeping forward with the rest of the troops. Corporal Chambers then gave the signal for the group to split up around the open area. Elijah followed behind Katanna in a two-person team fit for the most difficult of challenges. Katanna rushed around corners and climbed over rubble but found no enemy with her companion Elijah. As he breathed heavy while trying to keep up with updates from the radio on his back. His legs felt heavy from exhaustion as he caught up to her near a group of trees at a dead end of the street.

There was a tent at the end of the road with an assortment of things placed on a white plastic table beneath the tent. Katanna walked over to the tent with Elijah tailing close behind as the radio buzzed, "All units be aware we have heavy Zodia presence in the area." With hearing that Elijah felt a little nervous sitting in one spot like a duck circling in a pond.

"Katanna we need to get a move on," Elijah exclaimed while rushing her as she picked up the items on the table one by one; inspecting them as if they were murder weapons.

"Katanna!" Elijah screamed at her.

"Just give me one second," she retorted while picking up a sword from the table. It was a pink Katana, sharpened to perfection in its pink sheath. Then out of nowhere a Zodia member rushed out of the woods and threw a hubcap with razor blades mounted on its circumference at Katanna. It sliced through the air and pierced her side, a painful way to catch the soldiers attention as she fell to the earth by the table and Elijah took the shot, hitting the man in the stomach; knocking him on the ground as Katanna pushed herself back up and pulled the hubcap out of her side. Holding one hand on her side she walked over to the man who was screaming on the ground. Elijah walked up to him with her as she withdrew her pistol and pointed it at the man's face, forcing him to stare down the barrel.

"Do it!" he screamed at her before she pulled the trigger and his brains splattered across the earth. Elijah sighed to himself at the sight before trying to help Katanna move about.

"Get your hands off me, I can walk by myself!" she screamed at Elijah before falling to the ground in pain.

"Let me help you," Elijah insisted as she brushed his hands off him; but soon he got fed up with her attitude and walked off from her.

Just as he made up his mind to leave her sitting there the radio buzzed, "All units, be advised we are issuing a retreat. All units, I repeat; get out of there now and meet at the rendezvous point."

"You hear that? We have got to go," Elijah inquired after the radio had finished. He walked back to her and placed one arm around her shoulders, picking her up from the ground.

"Wait a second," she retorted while hobbling over to the pink sword and grabbing it before joining Elijah again, and they began to make their way out of the warzone. Bullets fired in the distance and the smell of death filled the air as they made their way back, trailing some of the ways through the woods instead of on the main road. To be injured, Katanna moved fast holding a sword in the hand around Elijah's neck and a rifle in the other. But progress was soon forfeited as Elijah's boot got caught in the mud, forcing him to stumble but not fall as they tallied along the path to the point of interest.

Mosquitos buzzed around their gritty faces as they swatted them away Elijah professed, "We need to get you patched up."

"Thanks for what you did back there," she exclaimed through grunts of pain.

"That's what I'm here for," he retorted while looking at her in the eyes. After about ten minutes of trailing through the muddy woods, they reached their destination, Katanna had lost a lot of blood and Elijah was wondering where the rest of the platoon was as they sat at the meeting point together with no one else in attendance. Elijah sat next to Katanna as he called his superiors on the radio but was only answered with static.

"HQ, this Private Elijah at the rendezvous point; I need emergency medevac on my position. Do you copy," he called into the phone of the radio. But time went by, and no response nor other soldiers came to their aid. The company was wiped out and it didn't take Elijah long to come to that conclusion.

"We can't keep waiting, we need to move," Elijah exclaimed while getting up on his feet; giving up on the radio and any hope of support. He pulled Katanna up again and placed one arm around his shoulder before hobbling down the road with her, looking for Zodia and any sight of allied troops.

Chapter Forty-six

November 10th, 2044. 5:00 A.M. Conroe, TX.

The group that left with Gayla had detoured through Conroe to avoid the Zodia in Kingwood, making there way to Houston step by step with Gayla commandeering the map. The horse's feet trotted at a steady pace as the walked beside the moving wagon attached to it, with Crunchy holding the reigns of the horse on foot as well. He dangled a carrot in front of its mouth, teasing the horse to the max. It nibbled while walking, stretching out its neck and showing its teeth as it tried to grab the vegetable. Finally, after a few minutes of teasing; Crunchy gave it to the horse.

It gobbled it down in mid-stride as Dr. Sherman exclaimed, "It's more humid than a dragon's breath out here." He wiped the sweat off his forehead with a white towel as Crunchy looked at him and shook his head.

"I'm sorry, Is there a problem?" Dr. Sherman inquired.

"You're not used to outside labor, are you?" Crunchy asked as he laughed to himself.

"I prefer to be in seclusion, with the comfort of a candle to light my craftsmanship," the doctor professed while placing one hand on his chest

"Craftsmanship?" Joe called out; "I built the wall back at the ranch."

"That's craftsmanship", he finished as Gayla rolled her eyes as they started to go back and forth.

"I'll have you know I am in the process of a breakthrough for our time," Dr, Sherman exclaimed.

"Oh boy, let's hear it," Crunchy muttered underneath his breath.

"I'm going to make medicine," he exclaimed with a smile.

"Is this another one of those ideas that you start to run with but eventually stop after it fails?" Joe asked.

Dr. Sherman cleared his throat before exclaimed, "The last few were attempts to improve the life at our compound, and I didn't have all the necessities or people trying to accomplish the task with me."

"Furthermore, It's entirely disrespectful to bring up such things anyways, on to a new subject," Dr. Sherman exclaimed as Joe and Crunchy looked at each other and chuckled to themselves.

"How much longer do we have until the next town," Dr. Sherman asked Gayla from behind.

"We should have about three more hours until we are in Spring," she retorted.

"Three more hours my lady and you gentlemen, let's keep it moving," he professed while grabbing the collar of his lab coat.

"Here's food for thought, where would be the perfect place to settle down," Joe said with cheer.

"An underground layer," Dr. Sherman added quickly.

"Southeast, Texas for me; maybe on another ranch like Patrice had," Crunchy said while kicking a round piece of rubber on the road.

"As long as we can set up a church there, I'm ok with it," Gayla exclaimed.

"A place safe from aggression," Joe said.

"Well aside from Crunchy most of you were vague, and my underground layer will have all of that," Dr. Sherman said while looking at them with a smile.

"No one is living in an underground hole", Joe exclaimed for the group, and after the following seconds of silence, Dr. Sherman concluded that the group was with him.

"You have to think of all the positives, your safe from savages number one. I'm sure I can even get us a garden to grow under the earth," the doctor said while folding his arms across his chest as he pondered the idea. Gayla shook her head at them all, muttering a prayer for strength as they made their way to Houston. As they tallied along to the light sound of a horse's feet hitting the cement, it wasn't long before they passed an apartment complex with the gate open.

"Maybe we should check that place for supplies," Joe exclaimed while pointing to a large house.

"I think you are right," Gayla retorted as she grabbed the horses reins and walked into the gate with the others.

"So how do you want to do this?" Crunchy professed.

Gayla then withdrew an arrow from it, "Just follow behind me, we will search from the bottom up." She strolled over to the first room with two others following closely behind as Crunchy tied the horse's reins to a guarding rail.

"The door is locked," she exclaimed as Joe stepped forward and kicked the door with his massive legs. It took two kicks before they were able to enter, storming in like paratroopers falling into battle. As they made their way through the apartment they inspected everything but moved as quietly as they crept about. Then all of a sudden, Gayla heard something rustle in the master bedroom.

"I don't think we are alone," Joe said while ceasing to move. Gayla then crept to the room with her legs bent at the knee, rolling her feet to make as little noise as possible. But to her surprise the master suite was empty, the only other place the noise could have generated from was the double-door closet in the left-hand side of the room. Gayla looked a Joe and he nodded his head as if he got the signal to open the door, he walked over to it slowly with Gayla standing behind him with the arrow ready to fire.

"Ready," he whispered as she nodded her head and he flung open the door and rushed out of the way. But the sight that was saw made Gayla drop her hunting bow and stare.

It was a little girl, she was not even a teenager yet; curled up in a ball in the bottom of the closet like dirty clothes.

"Where are your parents?" Gayla inquired as the little girl shrugged her shoulders in return.

"What is your name?" Gayla asked the girl.

"Sequoia," she retorted.

Chapter Forty-seven

November 12th, 2044. 11:00
A.M. Houston, TX.

Elijah and Katanna had been wandering throughout the city of Houston for a few days now and they had not caught glimpse of Zodia forces, let alone their platoon. Elijah had found a medkit on a dead medic and patched Katanna up nice and well. Katanna had her military jacket unbuttoned, showing her green muscle shirt beneath and silver dog tags; while still carrying the katana in one hand but hoisting the rifle over one shoulder. Elijah wiped the sweat off of his forehead as he switched the rifle in the other hand, they were two soldiers twisting in a twine; coming closer the more time they spent together. Katanna had begun to grow fond of Elijah, and Elijah scanned her head to two every chance he could get. He had forgotten all about Gayla and what they had gone through and did, now his eyes were on the prize, and he wanted the gold medal. His biggest character flaw was his lustfulness towards the sweets of life, the beautiful woman he passed on the day today. He wanted Katanna for some time now, and he was waiting for the right chance to strike like lightning snaking its way through the clouds. It was then that thunder from above roared in the sky and raindrops began to fall. Elijah and Katanna rushed down the highway to an abandoned car, to find it unlocked as they hopped in the back seat to beat the storm.

"It's pouring down outside," Katanna exclaimed while taking off her combat jacket, exposing the damp tan flesh exposed by her muscle shirt. Elijah then took off his jacket as well as he agreed with her in a joking fashion, seeing her smile warmed his heart as he sat the jacket down onto the floorboard of the vehicle. Katanna then dried herself with her jacket as Elijah watched her every move.

"See something you like," Katanna said while wiping the rainwater off her neck.

"I'm just wondering if it's as sweet as it looks," he retorted.

"Excuse me?" Katanna said while ceasing to dry herself.

"I mean, you are a very beautiful woman and a soldier like me would go through twelve platoons of friends just to get next to you," he exclaimed with a smile.

"Well that's just flattering but you're already next to me," Katanna said with a smile, before continuing to dry herself. He then sat up and got in Katanna face, and while looking her in her eyes he exclaimed; "Then how about a kiss."

Just like that, it happened; Katanna kissed him but it was Elijah who took it the extra mile. Feeling her body as the rain pelted the roof of the vehicle.

"I've never kissed a Black man before," she professed before Elijah continued to caress her.

"There's a first time for everything," he retorted as he engulfed her in lust.

1 Hour Later

Elijah pushed open the door of the foggy windows as the rain ceased and the sun began to poke out. He put on his combat jacket and looked across the roof at Katanna who was buttoning her pants with her body blocked by the automobile before he did the same. Elijah then asked for forgiveness for his actions in his mind, knowing that even our thoughts are not hidden from the Father's view. Once they had got themselves together they started walking again. Their shoulders rubbed together with every other step, they were as cute as two kittens playing in a field. Elijah then put his arm around her neck and she responded by snuggling closer to him, yes his lust snared her foot; but she loved being in the trap. Then something caught their attention, there was someone in the woods watching them. Elijah was the first to notice and pointed his rifle at the figure he saw standing not too afar. Katanna then stopped moving and dropped the katana, pulling her rifle off her shoulder as the person dashed into the woods and Elijah chased after him, with Katanna at the rear.

Man, this guy is quick, Elijah pondered while watching him jump over a fallen tree and disappear into the woods. Although Elijah could no longer see him he charged furiously in the last direction he had seen him go, then it hit him.

"Wham," Elijah flew onto the ground after taking a tree fat limb to the face.

Dazed and confused he lay on the earth like a turtle on his back as the young man tried to hit him again Katanna held up her rifle and loaded it, forcing him to stop in his tracks. He dropped the board and turned around, she could tell that he was just a kid.

"What are you doing out here by yourself?" she inquired while still holding the gun up to him.

"My parents are dead, those freaks killed them," the boy said.

"What's your name kid?" Elijah inquired as he got up from the earth.

"Stevenson" he retorted.

"Stevenson, don't ever hit me like that again," he exclaimed to the kid.

"Then, don't hold me at gunpoint," he professed while looking at him with a dumbfounded expression as Katanna dropped the rifle; seeing the boy was harmless.

Chapter Forty-eight

November 14th, 2044. 3:00
P.M. Houston, TX.

As Elijah and his group made their way through Houston, scavenging anything that could be of use to their well being; but supplies were growing thin and their bellies were beginning to grumble. Wandering in the wilderness like a pack of the nomadic beast, finding food here and empty basins there. Stevenson tapped on his leg as he walked, making a beat that was upbeat and groovy in an attempt to lift their spirits. Elijah even found himself starting to bob his head as they made their way down the street.

"I like that," Elijah exclaimed while continuing to groove to the young man's tune. Elijah then started rapping, "This you boy Elijah, spitting fire on the beat. You know were out here surviving, living on the streets."

"God's our only friend", Stevenson added in twice.

Elijah then hopping back into their new single, "This world is a mess, I mean why stress over bills if men kill.

They will spill your brains with a sandwich in their hand, does someone feel my pain or am I the only man".

"God's our only friend", Stevenson repeated twice while continuing to tap on his legs. The scene made Katanna smile as she admired them both. Elijah then stuttered as the beat continued.

"You fell off the beat," Stevenson said with a laugh.

Meanwhile

Gayla then stopped in her tracks, halting the others as she asked; "Did you guys hear that?"

Joe and Crunchy agreed as she withdrew an arrow from her quiver and crept away from the others towards the ruckus. Peeping around the corner to see Elijah from afar, forcing her to stop dead in her tracks.

"Elijah," she said to herself before she went chasing after him while screaming his name. The scene made Elijah, Katanna, and Stevenson stop walking away from them, turning around to see Gayla running towards them with the others following closely behind. She sprinted down the street to the man who once held her heart, flying straight into his arms, in a hug that even left Elijah speechless.

"Hands off my man nigrita," Katanna screamed while withdrawing the katana and placing it at the side of her throat. Her actions forced Gayla to let go of Elijah and withdraw an arrow and aim it Katanna as the group caught up to Gayla.

"Elijah what is she talking about?" Gayla inquired.

"Gayla we apart so long," Elijah started, "I didn't know if you were even still alive."

As the words pierced Gayla's heart she pieced the story together and became aware of Katanna and Elijah.

"I waited for you though," she said as a tear leaked from her eye and she dropped the bow and ran off, forcing Joe to chase after her. It was then that Elijah noticed Sequoia, standing behind all of them.

"Sequoia?" Elijah asked before rushing to her and scooping her up in a hug.

"Who is this?" Katanna asked as tears leaked from Elijah's eyes.

"This is my daughter," he professed to Katanna.

"I thought I lost you," he exclaimed to Sequoia.

"Well I hate to break up the family reunion here, but we are looking to find a place to settle down. Are you interested in forming a compound with us," Crunchy inquired.

Elijah raised from Sequoia and inquired, "Were at?"

"Houston", Crunchy professed as Katanna watched them both.

"We will need a wall," Elijah exclaimed.

"Our friend Joe can build it," Crunchy professed while stepping forward.

"I'm Crunchy, this fellow here is Dr. Sherman," he exclaimed before extending his hand to shake Elijah's.

"Gayla's told me a lot about you," Crunchy said.

"Well I hope what you heard was more good than bad," Elijah retorted.

"It was a mix of both," Crunchy responded before continuing; "What will we call this place."

"What about Hope," Dr. Sherman exclaimed before Crunchy added; "Beacon of Hope".

"I like that," Elijah said while looking at Katanna.

"Don't look at me, you have a love triangle to sort out. As a matter of fact, I'm removing myself from it. I'm sorry Elijah, `` she retorted before walking off.

Chapter Forty-nine

December 1st, 2044. 7:00 P.M. The Beacon of Hope Compound. Houston, TX.

As Elijah made his way through the compound the two groups co-founded. The wall was nearly complete and stretched nearly fifty yards, and upon its completion, it would wrap around an area that was the size of half a football field; a small start to a big project. The houses they constructed were made out clay and insulated with trash they found laying around the city; topped with a roof made of dead tree branches and leaves. The group had split up, Katanna had taken to starting a scout platoon to search the nearby area for goods. Elijah was now taking up farming, growing food for the others. Crunchy tended to firewood. The horse was tended to day in and day out by Joe until Katanna borrowed it for another scavenging mission or Joe was expanding the walls. Gayla was a hunter for the compound, killing the game in the wild outside the walls. Dr. Sherman then approached Elijah with his hands in his pockets as Elijah made his way across the fenced-in area.

"Hello," he said before Elijah greeted him as well.

"I expressed to the others, my interest in bettering the lives of those that live here. I'd like to use some of the supplies to make medicine," he expressed.

"Furthermore, I will need an assistant and I think Stevenson would be perfect, I have already spoken to him and he has agreed to help me in my pursuits for three chocolate chip cookies," he finished.

"What type of medication?" Elijah inquired.

"Penicillin and Moonshine," Dr. Sherman professed.

"I would like to set up a storehouse for the supplies gathered and for the medication, the last thing I want is for someone to drink up all of my hard work," Dr, Sherman exclaimed.

"I see no problem with that," he said as Dr. Sherman exclaimed before heading off with a smile, "Very well."

Elijah then continued his journey but stopped along the way as he passed Gayla's quarters. Things had been sore between them ever since she had found about Katanna and they had not spoken in weeks. He walked up to her door but what he heard from inside ripped him apart as he started to knock on the door. But he heard her voice loud and clear moaning Joe's name. Elijah dropped his hand from the ready position to knock on her door and headed off with his head hanging to the floor, and his stomach in knots. It twisted and turned and he was sick to his stomach. The woman he once longed for was making love to someone else. Gayla was gone, he no longer had her heart, and she no longer desired to be his.

Chapter Fifty

December 20th, 2044. The Beacon of
Hope Compound, Houston, TX.

B y now people were starting to show up at the
Beacon of Hope Compound. They seemed to
flock to it, like a herder to its sheep. People of
all shades and backgrounds, and the need to expand the
was upon them and the previous wall project was nearly
finished, only having about ten more yards to fill in. They
had decided collectively as a group to finish their current
project, and add on an expansion of another district under
their control attached to where the current wall was. Thus
from the sky, it looked like a geometric shape next to a
large triangular outline of the wooden post in the ground.
Over the construction project was Joe himself, along with
a team of new arrivals. Changes were taking place like
wildfires under Golden State sunshine. Elijah had begun
constructing a church in an abandoned building. Katanna
had found some two cans of paint, one full the other
almost empty. She also recovered old purple fabric on one
of her runs into the wild and Elijah was intent on fixing

the bag of ugly into a temple of worship. There were giant roaches infested in its crips, and paint chipped off the walls, and graffiti behind were Elijah wanted to place the pulpit. He knew they would have to find a minister, but the thought of setting up a place where others could come that also worshiped God made him smile, and he was intent on living out this vision. He painted the wall behind the pulpit yellow, leaving a cross shape space filled with graffiti. Along the crossbar, he then painted in the center with John 3:16 in black paint, then going outside the cross and filling verses in black paint. He had taken the liberty to have one of the men in the compound to make benches made of wood, he covered all seven of them in the fabric Katanna had brought back, adding the finishing touch of laying the last strip of it he had down the isle of the temple.

Chapter Fifty-one

December 21st, 2044. The Beacon of
Hope Compound, Houston, TX.

Dr. Sherman manned the reins of the wagon with his glassware apparatuses, a cooler and tables, heading for some destination outside the compound as a place to conduct his new research. Somewhere discreet, yet accessible to equestrians so he could transport some of the goods back to the compound. But first, a few things had to be established.

"So where are we going?" Stevenson asked Dr. Sherman as they rode out of the gate and off towards the woods of the wild.

"We are going to set up a laboratory," he said with a smile before exclaiming; "Somewhere outside the wall."

"And you have the cookies on you?" the boy asked Dr. Sherman.

"You will get your cookies," he exclaimed.

"I'm interested in your work ethic," the doctor professed as Stevenson turned away from him and looked straight.

"I'll work hard for you," he exclaimed as the started into the woods.

"I haven't had a chocolate chip cookie in forever," he professed as the wagon wobbled going across the rough earth. It was a very cold day for the area, the brisk winds made it worse as they both wore coats, but Stevenson's was too big for him and he looked awkward. After a few minutes of riding in silence, with Stevenson starring excitedly at his surroundings as if they fascinated him.

"You know Dr. Sherman, you're not that bad of a guy," he exclaimed to him with a smile on his face.

"There, there," he said to the horse before turning to Stevenson.

"I'd like for you to unload everything first," he exclaimed to the boy.

"Sure thing," he retorted while hopping out of the buggy and beginning to unload the contents. Dr. Sherman exited the buggy then as well, standing in the middle of a cleared area surrounded by trees.

He placed his hands on his hips and exclaimed, "It's perfect."

"What do you have in this thing, dead bodies," Stevenson professed while pulling out the cooler.

"Do be careful with that," Dr. Sherman exclaimed to him.

Before long the buggy was empty, Dr. Sherman walked over to the pile of unloaded things and picked up a shovel, handing it to the boy and exclaimed; "Well don't just stand there, dig." The boy then began to dig a gaping hole in the earth while Dr. Sherman put up the tables and set up the glassware. He positioned the flask and test tube holders to his liking, making sure everything was perfect.

After about fifteen minutes of digging, Stevenson exclaimed, "Is this hole deep enough". He leaned his weight on the shovel in the hole with a pile of dirt surrounding it. It was about waist high to the now perspiring child.

"Sure is," Dr. Sherman said while walking over to the hole, inspecting it closely.

"What do you need a hole for," the boy inquired as Dr. Sherman went over to other cooler and pulled out a block of dry ice. It steamed in the cool air as the boy crawled out of the hole and Dr. Sherman placed the block of ice inside.

"It's for storage, the medicine will have to stay cold," he professed.

"Where did you get dry ice from?" Stevenson inquired.

"My boy, I can get my hands on some of anything, you just have to know where to look," he retorted.

"Come on, let's go home," the doctor professed after the hole was filled in. The boy then ran to the buggy.

As Dr. Sherman crawled in it he asked about the cookies once again, but Dr. Sherman gave him the same answer. Something truly seemed fishy to Stevenson but he let it go and rode the whole way back without a word, his lips were glued together like two pieces of pink paper. But when they had made it out of the woods and reached the gate of the Beacon of Hope Compound he asked again about the cookies, but Dr. Sherman responded the same.

"No, give me them now!" Stevenson yelled at him. But Dr. Sherman remained silent.

After a few seconds, Stevenson yelled, "Give me the cookies!"

"I can't do that just yet," Dr. Sherman said.

"Well, why not!" the boy screamed at the man.

"Because I don't have them just yet," he professed while turning away from the boy; manning the reins and not giving him much attention. It was then that Stevenson did the unexpected, he lurched across the coach seat, grabbing Dr. Sherman by the next and knocking him onto the ground; he shook him as the ruckus made the horse trot off with the empty buggy. Joe and Gayla were standing nearby and happened to notice, running over to them both and separating the two.

"What is the meaning of this?" Joe inquired.

"This savage tried to attack me," Dr. Sherman blurted.

As Stevenson swung his arms, trying to fight to get out of Joe's grip and get to Dr. Sherman he yelled; "He cheated me out of my cookies."

"Ask him, he doesn't even have them!" Stevenson yelled with a flushed face and messy brown hair.

"Ok, were going to take a walk," Joe exclaimed while packing Stevenson off away from Dr. Sherman.

"You promised him cookies?" Gayla inquired.

"Something like that, but I told him I don't have them yet," he professed.

"You lied to him," she stated.

"I, well," he stuttered before sighing.

"I don't know what he did but make it up to him", Gayla exclaimed before walking.

"Come on, are you serious", Dr. Sherman screamed after her, only for her to turn around and give him a look before walking off.

Chapter Fifty-two

S tevenson sat on a workbench in Dr. Sherman's office, waiting on him to make up for the fruits of his labor. He kicked his legs which hung below the seat like an owner dangling a piece of meat to his cat; swinging back and forth because his feet could not touch the ground.

"Well then, I'm sure you are not too fond of me right now," Dr. Sherman said while sitting next to him; "But I would like to sincerely apologize."

"It was wrong of me to pull a blanket of guile over your eyes like that," he professed; "I used you".

"I forgive you", Stevenson exclaimed.

"Excellent, I have a token of my gratitude I would like to make you," he professed while looking into the boy's eyes.

"But first, some Shadow Mozza," Dr, Sherman professed while getting up and heading to a gas generator they had brought back from a scout patrol but Stephenson looked bewildered by the artist's name.

"This is absolutely rubbish, you don't know who Shadow Mozza is?" Dr. Sherman inquired before not giving him a chance to respond, "This will not do."

He then cranked up the generator, making the lights in his lab cut on. He then walked over to a speaker and plugged up an Infinity Music Pod Player to it. Instantaneously classical music started coming through the speaker as Dr. Sherman waltzed around the lab with an invisible person. The sight made Stevenson grin before Dr. Sherman walked over to the boy and grabbed his hand, stringing him up from his seat and into the waltz with him. They danced and danced to tune after tune, a sort of bonding Stevenson never expected. He only wanted his reward and cared little for the lying doctor, but soon enough he sat down Stevenson again and commenced to make him a prize.

"What are you making?" Stevenson inquired.

"Brownies with acorns in them," he professed before asking; "You're not allergic to nuts are you?"

"I don't think so," he retorted.

"Excellent," the doctor retorted.

"You know, we sure got off to a rough start, but you're not that bad at all," Dr. Sherman exclaimed, forcing Stevenson to crack a smile.

Meanwhile

Outside the gate stood a visitor from a compound in Galveston, upon being spotted he asked, "Who is your leader?" The men on guard duty then summoned Elijah,

Joe, Crunchy, and Gayla. They ordered them to open the gate and let him in.

"Greetings I suppose you are in charge here," the man said while looking at Elijah.

"Well it's more of a group of us," Elijah exclaimed while looking at the others. "But we are about to have a meeting right now, why don't you attend and tell us why you have come," he exclaimed while walking towards a building with Joe, Katanna, Crunchy, and Gayla going inside first. When they entered the group began to chat around the round table, deciding what to do about food since more people were starting to show up.

"Alright everyone, this is," Elijah exclaimed while stopping in mid-sentence.

"Oh, forgive me. My name is Excalibus, I am a trade emissary for the Galveston Rune compound and I have come with a proposition," the man professed while pacing back and forth with his hands behind his back.

"We are a group of magicians and soothe sayers looking to fuel our economy through trade," he professed.

"So what do you have to offer?" Katanna inquired in a dry tone of voice.

"Jewelry, food, spices, guns, ammo, the works", Excalibus professed.

"I like that idea, I mean we can always use more supplies," Gayla exclaimed as Crunchy agreed with her.

"Do you all also play games, like basketball for instance?" Joe inquired.

"No, unfortunately not basketball, but we do play football," Excallibus exclaimed.

"If you all would like to challenge us, we would be more than welcome to play against us. The game can be a sign of good relations between our two groups," Exallibus said.

"Would you mind stepping outside, we need to vote on the proposal before we take action and give you a definite answer?" Elijah asked Excallibus.

"OK, I understand," he said and added while leaving; "I will be awaiting your response."

After Excallibus left the room the group buzzed with excitement but Katanna cut the ruckus in two by exclaiming, "I don't trust him."

"What?" Gayla exclaimed before continuing; "We could trade extra wares for more food". Crunchy and Joe then agreed with her with a short saying and ahead nods.

"I just have a bad feeling about this, something doesn't seem right," Katanna exclaimed while folding her arms across her chest.

"This could be good for all of us," Joe exclaimed while standing up from his seat.

"Ok, everyone we need to tally a vote," Elijah exclaimed before continuing; "All in favor".

Elijah, Joe, Gayla and Crunchy then raised their hand in agreeance before Elijah exclaimed, "All opposed." Katanna then raised her hand, being the only one to not be in favor of the proposal.

"Then it's all settled," Elijah exclaimed with a smile.

"I can't believe this," Katanna professed while getting up from the table and walking outside, only for Elijah to follow her. As she walked past the emissary, not giving him the time of day, Elijah approached him.

"Excallibus, tell your leader we accept; and we will host the games as a sign of goodwill along with a feast to celebrate our union," Elijah exclaimed while shaking his hand.

"Excellent," he retorted.

Chapter Fifty-three

January 1st, 2045. The Beacon Of
Hope Compound. Houston, TX.

A team had been assembled to play in the football game and the potential players were gathering in a field inside the compound for the tryout. But they were short-handed and only had nine players show up, meaning they needed one more to have a complete offense.

"Boys step back, you are about to witness greatness in its prime," Stevenson exclaimed while picking up the reddish-brown football, he gripped its white laces as he squeezed it in his hand.

"I wonder who is going to be a quarterback," one of the players said while placing his hands on his hips.

"That would be me," Katanna's voice called back from behind him.

As the group turned around to see Katanna walk up Stevenson exclaimed, "Yeah right, girls can't play football with guys."

"Is that so," Katanna exclaimed while reaching her hand out for the football.

Stevenson gave her the ball as she said, "Reggie go out for a pass."

"Sure thing," the tall thin African American man exclaimed. He jogged out to the wide receiver position and bolted off like a dart in mid-flight. Katanna waited until he was about forty yards out before launching the ball like a bullet down the field, putting the ball right in his hands in mid-stride. The crowd was in aw, they didn't expect a woman to throw as good as she did. As Reggie brought the ball back Elijah was approaching from the distance. Reggie then bolted off again as Stevenson took his turn, waiting until he was about thirty-five yards out before launching the ball. But the pass was horrendous, it flew wide to the right, landing far outside the field of play after duck tailing and wobbling in the air.

"Ooooo!" the crowd exclaimed as Elijah made it the group.

"My fingers are a little sweaty," Stevenson said as he fumbled for excuses as Katanna smiled at him.

"Dude, she out threw you fair and square," one of the players professed.

"All right you all, calm down," Elijah exclaimed.

"I think I've seen all I need to see, I'm placing Katanna in the position of team captain. She will be coaching and leading you guys out on the field against the compound from Galveston," he exclaimed brightly.

"What!" Stevenson burst out loud in disagreement.

"My decision stands," he expressed to Stevenson.

"Katanna, you're in charge of the team, lead us to victory," he professed bluntly.

Chapter Fifty-four

February 2nd, 2045.12:00 P.M. The Beacon
of Hope Compound. Houston, TX.

"Ladies and gentlemen," The announcer
called into a wood grain megaphone before
continuing; "Welcome to the game of the
century". The audience in attendance was composed of
both compounds, some stood; others sat but everyone's
eyes were glued to the announcer in center field. Crunchy
had lined the lines on the field by placing dirt on top of
the grass. The announcer wore a white shirt and red vest,
with a black bow tie and slacks to match his shiny black
shoes. From his neck dangled a black mask and he had
on red lipstick. Elijah found it strange that many of the
members of the Galveston compound wore a mask or lots
of makeup. Even the brown women were powdered down
with the pancake pad. They wore their hair in elaborate
fashions, the women wrapped their hair around a stick.

"You have the pleasure of a lifetime, to see the greatest
grand finale of them all," he yelled; "We have traded,
communed, now for a little friendly competition."

"There are no referees, so we encourage both sides to express good sportsmanship. The first one to attain fifteen points wins the game," he said as the group in attendance began clapping their hands.

"In one corner, we have our brothers and sisters from the Galveston Rune Compound," he yelled with fire in his voice before a large portion of the crowd started cheering.

"On the other pole, we have our new friends from Houston, Texas. The Beacon of Hope Compound," he said with a smile as Gayla and Joe showed up and had a seat before starting to cheer as well.

"It is time for the coin toss," he professed in an exaggerated tone as he took out a gold coin and tumbled it between his fingers. Katanna then walked to the center of the field from the crowd as did someone from the other side as well. The Beacon of Hope team then walked up behind her, interlocking fingers and stopping a short distance behind her.

"We will give you the option," he said to her.

"Heads or tails my lady," he said before passing her the megaphone.

She thought for a moment and said, "We want heads."

"You heard her," he yelled before saying; "Let the games begin."

He then put the mask over his face and carried the megaphone with him as he disappeared into the crowd and the padless teams took the field. The Beacon of Hope Compound then took the field, they stood in two lines in front of Katanna, with the tallest in front bent over so the shorter players could see. But oddly enough, even some of the players of the Galveston Rune Compound wore a mask as they stood on the other side of the line of scrimmage staring at them. She didn't like them and wanted to beat them badly and she had no fear in her heart she walked up behind the center in the shotgun position.

"Blue, 1914", she yelled before Reggie changed positions on the field and was followed by a cornerback of the opposing team. He was a tall brown stocky man, looking more like a professional linebacker than a cornerback. She then tapped her leg one time and the center snapped the ball to her. The team scuttled all over and the line was busy pushing back and forth. Katanna held the ball close to her chest with her back arched as she scanned the field for potential targets.

"A, no. B, no. C, Bing," she said as she examined the routes the players ran; throwing the ball only for it to be swatted down by their other cornerback. Second down was here as the team reset and Katanna called the next play in front of the same shaped huddle.

"Ok guys, their tuff; but we can do this. Let's do Butterfly wings," she said as the team returned to the line of scrimmage. She tapped her leg one time and the ball was snapped to her, and as she scanned the field the unexpected happened. From nowhere, the cornerback came after her on a blitz and her back was turned to him. He knocked her onto the ground with his shoulder, and after she plopped onto the earth she rolled a few times but still managed to hold onto the ball.

Aching with pain from the blow she looked up at the aggressor as he yelled at her, "There aren't any referees to protect you. Your playing with the big boys now!"

He then rushed off to the other side of the field as one of the linemen for the Beacon of Hope Compound helped her stand up.

"Your bleeding," he said to her as she noticed the blood gushing from her elbow.

After the team assembled in a huddle, they could tell she was hurt, but they encouraged her as one of the players exclaimed; "There aren't any substitutes Katanna, the pain will subside I promise."

She huffed deeply and got on one knee, "I'm fine. Guys, we have to watch that backside," she exclaimed.

"The next play is Nathan Crisp," she exclaimed while looking at the team.

"Break!" they yelled as the team went to the line of scrimmage. She then tapped her leg as the ball snapped again and she backed down the pocket, scanning for targets once more. Then Reggie made a quick turn to the right in an out route, and Katanna took advantage of the wide-open receiver; launching the ball to him. He slipped and fell as he looked back at the bad pass, but his athleticism showed and he quickly pushed himself up and caught the ball; running past the cornerback and into the end zone as the Beacon of Hope Compound scored six points. Stevenson called the next huddle; he was the kicker and it was now time for the extra point.

"We got this Rune", the bulky black man said to his team as they both lined up. Katanna then tapped her leg two times and the ball was snapped to her, and Stevenson kicked the ball through a goal made of small oak trees and rope, scoring an extra point for their team. The other team then took the position at the center field, and Katanna and the Beacon of Hope team were now on defense. The Rune team had many players, some were big and others small; and the cornerback that hit her was the quarterback. When the Rune team snapped the ball Stevenson who was a poor example of a linebacker ran up to blitz through a small hole. However, the ball carrier, had the upper hand; with a low center of gravity as he knocked Stevenson down and was tackled by the Free Safety.

The next play was much different though, Katanna, who was the other linebacker, blitzed on the right and popped the quarterback just as he threw the ball. Knocking him onto the ground as Katanna said to him; "I don't need a referee to protect me."

The pass bobbled in the air just long enough for Reggie to intercept the pass and take off for the end zone. Katanna then took the position of lead blocker, taking down a man by a chop block, as Stevenson tried to keep up but couldn't. Through it all though, he made it into the endzone, and the other team was in a fritz. The Beacon of Hope team high fived each other as they celebrated in the end zone, it made the Rune Quarterback sick to his stomach.

Once the huddle had formed Katanna took a position in front of them, "Let's do Sneaky Seals," she said to them before they broke the huddle and took the position. Upon tapping both of her legs the ball was snapped to her and she took off running for the two-point conversion, juking one Rune player and spinning off two more to hurl into the end zone; and just like that they won the game. The Beacon of Hope Fans ran onto the field and grabbed

Katanna, lifting her into the air on two players' shoulders as everyone cheered.

1 Hour Later

As the feist was about to start and the people were gathering in one of the buildings.

The announcer of the football game wore the mask over his face, as he removed it in the center of the crowd he exclaimed, "I would like to do a trick, fit for the ages and passed down through my family lines," he said as the group of people watched him.

"There are three balls try to keep an eye on them," he said. He then threw them into the air and as they came back down he jumped up and swirled in the air and struck one of the balls, unleashing a huge black smoke cloud that made everyone choke on the air. As the smoke cleared Gayla noticed Elijah was missing and the Galveston Rune Compound was gone.

"Where is Elijah?" she called out as Katanna kicked at the door but it wouldn't budge.

"They put a chain on the door," Katanna said as she kicked the door again.

"I will kill them!", She yelled, "I knew we shouldn't have trusted them!"

"The door isn't going to open", Gayla exclaimed after walking to the door, "it's chained shut."

"There is treachery among us," Crunchy said with a bald fist.

Chapter Fifty-five

February 15th, 2045. 10:08 A.M. Tingleton Howard International Airport. Houston, TX.

Nightmare and the Don exited off a plane at Tingleton Howard International Airport, which was beginning to be surrounded by Zodia cult members. They were closing in swiftly like aligned birds in flight, with Luther Martin leading the pack with a slick grin smirked across his face.

"Welcome to Houston," Luther professed while stretching out his arms slowly outward before shouting in Latin and three Zodia members grabbed their bags from Nightmare and Don's hands.

"Today, you shall dine like kings at my table", Luther proclaimed to them both.

"Thank you Luther, but remember; this is about business", the Don said as Nightmare nodded his head in agreement.

In all truth, the Zodia always tripped Nightmare out, but Don was persistent in the belief that their partnership was essential to the survival of the Family branch in Mexico.

"Ah, right you are; and business we shall discuss," he exclaimed before continuing; "But first, follow me."

With that conclusion, they followed Luther into the airport, which was severely mangled and beaten by tides of war. In fact, in the west wing of the runway there was a plane rammed into the side of the airport; as if taking off from the ground took a tragic end. In the room they entered, there was a huge hole in the floor were four masked fiends ran around attacking each other over Neon Moon in the center of the hole, but in a deeper gape inside of the first crater. The Don was astonished to see the sights as Luther smiled at them both.

It was then that Nightmare inquired, "So this is what our partnership is funding?"

"Oh, this? It's just a little entertainment," Luther professed as the Don looked around the room and saw several sultry but beautiful concubines of different shades walk towards Luther carrying plates of nuts and bits of cooked meat. When they approached him he held out his hand with a fat silver ring on it, in which they all bowed before him and each woman kissed the ring while looking at the floor. The Don's lip began to quiver as he watched how the Zodia handled things but swallowed his long tongue to avoid causing a dramatic encounter.

"Are you hungry?" Luther asked them as he took samples from one of the plates of meat.

"No thank you, we ate on the plane," Nightmare said as the Don remained silent.

"Nonsense", Martin retorted back while holding up one hand and nearly cutting Nightmare off mid-sentence.

Then while still chewing the meat he approached the edge of the pit in the center of the circle he said, "Let us welcome our brothers from the Family by presenting a human sacrifice."

The Don quickly exclaimed, "Now, Luther there's no need for that." But he was too late, two Zodia members then grabbed a young man who started smiling as they drug him to the pit and they threw him in, forcing him to roll to the center hole near the Neon Moon.

Instantaneously the fiends stopped fighting and started sniffing in the air before darting towards the man in the center; savagely beating him all over his body with an occasional bite and scratch here or there. At first, he took the beating; but it wasn't long before he began to scream and the Don closed his eyes and asked the Lord for forgiveness. Although his hands were bloody, he still believed in God and the state of his hands made him pray more than the average person.

Though he knew no man was perfect except Jesus, and his faith and life choices weren't perfect it was then that he wondered, *what God would say to me during his judgment.*

As the Zodia man fought back he held one of the fiends by the shoulders as it sat on him choking him as the three others went for the Neon Moon. The Zodia man began to feel on the fiends mask finally pulling it off to reveal a face that was pale and as if it had been put in a cheese grater. The monster also possessed one white eye. It then screamed in his face and the fiend snapped the man's neck before he lay lifeless in the hole.

In Luther Martin's tent

Luther sat at the table stuffing slices of watermelon into his mouth, causing the juice to drip down his brown hairless chin as he smacked on its sheer deliciousness. The Don and Nightmare sat on his left and right side, not touching their plate of meat and eager to discuss the future of their partnership.

"Mr. Martin, if you don't mind? I like for us to start talking business now, `` Nightmare exclaimed as the Don resumed watching Luther Martin silently.

"You sure are eager to discuss matters, did you not just get here? Very well then, `` he expressed as he waved a hand in the air and three slaves cleaned the table before leaving them alone.

It was then that Luther stood and walked over to a giant chest near a purple canopy bed. The chest had gold trim and a lions head engraved where the key should have gone, but it was already unlocked. He then opened it and began to rummage through it before expressing,

"You know, a person can trust a friend; but if there is…...mistrust in the partnership. How valuable is it?"

"What are you trying to say?" The Don intervened while squinting one eye.

It was then that five armed Zodia members walked into the tent and grabbed the two mafia members, standing them up in front of Luther before kicking them in the back of the legs to make them fall on their knees.

"Hey take it easy with the Don!" Nightmare screamed in anger, but he stopped because they loaded their guns and pointed them in their faces.

Luther then walked over to them after taking off his shoes and placing them in the chest. He stuck out his hand before the Don, exposing the ring on his finger before his lips like he knew what to do. At first, the Don didn't budge.

It wasn't until they pushed a gun to the back of his skull that he inched forward to kiss the ring as Nightmare screamed, "No!"

However, this outburst did not stop the Don, as he commenced to lean forward and he kissed the ring with Nightmare followed in his footsteps. In utter shame, they were dismissed out of his sight despite their actions.

As they walked out Luther claimed that he saw, "seeds of disloyalty."

They bowed their heads to the earth like the slaves did as the Zodia members escorted them out of Luther's tent and into there plane before closing its doors.

"Don, I won't tell anyone what we did today," Nightmare said while placing one hand behind Don's seat.

After a few seconds, Don retorted calmly; "I'm not worried about you telling anyone, because I don't think either of us will live to tell the tale."

"What do you mean Papa?" Nightmare inquired.

"The pilot's door is open," he exclaimed as the plane started to take off down the runway.

"I'm going to pray," the Don professed before Nightmare then rose to his feet to see a Zodia member mashing the accelerator to the max.

Just as the plane lifted off the ground Nightmare screamed; "You're not the pilot!"

By the time the plane had reached over the metal gate surrounding the airport, though not very high off the ground. It burst into flames and broke into three pieces before exploding into flames as the planes fan blades ripped apart everything they came in contact with.

Nothing was left but a pile of the wreckage when armed Zodia scouts searched the scene a few minutes later.

Chapter Fifty-six

February 15th, 2045. 11:00 A.M.
Dr. Sherman's Laboratory. The
Beacon of Hope Compound.

As the generator cranked up, Dr. Sherman turned on a projector screen and broadcast a movie on the wall of the dimly lit lab. Though he had just placed green and blue Christmas lights upon the rafters to set the mood for the occasion.

Before he placed the JumpStart Flash Drive into the projector he read the title; "TailorMade's Greatest Hits."

The Projection on the laboratory wall

As a dark skinned man in a pink suit stood center stage in front of a mass crowd he announced, "Welcome to the kick off of the third annual Ginger Tour."

"Tonight I would like for you all to give this man a welcoming only Abuja could provide," he said with a smile.

"Up next we have TailorMade performing with DJ Naija in a song entitled, Mystery Girl!" he yelled.

TailorMade then took the stage, he was a milk chocolate toned man who had many piercings and wore a gold chain. He was followed by DJ Naija, a tall brown woman who wore a black silk gele, and her clothes were designer label Ash Gray attire.

TailorMade

As I sit with my pad & pen, I come dey
wonder wetin man go get If he gains the
whole world & looses his soul

To hell he goes, dead sea of soul
But i'm really being honest, this is really
on my mind

I no fit stop to think about the mystery
of mine
And I still flashback to the time when our
hearts intertwined
You be my world though you dey God
side
Wetin you call am, when man hale
everything

The house, cars, horse, garage, we could
really name it all
But it was all for the mystery
The one wey I said him sent to me
pardon my energy. but I no ignore this
synergy

And the way she makes me feel
Dey gimme reasons to think that we are
meant to be
But as I dey search hell for the soul wey
I no see
I come dey feel the pain of the lonely,
Now they know who be the mystery

DJ Naja

As I sit with my pad & pen, i come dey
wonder
Wetin woman go get if she gain the whole
world & looses her soul.
To hell she goes, dead sea of soul.
But im really being honest, this is really
on my mind.

I no fit stop to think about the mystery
of mine.
And I dey flashback to the time wey our
hearts intertwined.
God was my world and now I dey God
side.
Dem say Naija go love you die, no be lie.

Stay for your side, do wetin dey right
And when Jackals ride.
She will be down to pull the trigger,
Bonnie and Clyde.
I just dey try wrap my brain around wetin
dey blow my mind.

But there be a God dey, I cannot lie.
Though I must admit, you were my
beautiful flower and our souls split.
So there is a mystery, yet I dey happy as
can be.
Oluwa Oshey, you be the world to me.

In the Laboratory

The scene in view the backed out as the song began to end, forecasting the Beacon of Hope Compound, then the city of Houston, before closing with a view of the world spinning on its axis.